# THE TIME OF THE ANGELS

# THE TIME
# OF THE ANGELS

*By*

IRIS MURDOCH

1979
CHATTO & WINDUS
LONDON

Published by
Chatto & Windus Ltd
40 William IV Street
London WC2

*

Clarke, Irwin & Co. Ltd
Toronto


*First Published 1966*
*Second Impression 1969*
*Third Impression 1979*

ISBN 0 7011 0981 5

© Iris Murdoch 1966

Printed in Great Britain by
Redwood Burn Limited
Trowbridge & Esher

To
EDUARD FRAENKEL

The quotation at the beginning of Chapter Fifteen is from Heidegger's *Sein und Zeit.*

# Chapter One

"PATTIE."

    "Yes."

"Have you lit a fire in Miss Elizabeth's room?"

"Yes."

"It's so cold."

"What did you say?"

"It's so cold."

"Yes."

Pattie stretches out her plump arms, rich brown in colour, just a little darker in hue than a *cappuccino*, and with cramped chilled fingers claws at cinders in the bottom of the narrow grate. The whitish cotton smock, bulkily tucked up to the elbows, which she wears over her jumper and skirt is patterned with red strawberries. A flowery rayon scarf, not very clean now, contains her inky black hair.

"Pattie beast."

"Yes?"

"What's that funny noise that keeps coming?"

"It's the underground railway. It runs right underneath the house."

"The underground railway. I wonder if we shall get used to it."

Pattie crumples up crisp clean pages of *The Times* and lays sticks criss-cross above. She puts old rusty misshapen cinders on top of the sticks.

"Mind that spider, Pattie. Rescue him, would you. That's right. May I light the fire?"

The match flares, revealing on the crumpled back page a picture of some black men torturing some other black men. The paper blazes up mercifully. As Pattie sighs and sinks back on her heels, a ladder darts up her stocking like a little lizard.

7

"Don't forget those mousetraps, will you, Pattie. I'm sure I saw a mouse in my bedroom."

"Yes."

The sticks subside crackling into the inferno of blazing paper. Pattie picks small shiny lumps of coal out of a dusty coal-scuttle and drops them into the grate. The papery blaze warms her face.

"And, oh Pattie."

"Yes."

"If my brother Marcus rings up tell him I'm not available. If anybody rings up tell them I'm not available."

"Yes."

The rescued spider stops shamming dead and rushes underneath the coal-scuttle.

"How terribly dark it is inside. The fog seems to have got into the house."

"Yes, it is dark inside."

"Could I have some milk, Pattikins?"

"There isn't any milk. I'll borrow some from the porter."

"Well, never mind. Don't exhaust yourself, will you, sugar plum Pattie?"

"Someone's got to do the things."

The black cassock brushes the stretched stocking of her bent knee and a cold finger caresses the prominent vertebra of her inclining neck. Footsteps move away and the frou-frou of the cassock ascends the stairs. Without turning round, Pattie rises.

A huge glass-fronted bookcase which has not yet found its place in the new house stretches diagonally across the hall where Pattie has been lighting the fire. The floor in front of it is covered with books upon which she stumbles now as she steps back. Falling over *Sein und Zeit*, she loses a slipper and kicks *Sein und Zeit* petulantly with a cold stockinged foot. Pattie's shoes all become mysteriously too large for her very soon after she has bought them. A faint sound of music comes from above. Swan Lake. And for a second Pattie's body feels all feathery and light. Pattie has seen ballet, watching from far above the white figures moving like animated flowers. But I am fat now, she thinks at the next instant, I am a fat girl now.

The front door bell rings with a threatening unfamiliar sound and Pattie opens the door a little way. She does not open it properly because although it is very cold in the house it is even colder outside. Fog comes rushing in, making Pattie cough. In the yellowish haze of what is supposed to be early afternoon she can just discern a middle-aged lady with bright wide-apart eyes standing upon the pavement. Wisps of damp hair emerge from under her smart fur hat and cling streakily to her cheeks. Pattie scrutinizes, prices, and covets her coat of Persian lamb. Her suede boots leave clear imprints in the frost upon the paving stones as she tramples to and fro a little with the cold. Her la-di-dah voice comes as no surprise to Pattie. An enemy.

"So terribly sorry to bother you. My name is Mrs Barlow. I'm from the pastorate. I wonder if I could see the new Rector?"

"I'm afraid the Rector is not seeing anybody at present."

"I'd only keep him for a moment. You see, actually—"

"I'm sorry, we've only just moved in and there's such a lot to do. Perhaps you could call later."

Pattie shuts the door. In the foggy interior a youth of singular beauty and perhaps twenty summers walks or rather glides. His closely cropped hair is the colour which Pattie has learnt from her magazines to call strawberry blond. He looks about him with curiosity, starts to examine the books on the floor, and then seeing Pattie slinks back under the stairs in the direction of the kitchen. Pattie, who thinks that all young persons are sneering at her, notes with disapproval his pointed footwear. Another enemy appears.

"Oh, Pattie."

"Yes, Miss Muriel."

"Who is that frightfully good-looking boy I saw just now?"

"He's the porter's son."

"Oh, have we got a porter? What's his name?"

9

"I don't know. Some foreign name. Would you like a fire lit in your room?"

"No, don't bother, I'll go in with Elizabeth. There's the telephone, would you answer it, Pattie? If anyone wants me say I'm out."

A man's voice speaks, very hesitant and apologetic.

"Oh, hello. This is Marcus Fisher speaking. I wonder if I could speak to my brother, please?"

"I'm afraid the Rector is not available."

"Oh. Could I speak to Elizabeth, then?"

"Miss Elizabeth never comes to the telephone."

"Oh. Perhaps I could speak to Muriel?"

"Miss Muriel is not here."

"Oh. When could I get hold of the Rector?"

"I don't know, I'm sure."

"Who is that speaking, please?"

"Miss O'Driscoll."

"Oh, er, Pattie. I'm so sorry I didn't recognize your voice. Well, I suppose I'd better ring again, hadn't I."

"Goodbye, Mr Fisher."

A dark figure at the top of the stairs murmurs approval and a paper dart takes the air and sweeps down to tap on Pattie's smock a little above the heart and fall to the ground at her feet. Without looking up, Pattie smooths out the paper to put it on the fire, and as she does so reads the new address which is printed on it. *The Rector's Lodgings, St Eustace Watergate, London, E.C.* She still cannot quite believe that she is in London.

A soft voice above her sings "*Frère Jacques, Frère Jacques, dormez-vous?*" and an opening and a closing door releases a momentary whisper of Swan Lake. A train passes beneath and jolts everything in the house a millimetre or two and jolts Pattie's heart with a little reminder of death. She murmurs the poetry which takes the place of the prayer which took the place of the poor defeated magic of her childhood. Turn away no more. Why wilt thou turn away? The starry floor, the watery shore, is given thee till the break of day.

She goes into the kitchen where the strawberry blond is waiting to take her to see his father.

Pattie in the porter's room soon begins to feel a different person. The blond youngster, whose name is Leo, has mouched away and the porter, whose name is something odd which Pattie still cannot catch, is handing her a miraculous cup of tea. The porter, who is clearly a foreigner, has a gentle mournful face like an animal and thick drooping rusty-brown moustaches. Pattie likes men who look like animals and she takes to the porter for this reason and also because she is quite certain he is not sneering at her.

The porter has been explaining the heating system of the Rectory, after which he looks. The system is complicated and it occurs to Pattie that it seems to heat the boiler room and the porter's room and very little else. Pattie inspects the porter's room. It is a concrete box which looks like an air-raid shelter. There is an odd smell which Pattie imagines to be incense although she has never smelt incense before. A curious steel cage turns out to be two bunks, one above the other, only the lower one being made up as a bed. The upper one, covered by a board, supports the most extraordinary picture which Pattie has ever seen. It is painted on wood and partly with golden paint, real gold Pattie thinks it must be since it glows as if it were on fire. It shows three angels confabulating around a table. The angels have rather small heads and very large pale haloes and anxious thoughtful expressions.

"What's that?" says Pattie.

"An icon."

"What's an icon?"

"Just a religious picture,"

"Who are these people?"

"The Blessed Trinity."

Because the porter says "The Blessed Trinity" and not just "The Trinity" Pattie assumes that he believes in God. This reassures and pleases her. God is vague but important in Pattie's life and she is comforted when other people believe in Him.

"What *is* your name, please, I still can't get it."

"Eugene Peshkov."

"That's foreign, isn't it. What are you?"

He says with pride, "I am Russian," and then, "What are you?" She understands his question but how can she answer it?

"I am Pattie O'Driscoll."

# Chapter Two

"WHAT are you going to do about your brother?"

"I don't know. Has something got to be done about my brother?"

Marcus Fisher stood with his back to the warm cheerfully lighted room, looking out through a gap in the curtains. The fog had thickened the darkness and gauzed it a little with its own rusty yellow as if the fog itself were a source of light. The nearby sound of a ship's siren was stifled in the dense air. With satisfaction Marcus pulled the curtains together and turned back to the blazing coal-fire.

Norah Shadox-Brown, sturdy in tweed, loomed over the tea-table. Like so many of those whose only troubles are the troubles of others, she had carried her girlish looks well on into middle age, though her neat straight hair was now a sleek silver. Lamplight shone about her upon the stiff cloth of Irish linen in whose whiteness a tracery of shamrocks gleamed a very faint and pallid gold. Huge as a cheese, a segmented cherry cake revealed its creamy interior, studded with juicy cherries, Marcus noted approvingly, all the way up to the top. Toasted scones fainted limply under their load of melting butter. Greengage jam, called by its maker "greengage chutney" in order to indicate that it was very special and to excuse its being very expensive, formed an oleaginous mountain in a dish of Waterford glass. The tea-pot had just been filled and a sharp clear smell of hot water and Indian tea welcomed Marcus to the table. He sat down.

"I'm just afraid that there'll be some kind of scandal. So bad for the girls."

"I can't think what you've got in mind," said Marcus. "Of course Carel's terribly eccentric, but he got on all right at the other place, and I don't see why he shouldn't get past here. It looks as if it's a bit of a sinecure anyway."

"Precisely! I suspect the hierarchy have got your brother's measure and they've put him in a place where he can't do any harm!"

"What is his job, anyway, as rector of this non-existent church? There isn't anything of the church left, is there, except the tower."

"That's all. A bomb destroyed the rest. Such a loss. Wren, you know. And he never made anything prettier."

"The whole place looks as if it's been bombed now. I went down just before Carel arrived. They've knocked everything down all round the Rectory."

"Yes, it's that building site there was such a fuss about and letters to *The Times*."

"That skyscraper idea?"

"Yes. Planning permission was withdrawn at the last moment."

"*Solitudinem fecerunt* all right. But is there nothing but the Rectory and the tower? No church somewhere else?"

"No. I believe there's a church hall, but it's not consecrated. I gather the Rector can do as much or as little as he pleases. You remember, well perhaps you don't, the chap who was there before, an odd-looking crippled man. He never seemed to do anything at all. It's obviously a niche for problem children. I met a rather maddening woman called Mrs Barlow at the Oxfam office and she told me about it. I suspect she fancies herself as the power behind that particular throne. She seemed quite possessive about the place. You know what those city churches are like nowadays. Lectures and concerts and shut on Sundays. It should suit Carel down to the ground! He can leave it all to Mrs Barlow."

"Well then, why worry?" said Marcus, helping himself to greengage chutney.

"Because he'll never let well alone. He *likes* to scandalize people. You know how terribly unbalanced he is."

"Oh come!" Sensible straightforward Norah would never understand a complex inward character like Carel. Norah regarded all subtleties as falsehoods.

"And look at the way he refuses to see you and won't even let you see Elizabeth. After all, you and he were appointed her joint guardians when her father died. And he's never let you have any say at all."

Carel was Marcus's elder brother. Julian, Elizabeth's father and Marcus's younger brother had died many years ago of a mysterious illness during Marcus's sojourn in the United States. It was true that Carel had behaved as if he were the child's sole guardian.

"I wouldn't put it like that," said Marcus. "It's partly my fault. I ought to have taken a strong line from the start."

"You're afraid of Carel, that's what's the trouble with you."

Was he? Marcus's parents had died when he was still at school and Carel, head of the family at sixteen, had come to seem to him strangely like a father. Julian, youngest and always slightly ailing, had been for both his elders the object of love. But Carel had been the source of power.

"We were all very happy together when we were boys," Marcus mumbled, his mouth full of warm buttery scone and greengage.

"Well, it looks as if something came unstuck."

"I suppose it was just growing up. And then there was a girl. And, oh, various things."

"What did the girl do?"

"Oh, just made trouble. She was an ecstatic type, sort of in love with all three of us, and we were sort of in love with her. I escaped by rushing off to the U.S.A. Carel and Julian were already married then."

"Sounds messy to me."

"It was. She was rather an absurd girl, but awfully sweet. I thought her a bit of a joke. Funny, I can't even remember what she looked like now. She was a member of the Communist Party. That was all inconceivably long ago."

Marcus was more deeply disturbed than he had yet admitted to Norah by his brother's unexpected return to London. The parish in the Midlands had been sufficiently far off to seem inaccessible. There had been rumours of eccentricities. Marcus had made two brief and obviously unwelcome visits and it was now several years since he had seen either his brother or Elizabeth.

"How old is Muriel now?" said Norah, pouring out more tea. "Let me see, she must be twenty-four."

"I suppose so." Muriel was Carel's daughter and only child.

"And how old is Elizabeth?"

"Nineteen." Nineteen! He knew that. He had thought a lot about Elizabeth's growing up. He recalled her very clearly as a magical child of twelve or so, with her long, pale, wistful face and blonde hair, almost white, streaming on her shoulders. She had the self-contained maturity of a conscious only child, a conscious orphan. Of course she was a bit wild and tomboyish. Neither she nor Muriel had long enjoyed a mother's care. The two Mrs Fishers, Sheila and Clara, had borne each a girl child and died thereafter. Their fading images, now confused together, hovered in the background, wistful and faintly accusing presences, still endowed for the bachelor Marcus with the numinous and mysterious quality of a brother's wife.

"Elizabeth must be very beautiful now," said Marcus, helping himself to a piece of cherry cake. Although he had cravenly never asserted his rights over his ward, he still felt about her the curious excitement which had come to him when, after Julian's death, he had apprehended himself as the quasi-father of a very pretty and clever child. Carel had soon stolen the little waif away. But she had had her place in Marcus's most private dreams. While she was still a child he had corresponded with her regularly, and he had got used to connecting her with a certain vague warm sense of the future. Elizabeth was somehow in reserve, something still to come. He felt now in his bones the thrill of that old innocent possessiveness, mingled with an even more ancient fear of his elder brother.

"All that illness may have wrecked her looks," said Norah. "Some inherited defect there. Shouldn't be surprised if she died young like her father." Norah, whose good sense sometimes issued in judgments of a surprising callousness, had never liked Elizabeth: a sly, little fairy thing, she called her. "Quite apart from anything else, you ought to know more about Elizabeth's state of health."

Some four years ago Elizabeth had developed a weakness in the back, the sort of thing which is usually called a "slipped disc" at first. Her ailment had resisted diagnosis and treatment. She now wore a surgical corset and was under permanent orders to "take things very easily".

"You're quite right," said Marcus. He was beginning to feel a special pain which was the urgency of his desire to see Elizabeth again and to see her soon. She had been sleeping in him. Now she was waked. He felt guilt and puzzlement about his long defection.

"And then there's her education," Norah went on. "What do we know about that?"

"Well, Carel was teaching her Latin and Greek at one point, I know."

"I've never approved of teaching inside the family. It's far too emotional. Teaching should be done by professionals. Besides, a bit of ordinary school life would have done the girl good. I'm told she hardly ever goes out at all. So bad for her. With that sort of condition people simply must make an effort and help themselves. Giving in and lying back is the worst thing of all."

Norah, a retired headmistress, believed in the universal efficacy of self-help.

"Yes, it must be very lonely for her," said Marcus. "It's just as well she's always had Muriel for company."

"I don't like that either. Those girls are too much together. *Cousinage, dangereux voisinage.*"

"What on earth do you mean?"

"Oh, just that I think it's an unhealthy friendship. They ought to see more young men."

"It's a change to hear you prescribing young men, my dear

Norah! Actually, I've always had the impression those two girls didn't get on too well together."

"Well, Elizabeth *is* difficult and spoilt. And I'm afraid Muriel has changed a good deal for the worse. If only she'd gone to the university and got herself a worthwhile job."

"Well, *that* wasn't Carel's fault," said Marcus. He did not altogether like his elder niece. There was something a little sardonic about her which he mistrusted. He suspected her of mocking him. Muriel was however Norah's favourite, and had even been for a while, as a result of Marcus's good offices, a pupil in Norah's school. Though an exceptionally able girl, she had nevertheless refused the university place which she could easily have had, and had become, of all things which Norah abhorred, a shorthand typist. Marcus thought that Norah had been a little too urgently ambitious for Muriel. Perhaps she had been a little too fond of Muriel.

Marcus, who was himself the headmaster of a small independent school in Hertfordshire, had made Norah's acquaintance in the course of his professional duties. He liked and admired her. Only lately he had begun, imperceptibly and uneasily, to apprehend her as a problem. A woman of immense energies, Norah had been forced by ill health into an early retirement, and had installed herself in a decrepit eighteenth-century house in East London. Of course, she at once found herself other employments, far too many of them, according to her doctor. She did voluntary work for the local council, she was on library committees, housing committees, education committees, she busied herself with benefiting prisoners and old-age pensioners and juvenile delinquents. But she still gave the impression of someone restless and insufficiently absorbed. Emotions which had previously supplied the energy for her work now stalked and idled. Marcus noticed in her a new sentimentality which, ill-matched with her old persona of a brisk sensible pedagogue, produced an effect of awkwardness, of something almost pathetic or touching. She displayed a more patent affection for former pupils, a more patent affection, he nervously noticed, for himself. And just lately she had made the alarming and embarrassing suggestion that he should move into the vacant flat at the top of her house. Marcus had returned an evasive reply.

"I'm afraid Muriel is rather typical of the modern young," Norah was going on. "At least she's typical of the brighter ones. She's naturally a strong-willed high-principled person. She ought to make a decent citizen. But somehow it's all gone wrong. She has no social place. It's as if her sheer energy had taken her straight over the edge of morality. That's the sort of thing you ought to discuss in your book."

Marcus had taken two terms' leave from his school in order to write a book about which he had been reflecting for a long time, a philosophical treatise upon morality in a secular age. It would, he hoped, create a certain impression. It was to be a fairly brief but very lucid and dogmatic work, designed to resemble Nietzsche's *Birth of Tragedy* in its streamlined rhetoric and epigrammatic energy.

"I know what you mean about Muriel," he said. "I've seen it in other clever young people. As soon as they start to reflect about morals at all they develop a sort of sophisticated immoralism."

"Of course that doesn't necessarily make them delinquent. Delinquency has other causes, usually in the home. That Peshkov boy, for instance, seems to me a natural delinquent, if you don't mind my being rude about one of your former pupils! In his case—"

Marcus groaned to himself while Norah went on explaining her views of the causes of delinquency. It was not that Marcus was bored by this, but he did not like being reminded of Leo Peshkov. Leo was one of Marcus's failures. Norah in the course of her work on local housing problems had discovered the Peshkovs, father and son, in an unhygienic den from which she had moved them, first to a church hostel, and later, with the connivance of the Bishop, to their present quarters at the Rectory, just before the arrival of the odd-looking crippled priest beforementioned. Leo, then a schoolboy, had been attending a rather unsatisfactory local institution, and Norah had asked Marcus to make a vacancy for him at his own school. In fact, Marcus and Norah had paid for Leo's education, but this was not known to the Peshkovs.

Once at the school, Leo had played the clever wayward boy in a style which somehow got through Marcus's professional defences. Marcus was not deficient in self-knowledge and he was not ignorant of the more sophisticated hypotheses of modern psychology. Tolerant of himself, he was well aware of the subtle and important part which is played in the make-up of the successful teacher by a certain natural sadism. Marcus had taken his own measure as a sadist, he understood the machinery, and he had perfect confidence in his expertise. He was a good teacher and a good headmaster. But a sadism which in the ordinary hurly-burly of human relations remains within rational limits may surprise its proprietor as soon as the perfect partner appears on the scene.

Leo was the perfect partner. His particular brand of cunningly defiant masochism fitted but too well the peculiarities of Marcus's temperament. Marcus punished him and he came back for more. Marcus appealed to his better feelings and attempted to treat him as an adult. Too much emotion was generated between them. Marcus was confiding and affectionate, Leo was rude, Marcus was blindingly angry. Leo stayed out his time, a troublemaker of genius. Marcus had destined him for the university, to read French and Russian. At the last moment, and with the connivance of the mathematics master whom Marcus, exasperated with himself, fell to treating as a rival, Leo went to a technical college in Leicestershire to study engineering. He was rumoured not to be doing well.

"It's all part of the breakdown of Christianity," Norah was concluding. "Not that I mind its disappearing from the scene. But it hasn't turned out as we thought when I was young. This sort of twilight-of-the-gods atmosphere will drive enough people mad before we get all that stuff out of our system."

"I wonder. Do we really want to get it all out of our system?" said Marcus, banishing the image of the disastrous boy. He found Norah's brisk sensibleness of an old Fabian radical a bit bleak at times. The cleancut rational world for which she had campaigned had not materialized, and she had never come to terms with the more bewildering world that really existed. Marcus, who shared many of her judgments, could not help being a little fascinated by what she had called the twilight of the gods. Could it be that the great curtain of huge and misty shapes would be rolled away at last, and if it were so what would be revealed behind? Marcus was not a religious believer, but he was, as he sometimes wryly put it, an amateur of Christianity. His favourite reading was theology. And when he was younger he had felt a dark slightly guilty joy in having a priest for a brother.

"Yes we do," said Norah. "The trouble with you is that you're just a Christian fellow-traveller. It's better not to tinker with a dying mythology. All those stories are simply false, and the oftener that is said in plain terms the better."

They had differed about this before. Indolent, unwilling now to argue, Marcus realized sadly that his tea was over. He turned a little toward the fire, wiping his fingers on a stiff linen napkin.

He murmured, "Well, I shall go and see Carel tomorrow and I shall insist on seeing Elizabeth."

"That's right, and don't take no for an answer. After all, you've called three times now. I might even come with you. I haven't seen Muriel for some time and I'd like to have a straight talk with her. If there's any trouble about Elizabeth I really think you should consider taking legal advice. I don't say that your brother should be unfrocked or certified. But he must be made to behave a little more like a rational being. I think I'll have a word with the Bishop about it, we often meet on the housing committee."

Norah had risen and was gathering up the plates, now furred with golden cake-crumbs and greengage jam. Marcus was warming his hands and wrists at the fire. It was colder in the room.

"I wonder if you heard that odious rumour about Carel," said Norah, "that he was having a love affair with that coloured servant."

"Pattie? No. It's impossible."

"Why is it impossible, pray?"

Marcus giggled. "She's too fat."

"Don't be frivolous, Marcus. I must say, I can't get over her being called O'Driscoll when she's as black as your hat."

"Pattie's not all that black. Not that it matters."

Marcus had heard the rumour but had not believed it. Carel's peculiarities were not of that kind. He was a chaste man, even puritanical. Here Marcus knew his brother because he knew himself. He rose to his feet.

"Oh, Marcus, you aren't *going* are you? Why not stay the night? You don't want to go all the way back to Earls Court in this frightful fog."

"Must go, work to do," he mumbled. And when, some ten minutes later, he was walking over pavements sticky with frost, his lonely steps resounding inside the heavy cloak of the fog, he had forgotten all about Norah and felt instead the warm seed of joy in his heart which was the prospect of seeing Elizabeth again.

# Chapter Three

"So sorry to bother you. My name is Anthea Barlow. I'm from the pastorate. I wonder if I could see the Rector for a little minute?"

"I'm afraid the Rector is not seeing anybody at present."

"Perhaps I could leave him a note then. You see I really—"

"I'm afraid he hasn't got round to dealing with any letters yet. Perhaps you could try again later."

Pattie closed the door firmly upon the faintly wailing, faintly fluttering figure in the fog. She was a hardened door-keeper. Used to this sort of scene, she had forgotten it the next moment. Upstairs she could hear the sound of the little tinkling hand-bell which Elizabeth used to summon Muriel. Retrieving the slipper which had come off as she crossed the hall, Pattie flip-flopped back towards the kitchen.

Pattie was nervous and uneasy. The constant noise of the underground railway jolted her by day and disturbed her dreams by night. Ever since their arrival the fog had enclosed them, and she still had very little conception of the exterior of the Rectory. It seemed rather to have no exterior and, like the unimaginable circular universes which she read about in the Sunday newspapers, to have absorbed all other space into its substance. Venturing out on the second day she had, to her surprise, been unable to discover any other buildings in the vicinity. The fog hummed intermittently with mysterious sounds, but there was nothing to see except the small circle of pavement on which she stood and the red brick façade of the Rectory, furred with frost. The side wall of the Rectory was of concrete, where it had been sliced off from another building during the war. Pattie's gloved hand touched the corner where the concrete met the brick, and she saw a shape to her right which she knew must be the tower built by Christopher Wren.

23

She could just see a gaping door and a window in the dark yellow haze.

Walking along a little further she found herself in a waste land. There were no houses, only a completely flat surface of frozen mud, through which the roadway passed, with small humps here and there under stiff frozen tarpaulins. It seemed to be a huge building site, but an abandoned one. Straying from the pavement, Pattie's feet crunched little cups of ice and frozen weeds which looked like Victorian ornaments under their icy domes. Frightened of the solitude and afraid of losing her way she trotted hastily back to the shelter of the Rectory. She passed nobody on the road.

The problem of shopping still remained unsolved. Shopping was for Pattie a natural activity, a fundamental form of her contact with the world. Never organized or systematized, it had been a daily ritual, and rushing out again for something forgotten a little busy pleasure. Without it she felt like a hen in a battery. Some instinctive bustling movement was denied her. It appeared that there were no shops anywhere near the Rectory, and she had not yet been able to discover anyone who delivered. She had still to rely upon Eugene Peshkov who strode out into the haze each morning bearing Pattie's list and returned later with all her requirements. The sight of the big man, smiling for her approval, with the bulging shopping bags one in each hand, was very consoling, only now Pattie had to be more business-like and make sure she did not forget anything. The needs of the household were in fact simple, even Spartan. Carel was a vegetarian and lived on grated carrot and eggs and cheese and whole-meal biscuits. His meals were, at his own wish, of an unvarying monotony. Pattie herself lived on beans on toast and sausages. She did not know what Muriel and Elizabeth ate. Elizabeth did not like to have Pattie in her room, and the girls, following a long tradition, cooked their own meals over a gas ring. It was another sign of their tribal separateness.

Pattie had been born thirty years before in an attic room in a small house in an obscure industrial town in the centre of England. She had not been a welcome visitor to her mother, Miss O'Driscoll. Miss O'Driscoll, who had herself arrived in the world under similar auspices, knew at least that her own father had been a labourer in Liverpool and her maternal grandfather had been a peasant in County Tyrone. Miss O'Driscoll was a Protestant. The identity of Pattie's father had been, during Miss O'Driscoll's pregnancy (it was not her first), a matter for interesting speculation. The arrival of the coffee-coloured infant settled, up to a point, the question of paternity. Miss O'Driscoll distinctly remembered a Jamaican. As she could never, being much given to the drink, recall his surname the notion of Pattie's bearing it had never arisen. In any case her father was a spectral entity who had, while Pattie was still a pinpoint of possibilities inside Miss O'Driscoll's belly, departed to London with the intention of taking a job on the underground.

Pattie was soon "in need of care and protection". Miss O'Driscoll was quite affectionate as a mother but far from single-minded. She shed her usual tears and heaved her usual sigh of relief when the little brown brat was taken away from her and put into an orphanage. She occasionally visited Pattie there to shed more tears and to exhort her to be a good girl. Miss O'Driscoll was given to being Saved at intervals, and when these fits were on would discourse fervently about the Precious Blood at the orphanage gates, and even burst into pious song. After a while, being once more in the family way, her visits ceased and she died of a disease of the liver, together with Pattie's unborn younger brother.

Throughout her childhood Pattie was sick with a misery so continual that she failed to recognize it as a sort of disease. No one was especially unkind to her. No one beat her or even shouted at her. Bright brisk smiling women dealt with her needs, buttoning and unbuttoning her clothes when she was little, issuing her with sanitary pads and highly simplified information about sex when she was older. Although she was very backward her teachers were patient with her. Classified as mentally retarded, she was moved to another school where her teachers were even more patient with her. Of course the other children teased her because she was "black", but they never actually bullied her. Usually they ignored her.

From the moment when the uniformed man had carried her away in his arms from the alcoholic sobbing of Miss O'Driscoll nobody had loved her. Nobody had touched her or looked at her with the close attention which only love bestows. Among a mass of children she had struggled for notice, raising her little brown arms as if she were drowning, but the eyes of adults always passed vaguely over her. She had not, like more fortunate children, been licked into shape by love, as a bear licks its cubs. Pattie had no shape. Her mother, it is true, had once provided a sort of love, an animal clutch, which the adolescent Pattie recalled with an uncomprehending wistful gratitude. She carried this shred, which was scarcely even a memory, about in her heart and prayed for her dead mother nightly, trusting that, though her sins were as scarlet, the Precious Blood had proved as efficacious as Miss O'Driscoll could have hoped.

And well, of course, God loved Pattie. The brisk women had taught her this very early on, turning her over as it were to God when they had, as they usually had, other things to do. God loved her with a great big possessive love and Pattie of course loved God in return. But their mutual affection did not stop her from being, nearly all the time, brutalized by unhappiness into a condition which resembled mental deficiency. Much later some merciful power out of the darkness which Pattie had worshipped in ignorance drew an oblivious sponge over those years. Adult, Pattie could scarcely remember her childhood.

When she was fourteen, still hardly able to read or write, she left school, and as she seemed incapable of further training she went into service. Her first employers were a continuation of her teachers, lively enlightened liberal-minded people who seemed to a more resentful, more conscious Pattie to be always converting her misery into their cheerfulness by a relentless metabolic process. In fact they did a lot for her. They taught her to live in a house, they convinced her that she was not stupid, they even put books in her way. They were very kind to her; but from their kindness the chief lesson she learnt was the lesson of the colour bar. As a child she had not distinguished between the affliction of being coloured and the affliction of being Pattie. As a girl she took stock of her separateness. Her employers treated her in a special way because she was a coloured person.

Pattie now began to feel her colour, to feel it as a physical patina. She constantly read it too in the looks of others. She exhibited before herself her arms, so indelibly dyed to a dark creamy brown, and her hands with the greyish pallor upon the palm and the slightly purple tint upon the nail. She looked with puzzlement, almost with astonishment, into mirrors to see her round flat face and her big mouth set upon a scarcely perceptible arc so that when she smiled almost all her gleaming white teeth were visible together. She fingered the curls of her very dry black hair, pulling them into straightness and watching them return like springs into their natural spirals. She envied proud delicate-featured Indian girls in saris with jewels in their ears and noses whom she sometimes saw in the street, and wished that she could wear her own nationality with such an air. But then, she realized, she had no nationality except to be coloured. And when she saw *Wogs go home* scribbled upon walls she took it to herself as earnestly and piously as she took the sacrament at the church which she attended on Sundays. Sometimes she thought about Jamaica, which she pictured as a technicolour scene in a cinema when soft music weaves together a vista of breaking waves and swaying palms. In fact, Pattie had never seen the sea.

Of course there were other coloured people in the town. Pattie began to notice them and to observe with a sharp eye their features and their different shades of colour. Now it was as if there were only two races, white and black. Not all the half-and-halfs were as dark as herself; her father must have been a very dusky man indeed to have injected so much of darkness into his half-Irish daughter. Pattie brooded upon these distinctions, though she did not know what value she set upon them. She felt no sense of unity with the other coloured people, even when they were most evidently akin to herself. Whiteness seemed to join all the white people together in a cosy union, but blackness divided the black, each into the loneliness of his own special hue. Pattie's clear apprehension of this loneliness was her first grown-up sentiment. She recalled a little poem which had troubled her at school: "And I am black, but oh my soul is white"; and Pattie decided that she was damned if her soul was white. If she had a soul and souls had a colour, hers was a creamy brown a little darker in hue than a *cappuccino*. She had found in herself after all a little nugget of pride, something which she had brought along perhaps wrapped up in that shred of love which poor Miss O'Driscoll had blindly given to her little wisp of a daughter. Pattie began to think.

She learnt to read properly now, teaching herself in her room in the evenings. She read a lot of romantic novels, including some she had been taught to call classics, she read the women's magazines from cover to cover, and she even read some poetry and copied pieces of it into a black notebook. She liked poems that resembled songs or charms or nursery rhymes, fragments that could be musically murmured. The Spartans on the sea-wet rock sat down and combed their hair. Pattie felt with this that she knew all that she needed to know about the Spartans. The world of art remained fragmented for her, a shifting kaleidoscopic pattern which yielded beauty almost without form. She amassed small pieces of poems, of melodies, faces in pictures, Laughing Cavaliers and Blue Boys, scarcely identified, happily recognized, easily forgotten. She took no concepts away from her experiences. For the rest, a devout Low Church Christianity provided her cosmology. Lo where

Christ's blood streamed in the firmament. The idea of redemption, vague, and yet somehow for her entirely factual, stayed with her as a consolation of a special kind. All manner of thing might not be well, might never be well, but the world could not be quite as terrible as it often seemed.

During this time Pattie led a life which was appallingly solitary. She did not even conceive of finding company, and when her employers tried to encourage her to join a social club she shrank from the idea in horror. She was seventeen. She put on make-up and did a great many of the things which her magazines told her to do and went regularly to a hairdresser to have her hair straightened, but these were entirely private rituals. Black men looked at her furtively, with a kind of yearning hostility which she understood. White men of a kind she found repulsive whistled after her in the street. And then one day her kind liberal-minded employers told her that they were going to move to London. They had no further need for her services, but they would give her an excellent reference. An employment agency recommended her to a post at a country rectory some way distant from the town and Pattie walked through a door into the life of Carel Fisher.

At the time of Pattie's arrival Elizabeth was six and Muriel was eleven. Elizabeth's parents were both dead, but Carel's wife Clara was still alive. Pattie could not recall being interviewed by Clara. It seemed to her in retrospect that she must have been welcomed instantly by Carel, as if a long arm had come through the doorway and a reassuring hand had caressed her before she was over the threshold. She entered into Carel's presence as into the presence of God, and like the souls of the blessed, realized her felicity not through anything which she distinctly saw but by a sense of her own body as glorified. Carel immediately touched her, he caressed her, he loved her. Indeed Pattie's dazed senses could scarcely have distinguished these things from each other. Carel took her into his possession with a beautiful naturalness and tamed her by touch and kindness as one might tame an animal. Pattie flowered.

Carel's divine hands created her in her turn a goddess, a dark swaying being whose body glowed with a purple sheen, glorious as Parvati at the approach of Shiva. For a year Pattie laughed and sang. She was fond of the other members of the household, especially of Elizabeth and, accepted them naturally as the properties of her master. She attended to the children and obeyed Clara. But what built the house and made it topless as the towers of Ilion, what constructed the hollow golden universe all ringing with joy, was Carel's sweet affection, his quick touch upon her arm as he spoke to her, his finger tracing out the bones of her neck, his tug at her hair, his clap to her behind, his strong grip sometimes upon her wrist, his playful flick at her cheek. Pattie felt she could have been happy so forever. And then one day, with the same beautiful naturalness, Carel took her to bed.

How this event was straightway known to the household Pattie never found out. But it was at once sombrely apprehended as if the whole place had been dyed with a dye as dark and indelible as the pigment in Pattie's skin. The children knew it in their own way and withdrew into a merciless childish silence. Clara knew it and changed oh so scarcely perceptibly and yet entirely in her treatment of Pattie. Nothing was said, but the condemnation was absolute. Pattie scuttled from place to place, seeking a reassurance, an explanation, even a direct glance, but found none. Henceforth she was to be alone in the world with Carel.

Pattie was so intensely surprised at what had happened and so confused by her new experience and so frightened of its consequences that it took her some time to become aware that Carel was really in love with her. When she realized this a dreadful happiness took possession of her, a dark exotic happiness, not like the innocence of her joy, but very strong. A darkness entered into her like a swarm of bees. Pattie strengthened and hardened. She lifted her crest and faced the household, henceforth prepared to be their foe. She felt some guilt, but she wore it boldly as the badge of her calling.

Whether Clara ever fully called her husband to account Pattie never knew for certain. Pattie would never have dared to question Carel, whose silence about everything to do with his family was authoritative and bland. But Carel managed his affair with a kind of confident grace which persuaded Pattie that as he so evidently did not feel, so he had never been made to enact, a guilty person. Also everyone in the house was a little afraid of Carel, and now that their relations were no longer innocent Pattie soon began to be afraid of him too.

Clara became ill. Arriving with the tea-tray, the dinner-tray, Pattie was silently reproached by eyes which became ever more large and luminously sad. Pattie responded with the blank hard look which she turned now upon everything that was not Carel. Carel sat upon his wife's bed, stroking her hand and smiling at Pattie over the top of her head. The head sank lower on the pillow, the doctors talked in low voices with Carel in the hall. Carel told Pattie that he would soon be a widower and that when he was free he would make her his wife.

Pattie did not grieve for Clara. She did not grieve for the children who came weeping out of the room where Clara grew daily thinner. Pattie held her head high and with a ferocity of will stared past the horror of the present into the all-justifying all-reconciling future when she would be Mrs Carel Fisher. Her destiny bore her stiffly up, a stronger force than sentiment or guilt. She was the elect, the Crown Princess. She would become what she had been born for, and let a million women die and a million children wring their hands.

Clara died. Carel changed his mind. Why he changed it Pattie never knew. She must have made some mistake. What could it have been? This brooding upon the awful "only because" was to be Pattie's daily bread in the years that followed. She had smiled at Clara's funeral. Could it be that? Or was it after all her colour, which Carel could tolerate in a concubine but not in a spouse? Or was it her lack of education or her voice or something to do with personal hygiene or having had an inopportune cold? Or letting Carel see her once in her underclothes? (He was puritanical about the peripheries of love-making.) Or was it just his pity for Clara at the last, or that Muriel, who quietly hated Pattie, had somehow persuaded her father of his folly? Pattie never discovered and of course she never asked. Carel's bland silence covered it all like the sea.

Carel came to her bed as before. Pattie still trembled at those macabre unrobings when the dark cassock unsheathed the naked man. Pattie loved him. He was, as he had been before, the whole world to her. Only now there was a kind of resignation in her surrender to him. She began to know, first vaguely and then more consciously, what it was like to be a slave. She became capable of resentment. Carel had instituted a sort of cult of Clara, photographs everywhere and references, half ironical, half in earnest, to his late espoused saint. Pattie resented too, what before she had scarcely noticed, Carel's assumption that Muriel and Elizabeth were socially her superiors. But this sharpening consciousness brought with it no impulse to rebellion. She lay beside him, Parvati beside Shiva, and with her eyes wide open in the night occupied herself with her guilt.

Pattie's guilt had bided its time. As soon as she knew that Carel would not marry her she began at once to feel more guilty. A crime for a great prize seems less wicked than a crime for no prize. She twisted her hands in the night time. She knew that she had caused Clara a great deal of pain. Clara had died in grief and despair because of Pattie. And there remained still, like a sentence held up in front of her face, the implacable hostility of the two girls. This hostility had not troubled Pattie at first, but now it became a torment to her. Her intermittent, feeble and vain efforts to reconcile her foes by flattery and humility only led her to dislike them more. Elizabeth especially, indulged and spoilt by Carel, seemed to Pattie a living insult to her own menial blackness. As the girls grew older and as they fell, with Elizabeth's illness, more closely into each other's company, they constituted a menace, a united front of ruthless condemnation. Those two pale cold unforgiving forces haunted Pattie in the night. Pattie wilted. Pattie repented. But she repented alone, could do nothing with her repentance, and it was in vain that she murmured, Didn't my Lord deliver Daniel, so why not every man?

Then one day, as mysteriously and as naturally as they had begun, Carel's attentions ceased. He left her bed and did not return. Pattie was almost relieved. She fell into an apathetic sadness which had a kind of healing in it. She neglected her appearance and became aware that she had grown fat. She moved about slowly and grunted as she worked. She had, during all this time, never ceased to practise her religion. She said her prayers each night, repeating her childhood solicitations. Jesus, tender shepherd, hear me. Perhaps a child's God would be able to preserve a place of innocence in her. She had knelt each Sunday to take communion from the hands which had glorified her and had not felt herself a blasphemer. Carel's own faith had always been, like so many other things about him, a mystery to her, but she had had faith in his faith as she had had faith in God. That he had never seemed to doubt himself as a priest, equally confident in church and in bed, had given Pattie at first a sort of moral insouciance which was like a kind of sublimated cynicism. When Carel was no longer her lover and Pattie could repent more laboriously and with impunity she became for a while both more pious herself and more puzzled about him.

Carel, who had been hitherto a minimally correct though unenthusiastic parson, began about this time to develop those small but unnerving eccentricities which contributed to the reputation which had preceded him to town. He became a recluse, refused to see callers or to answer letters, leaving it to Elizabeth, who sometimes acted as his secretary, to amass a pile of correspondence and send out replies at intervals. He introduced curious variations of his own into the ceremonial of his services and even into the liturgy. He began a sermon by saying, "And what if I tell you that there is no God?" and then left his congregation to fidget uneasily during a long silence. He once conducted a service from behind the altar. He was given to laughing in church.

These manifestations frightened rather than embarrassed Pattie. As Carel was endowed for her with an ineradicable grace she could not see his antics as other than somehow natural. Yet she felt frightened of something which was happening in his mind. What she could only express as his dryness appalled her. Amid all his oddity he remained a cool, temperate even circumspect person. He had, she thought, no excesses except the great one, and what that was she could not name. More simply she supposed that Carel was losing his faith. Pattie did not therefore lose hers; but it became for her more of a talisman than a simple fact. Her universe had altered and was altering. "Life has no outside," she said to herself one day, scarcely knowing what she meant. Her morning prayer on waking, her prayer that eased that nightly load of horror, became something vaguer and more formal. The Precious Blood had lost some of its magic power, and Pattie no longer felt on easy personal terms with God, although a veiled figure still towered to call the lapsed soul.

Occasionally now she thought about leaving Carel; but the thought was like a prisoner's dream of becoming a bird and flying over the wall. Love and passion and guilt had wrapped her round and round, and she lay inert like a chrysalis, moving a little but incapable of changing her place. She was very unhappy. She worried interminably about Carel and the feud with the two girls poisoned her existence. Yet she did not conceive of leaving Carel for an ordinary life elsewhere, and although she was sometimes conscious of an acute clear wish to be the mother of children she did not really picture another world where she might love in innocence. She felt she was irrevocably soiled and broken and unfitted now for ordinary life. In past days someone like her would have found refuge in a nunnery. She sometimes tried to imagine some modern equivalent. She would go far away and dedicate herself to the service of humanity and be Patricia for ever and ever after, Sister Patricia, perhaps Saint Patricia. She read the newspapers and represented to herself the vast sea of human misery. With this she associated a vision of herself, purified and unworldly, ministering to the wretched, an anonymous and yet oddly mysterious figure. Sometimes she even thought of herself as being nobly martyred, eaten perhaps by black men in the Congo.

Pattie really knew the falseness of this dream. She knew it as with the passing of time she realized that her bond with Carel was now stronger than ever. She was not left to herself. The physical connection between them still cobwebbed the house with its electric silk. Carel who had once danced with her, danced alone now to the Swan music, a shadowy figure moving in the darkness of his room, whose door for some protection he usually left a little open; but she felt sure that he danced for her, that he was her, dancing. She was aware of him and he was aware of her. By other means she was his mistress still. And Carel seemed to need her more than before. They did not talk a great deal, but they had never talked a great deal. They existed together in a constant sort of animal communion of looks and touches and presences and half-presences.

It was in this closeness that Pattie apprehended at last something like a great fear in Carel, a fear which afflicted her with terror and with a kind of nausea. It seemed to her now that, for all his curious solitary gaiety, she had always seen him as a soul in hell. Carel was becoming very frightened and he carried fear about with him as a physical environment. His fear had some curious manifestations. He saw animals in the house, rats and mice, when Pattie was sure there were none. He complained of a black thing which kept whisking out of sight. Pattie was aware that such imaginations could come from drinking, only Carel did not drink. In any case Pattie knew that what frightened Carel did not belong to the material world even in the sense in which pink elephants did.

And then there had come, quite unexpectedly, the move to London. This had been terrifying in prospect, terrifying in the event. Pattie realized then how much her weird world depended on the solid simplicity of its surroundings for its semblance of a decent reality. Like the Hindu mystic who used to conceal the supernatural glowing of his body in a closely wound sheet, so Pattie would don her three-quarter length coat and put on her red velour hat and her suede gloves to visit the Supermarket. It had mattered to her that she shopped in certain shops, gossiped with certain women, went to a certain picture house, had her hair straightened at a certain hair dresser's where there were certain magazines. There was a whole reassuring domain where Pattie was known in her ordinariness and where the lurid purple glow was veiled. There had once been a trifle of speculation about her and Carel, but it had died down and no one had been unpleasant to her. Pattie existed in this everyday world and had her title there. She had heard a woman utter it one day as she was coming out of church. "Who is that?" "The coloured servant at the Rectory. They say she's a treasure."

Pattie was afraid that, like some relic which turns out in the end to be composed of dust and cobwebs, her existence with Carel might suddenly fall to pieces if they were removed to another place. In her agitation all difficulties seemed equally charged with menace. Where should she go now to have her hair straightened? And where would she ever find a charwoman as good as Mrs Potter? And how on earth in the extraordinary desert in which the Rectory seemed to be situated was she even to *feed* Carel? Eugene Peshkov was still unable to procure any carrots. Eugene, big, friendly, calm and reassuringly unamazed by the phenomenon of Pattie, was in fact the only consoling feature in the situation.

The fourth day had brought no diminution of the fog. It was dark even at noon, and the house remained exceedingly cold even though Eugene assured her that the central heating was in working order. Pattie had shut Mrs Barlow out and forgotten her. And now the front door bell was ringing again.

Pattie opened the door a crack and saw outside Marcus Fisher, who had already called several times, accompanied by a woman whom Pattie vaguely recognized. The woman spoke.

"Good morning, Pattie. I am Miss Shadox-Brown, you remember me, I visited Muriel at the place where you lived before. I've come to see her now, if you please. And Mr Fisher has come to see the Rector and Elizabeth."

Pattie put her knee behind the door. "I'm afraid Miss Muriel is out. And the Rector and Elizabeth are seeing nobody."

"I'm afraid we can't quite take that for an answer, Pattie," said Miss Shadox-Brown, moving up on to the top step. "Suppose you just let us in for a minute and we can talk about it more sensibly inside, eh?"

"I'm sorry," said Pattie. "We aren't having any visitors today." She shut the door flatly against Miss Shadox-Brown's nose. A sturdy foot, which had begun to insert itself in the crack of the door, narrowly escaped being crushed.

Pattie turned back into the dark hall. *Frère Jacques, Frère Jacques, dormez-vous?* She caught at the white flash of the paper dart and crumpled its crisp wings in her hand. She looked up at her master, tall and dense in his black cassock as a tower of darkness. An underground train rumbled beneath them, possibly bearing Pattie's father about his daily work.

# Chapter Four

"**M**URIEL."

"Yes."

Requested when very small to call her father "Carel" and finding herself unable to do so, Muriel had been thus early deprived of the ability to call him anything.

"Could you come here for a moment?"

Carel always said "Come here" as if his presence were a definite locality. There was also a certain menace in the phrase as if a blow were to be expected.

Muriel stood uneasily in the doorway. She feared her father.

"Come nearer, please."

She moved into the study. The books, shifted now from the hall, covered the black horsehair couch and half of the floor with an indistinct dark fungus. A single adjustable reading-lamp revealed upon the desk a circle of scored red leather and a glass of milk, and showed beyond and above, more dimly, Carel's handsome face, always seeming to Muriel a trifle glazed and stiffened. The troll King.

"I was wondering what arrangements you proposed to make, Muriel, about finding yourself employment in London."

Muriel thought quickly. She had no intention of telling her father the truth, which was that she intended to remain unemployed for six months and devote all her time to writing poetry. Muriel, a composer of verses since childhood, had long been tormented by the question: am I really a poet? In these six months she would find out, one way or the other, forever. She would give a last chance to the demon of poetry. After all, the only salvation in this age was to be an artist. At the moment she was engaged on a long philosophical poem, in the metre of the *Cimetière Marin*, of which she had already composed forty-seven stanzas.

"I'll start looking round," she said.

"That's right. You should find no difficulty in obtaining a secretarial post in the city." Carel said "obtaining a post" and not "getting a job". It was part of a bureaucratic manner which, Muriel noticed, he kept reserved for her.

"I'll look around."

"Are you just going in to Elizabeth?"

"Yes."

"That's right. I think I hear her bell ringing now. Go along then."

As Muriel reached Elizabeth's door she heard the voice behind her calling softly "Pattikins". She frowned, knocked carefully upon the door and then entered.

"Hail to thee,"

"Hail to thee."

Elizabeth was sitting on the floor, smoking a cigar and engaged on the enormous jigsaw puzzle which had occupied the girls now for nearly two months. It had been brought to London in its half-finished state precariously in the boot of the hired car.

"These bits of sea are so difficult, all the pieces look alike."

The picture on the puzzle represented sailing-ships in a sea battle. The girls had not been able to identify the battle.

Elizabeth continued to smoke and to fiddle with the pieces, while Muriel sat down against the mirror of the French wardrobe and watched. She liked to see the thick brown cylinder of the cigar twisting between those thin paper-white fingers.

Elizabeth was in full beauty. Since her illness she always dressed simply, in black trousers and a striped shirt, and yet continued to have the slightly exotic feathered appearance of a favourite page. Her straight pale yellow hair fell in even pointed locks to her shoulders, metallic and decorative as a mediaeval head-dress. Her long narrow face was pale too, seeming sometimes to be almost white, but with the golden white of a southern marble. Her indoor life had bleached her, like a darkened plant, yet there was radiance in the pallor. Sometimes her whole head seemed to have been whitened as if a very cold light shone upon it. Only her large eyes, a dark grey-blue, glowed more richly, as if one should see a stormy sky through the empty eyes of a statue.

"Sorry to ring. I was just bored. Not a nuisance?"

"Not a bit."

"Any news *là-bas*?"

"Nothing special. That awfully nice Russian man has brought us some more grub. He's cottoned on at last to the fact that Pattie and I are separate institutions."

It was a matter of pride to Muriel not to let Pattie serve her. Pattie rejoicing at Clara's death had engendered a hatred in Muriel which time had merely dulled into a habit. When she was younger she had made one or two formal attempts to forgive Pattie, but there is no grace-aided sacrament of forgiveness. She pitied the pathetic brown animal sometimes, that was all. She had also tried to perceive her father's fault. But some mechanism of her universe made Carel's fault invisible. What she did grimly observe was that her father seemed to get some sardonic amusement out of the feud between his servant and his daughter.

"You've lost my place, damn you."

Muriel had automatically closed the volume of the *Iliad* which lay beside her on the floor. Knowledge of Greek hung upon Elizabeth as an extra grace. Muriel regretted now that she had not learnt Greek. She regretted that she had not gone to a university. She felt old and regretted many things.

"Sorry. I'm a bit nervy. It's like being besieged here just now. The fog's as thick as ever."

"I know. Rather exciting actually. I haven't even bothered to draw the curtains back. It might as well be night."

Elizabeth's new room, brightly lit with several lamps, had already begun to resemble Elizabeth's old room. It was, like the latter, L-shaped, with Elizabeth's bed in the recess, partly concealed behind a Chinese screen. Turning her head a little, Muriel could see in the mirror the very end of the bed. The sheets were trailing untidily, but the effect was of a nest of feathery silky stuffs composing a sort of Oriental couch. A long bookcase, already filled and ordered, occupied the nearer wall. Elizabeth's work-table, with her little wireless and her typewriter which she called "the dog", stood between the wardrobe and the door. Facing the fireplace where a sulky fire was burning, and now supporting Elizabeth's back as she rested from the puzzle, was the chaise-longue in pink velvet which Elizabeth had insisted on having, and which Carel had bought for her with care and expense, when she had first become ill. "If I'm going to be an interesting invalid I *must* have a chaise-longue," Elizabeth had said then. Muriel admired, was always admiring, her courage and the almost uncanny cheerfulness with which she endured her narrow lot.

"What did Carel want? I thought I heard him calling you."

It still gave Muriel a slight shock to hear her cousin call him "Carel". This she had done, and so addressed him too, from an early age with every naturalness. The girls never discussed Carel except at the level of speculating whether he might not be carried off to hell one day by the devil in person.

"He asked me about getting a job."

"You didn't tell him about the poetry jag?"

"No."

Elizabeth never asked to see Muriel's poetry, and when Muriel occasionally showed her something she made small comment. Muriel, who would have been very upset indeed by an adverse criticism, still hoped for a little more encouragement.

In these days Muriel felt in an almost physical way the altering proportions of her relationship with Elizabeth. The five years which divided them had signified at different times different things. Elizabeth had always been somehow the delicate pure heart of the household, its kernel of innocence. No shadow had ever seemed to fall upon the gaiety of the orphan child, a gaiety curiously invincible and purged. Even Pattie had loved her. Muriel had felt both gauche and tenderly protective as Elizabeth pulled her impetuously forward by the hand through the years of childhood. Muriel, who had a solid and even relentless confidence of her own, had naturally cast herself as Elizabeth's teacher. Elizabeth had been apt, affectionate and loyal. Now of late Muriel had felt the balance shifting, and felt her five years' lead diminish. As a cultivated educated person her cousin was nearly her equal, and Muriel now intuited in the almost grown-up Elizabeth a strength of character not inferior to her own. Intuited, because this power was never deployed against her, scarcely even shown in her presence. Elizabeth still acted the gay dependent child for Muriel's benefit, and indeed for Carel's, but now with a kind of spontaneous feigning. What had been, what still seemed, so adorably soft and silky now showed an occasional glint of steel.

This quiet hardening had, to Muriel's mind, completed Elizabeth's beauty. The pale face was sadder, seemed stretched a little longer, as if some authoritative structure had been scarcely perceptibly introduced behind. The dark blue-grey eyes were more veiled now, looked out of a more consciously inhabited, more formidably defended fane. Muriel had always accepted that Elizabeth was "the pretty one", and there was no shadow of envy in her admiration of her cousin's good looks. Muriel, who never tended in any way to underestimate herself, knew that she was not unattractive. Her face in fact notably resembled Elizabeth's, but without the extreme pallor and distinction of feature. Her hair, which she cut short in a boyish way, was a stripy golden brown and her rather narrow eyes were a dark and speckled blue. Muriel did not doubt her own handsomeness. But here she was content to be good and to delight in Elizabeth as excellent.

With things of the mind of course it was different. Elizabeth was bright rather than reflective, a clever but hardly a creative mind. Elizabeth had rapidly mastered Greek, and her Latin was now better than Muriel's. But Muriel had approved and ratified Carel's decree, issued partly on grounds of health, that Elizabeth should not go to a university. Elizabeth had been unmoved, confident, as Muriel had been at that age, in her power to educate herself, and Muriel had been pleased to be able to continue to form and inform a mind for whose future development she still had detailed plans. Muriel knew that she must continue, where her cousin was concerned, to be the boss; and indeed Elizabeth had never been, and she was sure could never be, a menace to her consciousness. There had never been anything approaching a conflict of wills between them. Their relationship, as they had so often had occasion to exclaim to each other, was remarkable, was perfect.

Muriel worried sometimes about the degree of seclusion which Elizabeth seemed to accept as natural. In the Midlands they had had a small circle of friends whom the two girls had invariably regarded as their inferiors, teasing and bossing them in their presence and mocking them in their absence. Any young person other than their two selves was sooner or later voted "awfully dim". In fact they treated their friends as a pair of sophisticated young princesses might have treated the children of their servants. Better company might perhaps be hoped for in London, but it would take a long time to find suitable friends for Elizabeth. Carel never made any attempt to procure her society, and Elizabeth herself seemed curiously indifferent to her solitude. Muriel had watched the adolescent Elizabeth a little anxiously for signs of interest in boys, for any incipient clutching at the other sex, but Elizabeth had done no more than laugh at her few male acquaintances. Muriel had listened in vain for any inward echo of a need, and she did not think there was in the crippled girl's acceptance of her present life a single grain of despair. Only of late, and in an uncanny silence, she had felt in Elizabeth the growth of a passionate nature.

Muriel, long ago convinced that she herself was exceptional, had lately begun to assume that she was not destined for any conventional love-life. Muriel was not only still a virgin, she was not even worried about it. She had never met a man of her own age who did not seem a very small object compared with herself. She had occasionally become attached to older men in what she thought of as a silly sentimental way. She had been in love with her Latin master and with a senior partner of the firm where she worked. Unrequited, and indeed unnoticed, her affections had died quiet deaths. She did not think that the great convention of passionate love was for her. She would be sombrely contented with the solitary destiny of the artist and thinker. And of course it was also true that the energy of her heart was perfectly distributed and used up in the system formed by her relationship with Elizabeth.

But for her cousin, Muriel perceived with a realism whose painfulness she found oddly invigorating, it might well prove in time to be different. Elizabeth's fate was not, like Muriel's, marked as the exception. One day Elizabeth would move into the happiness of ordinary life as into her birthright. She was far too delicious to be endlessly wasted in the dark unvisited cavernlike environment which Muriel's father increasingly created round about himself and in which Elizabeth was indeed the only centre of light. Of course, Muriel had thought of taking Elizabeth away; at least the thought had visited her, but had always been turned off as somehow improper and premature. There was a point of fragility, not in her relation with Elizabeth but somewhere in the situation, which would not brook such a violence. Elizabeth after all had paid the price of her seclusion. She was not yet ready to face the world. But it was possible that one day her prince would come. Or rather, should it ever become clear that a prince was required Muriel was determined to select and train him herself. She did not envisage marriage as the loss of Elizabeth. After these many years Elizabeth could not be lost. Between them they would manage Elizabeth's husband.

In thus setting her own destiny apart from her cousin's, Muriel affirmed a superiority which she knew would bring its own burdens. She had, as she slowly glided away from the shores of ordinariness, her moments of panic. It felt like a loss of innocence; and there were times when she weakly yearned for she knew not what reunion with simple innocent things, with thoughtless affections and free happy laughter and dogs passing by in the street. She could not think why her asceticism seemed so like a kind of guilt. Yet there had always been, even in her long friendship with Elizabeth, a secret melancholy. The idea of suicide was not forced upon her by circumstances or disappointments, it was entirely and deeply natural to her, and she had early provided herself with a stock of sleeping-tablets sufficient to remove her promptly and painlessly from the mortal scene should she choose at any moment to quit it. The thought that she stayed on provisionally, and because from day to day she chose to, gave her a reviving thrill as she clutched and shook in their little bottle the precious liberating tablets whose existence she had not revealed even to Elizabeth. Well, she might go some day. But she was certainly not disposed to go just yet.

"Muriel, Ariel, Gabriel."

"Yes, darling."

"Did old Shadox-Brown turn up like she said she would?" Elizabeth ground the cigar into the ash-tray and began to pick the leaves apart with restless fingers.

"Yes, she came this morning with Uncle Marcus. I heard Pattie turning them away."

"I suppose Carel can't keep them out forever. I can't say I much want to see Uncle Marcus though. Do you want to see Shadox?"

"Good God no. That woman of principle. Did I show you her letter? All about facing up to things and getting a worth-while job."

"I hate facing up to things, don't you?"

"Hate it. What's more, I won't."

The girls prided themselves on being theoretical immoralists of some degree of refinement. Being high-minded and superior and tough made them by a natural development non-moral and free. They were not themselves tempted by excesses. They lived indeed the strictly ordered life which Muriel imposed and Elizabeth accepted. But they took it for granted that all was permitted. They despised a self-abnegation which called convention duty, and neurosis virtue. They had disposed of such self-styled morality long ago in their discussions, just as they had at an early age convinced each other that there was no God, and then dropped the subject forever.

"I can't stand that world of do-gooders," said Elizabeth.

"Neither can I. They're just gratifying a sense of power. And so pleased with themselves. It's a kind of snobbery. Shadox is a snob."

"Talking of do-gooders, has dear Anthea called again?"

"Yes, dear Anthea called this morning. She is a daily visitation."

Mrs Barlow had already become a joke to the girls.

"I think I'll just hoist myself up."

Elizabeth rose from the floor with a series of slow measured movements and adjusted herself on the chaise-longue, stretching out her long black-clad legs. Muriel watched her and did not move. Elizabeth did not like to be helped.

"Did you sleep all right last night, sweetheart?"

"Like a log. Did you?"

"The noise of those trains kept disturbing me."

Muriel had had her terrible dream last night. It often recurred. She was in a lonely place, it might have been a temple, beside a marble pillar, and threatened by something dark coming out of the ground which reared itself up and up. She could not recall what happened at the end and always awoke in terror. She had never told Elizabeth about this dream.

"I felt so damned tired," said Elizabeth. "I went to sleep at once."

"You haven't been *lifting* things, have you, darling?"

"No, no. I put the books in one by one. I must admit it took ages."

"I hope you haven't got my cold."

"I gave you that cold, my pet!"

"How are you feeling at the moment?"

"Oh, middling."

Elizabeth's illness, still a mystery to the doctors, fascinated Muriel and even charmed her. It was as if all attributes of Elizabeth, even this one, were turned into sweets and favours. Elizabeth herself observed a reticence on the subject which she wore as a chaste air, a kind of modesty which captivated Muriel while it also provoked her. Elizabeth had withdrawn a little behind the secret of her illness. She never now allowed Muriel to see her undressing or undressed. It was an occasional privilege to see her long-barelegged in a shirt or regal in bed in her mauve nightdress with the little pearl buttons like milk teeth. Only an elaborate knock and a firm reply gave access to her room, her door was often locked, and at certain times Muriel had to await the summons of the bell. Also Elizabeth had become untouchable. Muriel knew this not through any words but through the complex language of movement. She had become aware of an electrical barrier which now shielded her cousin from her. This troubled Muriel, although Elizabeth's own awareness of the barrier had in fact made it into a form of communication. There were swift tensions between them, pauses and falterings which had a grace of their own, the moments when Muriel wished to take her cousin in her arms and could not do so.

Muriel conjectured that what made this situation was the surgical corset. She would have liked to touch Elizabeth's side and feel the corset. In fact this object, which she had never been allowed to see, occupied her imagination to a remarkable degree. Elizabeth had been prepared to talk a little about the corset at first, and had even made jokes about it, referring to herself as "the iron maiden", but later she had observed and imposed silence on the subject. The only fact which Muriel knew about the corset was that, since Elizabeth felt more comfortable in trousers, she wore the "male version" of the corset, though what made it male had never become clear. Muriel often wondered whether she ought not to force Elizabeth to show her the thing. So much reticence might be somehow damaging to Elizabeth herself. However, she still hesitated to bully her now more formidable cousin in so delicate a matter. She only wished that she could in some way remove the trouble from her own mind.

As Muriel watched Elizabeth shifting restlessly upon the chaise-longue her gaze passed behind the bleached golden head to a point on the angle of the wall where a long crack had opened in the wallpaper. Elizabeth's room, once much larger, had been rendered L-shaped by two hardboard partition walls which composed another little room, now opening separately onto the corridor, which had been designed as a linen-room, and was already so employed by Pattie. Exploring the house soon after her arrival, Muriel had entered that room and had seen a chink of light in the corner where the two partition walls joined. Through this chink it should be possible to see into Elizabeth's room and even, with the aid of the big French mirror, into the recess where Elizabeth slept. Muriel, amazed at the speed with which this idea had come to her on seeing the chink of light, had immediately left the room as if to avoid some appalling temptation. Of course she could not dream of thus spying on her cousin.

To take her attention off the still suggestive spy-hole Muriel turned round to face the mirror. The room appeared again, but altered, as if seen in water, a little darkened in a silver-gilded powdery haze. The mirror showed her her own head and just behind it the streaming hair of Elizabeth who had turned to pummel her cushions, and behind that a large part of Elizabeth's bed, tousled and feathery, in the twilight behind the screen. Muriel now looked into her own eyes, bluer than Elizabeth's but not so beautifully shaped. As she saw that her breath was blurring the glass she leaned closer and pressed her lips to the cold mirror. As she did so, and her mirrored lips moved to meet her, a memory came. She had once and only once kissed Elizabeth on the lips and then there had been a pane of glass between them. It was a sunny day and they had gazed at each other through the glass panel of the garden door and kissed. Elizabeth was fourteen. Muriel recalled the child's figure flying then down the green garden, and the cold hardness of the glass to which her own lips had remained pressed.

She shifted now and quickly wiped the minutely textured cupid image from the surface. Elizabeth, finished with her cushions, turned and smiled at Muriel's reflected face. Unsmiling Muriel still gazed into the mirror as into a magical archway in whose glossy depths one might see suddenly shimmering into form the apparition of a supernatural princess.

# Chapter Five

"PATTIE."

"Yes."

"Shall I make the tea or will you?"

"You make it, please."

Eugene Peshkov thrust his thick fingers into the tea-caddy. The tea was very fine, like sand, and ran through them. He closed his fingers tightly, making a little lump of tea, and transferred it to the pot. Only a few specks fell onto the furry green table cloth.

Eugene was unhappy because he had just had a quarrel with his son. Eugene did not suffer much from anxiety. He had spent too long sitting at the bottom of the world and hoping for nothing to suffer from any precarious play of tempting aspirations and glimpses. No object lay just beyond his grasp since he had long ago ceased grasping. He had never even been really anxious about Leo. But his son made him suffer, and especially of late. There was a constantly reiterated pain, like a repeated blow, uncomplicated and as it were external, but positively there, a pain, a presence.

They had quarrelled over nothing because Leo wanted to quarrel. Leo had made some malicious remarks about the people of the house, and Eugene had checked him, and Leo had said that Eugene had the mentality of a servant and Eugene had been angry and Leo had gone off slamming the door. Such things often happened now, and each time gave Eugene the primitive shock of realizing that a son could be so disrespectful to a father, and the pain which was the mature knowledge that a son could hate a father. Eugene had lived in great simplicity with his son, and Leo had been a very loving child. They had been together all the time since Tanya died and Leo was two years old. For years Eugene had carried Leo and led Leo everywhere he went. He had to. There was no one else to attend to the boy. Leo had lived on his shoulder and against his side like a baby animal that clings to its parent's body. Out of such a close and loving communion how could any hatred come?

Of course it was natural that now that he was grown up the boy should not want to live at home. His grant was not enough to pay for separate lodgings and of course he chafed. It was only for a while, as Eugene told him, it was not much to bear. But there was more than natural irritation in the child, there was some deep ferocious resentment. What had Eugene, who had been his minister and protector, almost his servant, all the days of his life, ever done to merit this? He had corrected him, but never harshly. He had criticized him a little. Eugene was aware that his precocious son was casually promiscuous with women, and this continued to grieve and shock him. There had been at least one pregnancy. Eugene had spoken to Leo once about this, in what he hoped was a prudential rather than a disapproving tone. Was he being hated for this, punished perhaps for this? For some time now Leo would not speak Russian with him, and if he spoke to him in Russian the boy would reply in English. This hurt Eugene more than a direct insult. He could apprehend a work of deliberate destruction going on in that resentful mind. Leo would destroy in himself if he could the precious inbuilt structure of the Russian language, he would destroy the tissue of his Russianness, he would forget if he could that he was a Russian.

Eugene was consoled to see Pattie. She had quite often dropped into his air-raid shelter room to ask him for things, but this was the first time, since he had formally invited her to tea and she had accepted, that she was likely to stay for a good while and talk. He felt at ease with her, as he usually did with people who had no pretensions and no position. Eugene suffered from no sense of inferiority. He was filled and stiffened by his Russian essence, just as he knew that English people were filled by their Englishness. English or Russian, more than any other people in the world they quite calmly and quietly knew themselves to be the best. There was no fuss. It was simply so. Eugene had lost, in his long battered exile's life, not a single grain of this confidence. But he was a realist and he sometimes surveyed this monstrous self-satisfaction, which was far too relaxed to be called pride, a trifle sardonically in its context. He had never made himself a place in English society, he had never even got a foot onto a ledge or a finger into a cranny. His friends were exiles and misfits like himself. There were enough people left outside to make a society themselves, perhaps a better one. In Pattie he recognized a fellow-citizen.

He looked at her now. She was sitting a little nervously, with her shoulders hunched, upon the lower bunk. The icon blazed above her head like a star. The room was brightly lit, perhaps too brightly and glaringly lit, and Pattie was shrinking and blinking. Perhaps she was someone who always wanted to hide. With its high ceiling and plain concrete walls the room seemed heavy, as if it were sinking into the earth, and it was indeed a little below ground level. A long narrow window had been opened the whole length of one wall, up near the top, uncurtained and now full of foggy darkness. Below in the well of the room was Eugene's double bunk, his table with the furry green cloth with its deep fringe, an armchair of modern design, a wooden chair, and a yellow porcelain stand, waisted and bosomed like a girl, upon which stood a potted plant. Eugene did not know what kind of plant it was, although it had been with him for many years. It had long drooping branches and very glossy heart-shaped leaves some of which very occasionally became brown and dry and fell off. It disliked both water and light. Eugene loved it dearly, and together with the icon it constituted his property. The rest of the stuff just happened to be there.

Eugene adjusted the electric fire so that its heat should shine on to Pattie. The fire was just for cosiness, since the room was already quite warm because of the proximity of the boiler. Pattie was fingering her cup timidly, stirring the tea for the fourth time. On the table on the furry green cloth was a plate of hot buttered toast, whose buttery brown smell pervaded the room, and a plate of cakes with decorated sugary outsides and soft spongy insides. Pattie had taken one of these on to her own plate beside her on the bed, but seemed too shy to eat it. Eugene contemplated her.

He had seen plenty of West Indian girls on buses and on the underground but he had never studied one close to or for long. He liked the flatness and width of her face which reminded him of a Russian face. Her ample figure too reminded him of his home. She was as a woman ought to be, large-bosomed, monumental. Her hips curved in a hesitant and then in a huge confident parabola and there was plenty behind. Her breasts, revealed now by a rather tight pink jersey, were big and perfectly round, two great firm spheres let into her body. She sat, her legs a little apart, showing a line of slightly tattered petticoat where her skirt was stretched over her knees. He liked the rather untidy, tousled, unkempt femininity of her and the way her shoes were always falling off. He wished she would smile at him more, he liked that sudden display of magnificent white teeth. She was much given to looking at him and the gravity of her eyes disturbed him. He was disturbed by her very dark eyes with the spots of fiery red at their points, and by the curiously straight dusky hair which floated about her head as if it were not really attached but simply followed by a kind of magnetism.

"Is it always dark like this here at this time of year?"

"The fog? Yes, it's often foggy, though usually not for so long. It'll let up soon."

"It rather frightens me. And the trains make such a strange noise underneath."

"You'll soon stop hearing the trains. I never hear them at all, I've got so used to them. You'll feel better when you've found your own way to the shops." Eugene was getting a little tired of doing the shopping for the entire household.

"I'll come with you tomorrow."

"Do eat your cake. It's feeling sad because you haven't eaten it."

The wonderful white smile, and then the teeth close a little shyly still over a very small morsel of cake.

"I expect you'll be busy soon. Parties and dinners and things. Once you've settled in."

"Oh no. The Rector never entertains."

Eugene was not sure if he was glad or sorry. He had debated with himself whether, if he were asked to act as butler, he would say yes or no. He had been a butler in his time. At least he had acted the part of a butler with some success. All who saw him had taken him for a butler and even a good one. Eugene had not felt demeaned by this masquerade. He had also, in his time, acted the part of an odd job man in an hotel, a liftman in a shop, a porter in a school, and, for a short while, a barman. In fact his present job suited him well, though there was little money in it. He liked definite simple manual work and keeping things clean and tidy and being left to himself in his own corner. The job carried a tiny wage, besides the excellent rooms for himself and Leo. There was also a refugee organization which paid him a small stipend. He got along. The previous Rector had required very little of him and Eugene had got into pleasant habits of idleness. He liked to do something which he called meditating but which he knew was more like day-dreaming. He possessed no books except a few paperback novels, but he was a regular reader of historical bio-graphies which he got from the library. He also had a little wireless set on which he absently listened to music. Yet he was interested in his new people and suddenly a bit disappointed that he would not be able to do his act as a butler for them.

"And Miss Muriel, does she entertain?"

"No, no. She keeps—to herself."

Eugene was not sure that he liked this self-assertive thin girl with her boyish head and her sharp curious eyes. She had asked him a lot of questions about himself rather too soon.

"The priest, the Rector—is he often ill like this?"

"He's not ill."

I have said something wrong, thought Eugene. He had assumed the priest was ill, as no one had been admitted to the house since he came, and he was often in bed in the mornings. Also his face was odd in some way. He alarmed Eugene a little, though he had been entirely if vaguely kind at their rare meetings.

"Oh, well, good—I heard you turning Mrs Barlow away again this morning and I thought— Are you glad you've come to London, Pattie? Do eat up your cake."

"Yes. I don't know. I haven't really seen London yet. It's nice to be near the river. Can you see the sea down the river?"

"Oh no. The sea's miles and miles away."

"I've never seen the sea."

"Never seen the sea!" How could anyone not have seen the sea? Surely the sea must somehow belong to the happiness of every child. He pitied her suddenly for that loss, as if in the deprivation of that essential experience she had dried up into a little wrinkled nut. "How dreadful—I suppose when your parents came from the West Indies—"

"My father came from Jamaica. My mother was white, she was Irish."

I ought to have guessed, thought Eugene. She isn't all that dark. I am hurting her. "Is it your mother's name then—"

"Yes.—I mean you'd know, wouldn't you. My parents weren't married."

She minds, he thought. And she thinks I'm somehow getting at her. How can I tell her that it doesn't matter at all. He wanted to reach over and touch her plump arm just above the wrist where it emerged from the tight pink jersey. He said, "It doesn't matter at all."

"I know it doesn't matter. Well, it does, it did. I had an awful time when I was little."

"Tell me about it."

"I can't. It's too awful. And anyway I've forgotten. Tell me about you, about when you were a little boy."

"Me—ach—"

"If you don't mind—"

"No, I don't mind." It was a very long time since he had talked to anyone about himself, and almost as long since he had talked to a woman. Talking so naturally to Pattie he realized how rarely now he ever met a woman, apart from the wives of his friends, and even them he had scarcely seen since he came to live at the Rectory. He thought suddenly, I have a woman with me, alone with me in my room.

"Where were you born?"

"In St Petersburg—Leningrad, that is."

"Was that before they changed?"

"Before they changed—Yes. I was six when they changed."

"Were your parents rich people?"

"Yes." It was odd to say it like that. His parents had been rich people, very rich by any standards of today. But there had been a naturalness about their wealth which made it strange even to mention it.

"So you grew up in a grand house with servants and all that?"

"Till six, yes. We had two houses, one in St Petersburg and one in the country."

He remembered it all so very clearly. His Russian memories came in brilliant colour. All his other memories were monochrome. He could see the pink front of the big house by the Moika, with the fat curves of the stucco decorations, painted cream, dusty in the summer, crowned with snow in the winter. And the tall uncut grass at their country house, reddish with its flowers, almost concealing the long low wooden façade from the gaze of the hidden child. He hides in the grass while his mother calls him from the verandah. He sees through the rosy plumes of the grass her white spotted dress and the fringes of her slowly turning parasol.

"You do speak such beautiful English."

"I learnt it at home as a small child. We all spoke English. I could speak it fluently before I left Russia."

"Were you happy as a child?"

"Happy? In paradise." It was true. He had been conceived and born in happiness, he had come to consciousness deep in a happy sea. He loved his parents. He loved his sister. He loved the servants. And everybody loved him and spoiled him. He was a little king. In the country he had his own pony and groom. In St Petersburg he had his own special sledge, with its horse Niko, and a servant, Fyodor, who always drove him when he went to see his friends. His boot crushes through the crisp sparkly surface of the snow and he climbs in. The brass fitments shine dazzling in the sun as if little lights had been placed here and there upon the sledge. The big fur rug is adjusted so that only his nose and eyes appear underneath his fur hat. The black leather belt which Fyodor is fixing is soft and smells of a special polish which is bought at the English shop on the Nevsky Prospect. The horse strains for a moment. Then there is effortless movement. The sledge skims, it flies. There is a faint singing. Faster, faster, dear Fyodor. The sun shines upon the snow of the road, creased and lined with the marks of other sledges. The sun shines upon the gilded dome of St Isaac's and upon the slim finger of the Admiralty spire.

"How lucky you are to have happy memories. That at least they can never take from you."

"They—yes." They had taken almost everything else. But it was true that those six golden years remained an endless source of light. Their radiance did not pain him by any contrast. Rather he gratefully received a warmth from them even now. It was as if he had woven the duller, darker stuff of his life round and round that dear early time, like a sombre egg containing in its centre some glittering surprise, a jewel made by Fabergé.

"But what happened then, when you were six?"

"The Revolution happened. My parents fled to Riga with my sister and myself."

"And you left everything behind?"

"Everything except some jewels. But they were worth a lot of money. We weren't really poor in Riga, not at first anyway." The memories are darkened now. Grown-ups whisper anxiously and fall silent when children approach. A round-eyed bewildered child gazes at a grey sea.

"You must feel very bitter against those people who drove you out."

"I suppose we could have stayed. Well, it would have been difficult. No, I don't feel bitter. Things were so dreadful before. Some people so rich and other people so poor. I expect it had to happen." It was true that he did not feel bitter. There was a kind of cosmic justice in the ending of his happy world. Yet something was unjust, or perhaps simply unutterably sad. He loved his country so much.

"Where is Riga?"

"In Latvia. On the Baltic Sea."

"Oh. And how long did you stay there?"

"Till I was twelve. My father was afraid that the Soviets would annex Latvia. They did in the end, but we were gone by that time. We went to Prague."

"Prague. In Czechoslovakia. Were you poor then?"

"We were poor then. My father got a sort of clerical job with a firm of lawyers that knew our family. My mother gave Russian lessons. I gave Russian lessons too when I grew up. I went to the university in Prague." Shut-in Prague. It had always seemed to him like a trap, a beautiful sinister cage. The big over-weighted buildings descended in cliffs of towers to the cooped-up river. They had had lodgings in a narrow street below the Strahov monastery. Being desperately, endlessly, cold in winter and listening to bells. Bells, bells in the cold.

"So you're a university man?"

"Yes, I suppose I am a university man. But it was so long ago."

"Could you make enough money?"

"Well, just. My father died when I was about twenty and things got more difficult. We all worked. My sister made clothes. Of course, there were a lot of Russians in Prague. We helped each other. We carried Russia with us. It lasted till then. But it was a sad time." His father's coffin tilts as it is carried up the steep street. The street is too narrow for the hearse. His mother and his sister stumble and weep but he is dry-eyed, hardening himself against pain. The hearse jolts on the cobbles. Bells.

"And what happened then?"

"Well, Hitler happened then. He cut short my studies."

"Hitler. Oh yes. I'd forgotten. Did you escape again?"

"We tried to, but our papers weren't in order. We were stopped at the frontier. My mother and my sister were sent back to Prague. I was directed to work in a factory. Later on I was sent to a labour camp."

"Was it dreadful? How long were you there?"

"I was there till the war ended. It was fairly nasty, but others had a worse time. I worked in the fields. There was enough to eat."

"Poor—poor you."

"Look, I've been calling you 'Pattie' for days. Won't you call me by my name, 'Eugene'?" He gave it the English pronunciation of course. It had been a long grief to him that English people mispronounced both his first name and his surname. The beautiful Russian sounds had become a secret. Now he took almost a grim pleasure in the enforced incognito.

"Well, yes, I'll try. I've never known anyone with that name."

"Eugene."

"Eugene. Thank you. What happened to your mother and sister?"

"My mother died of a stroke fairly soon. I never saw her after that time at the frontier, though I had some letters. My sister— I don't know—she just—disappeared."

"You mean you don't know what happened to her?"

"Well, people did just disappear in the war. She disappeared. I kept hoping, for a while."

"Oh, I am sorry. What was your sister's name?"

There was a silence. Eugene had suddenly found himself unable to speak. A great lump of emotion rose inside him and seemed to surge out into the room. He gripped the edge of the table. It was years and years since he had spoken of these things to anybody. He said after a moment. "Her name was Elizabeth. Elizaveta in Russian."

"I'm terribly sorry," said Pattie. "I shouldn't have asked you to talk. Please forgive me."

"No, no. It is good for me to talk. I never tell these things. You do me good. Do go on asking me. I can answer any question you ask."

"What happened then when the war ended?"

"I was in various refugee camps. Eventually I was in a camp in Austria."

"And how long were you in the camps?"

"Nine years."

"Nine years? Why so very long?"

"Well, it was difficult to get out. There was so much muddle and one was pushed from one place to another. Then later on I married my wife in the camp. Tanya was her name. Tatiana, that is. She was Russian. And she had T.B. And no one would take us with the T.B. It was a matter of finding some country that would take us, you see." He had never intended to marry Tanya. It was Leo who had decided that matter.

"And what did you do all those years in the camp?"

"Nothing. Well, a little black market. Mainly nothing." He recalled the long wooden hut among the pine trees. His bunk was in the corner. The thing was to get a corner. Later he and Tanya shared a small hut with another couple. They had arranged a few things round them, pinned pictures to the wall. He had not been too unhappy, especially when there was Leo. It was odd, after seven years of killing work, nine years of idleness.

"Did you ever think of going back to Russia?"

"Yes. I did think of it then. Tanya didn't want to. I think I would have been afraid to anyway. And then there was religion." He lifted his eyes to the icon. With gentle inclined faces the Father, the Son, and the Holy Ghost conferred around their table with the white cloth. Their golden wings overlapped, entwined. They were melancholy. They knew that all was not well with their creation. Perhaps they felt that they themselves were drifting quietly away from it.

"Oh, you're a Christian, Russian Orthodox Church."

"No, not now. I'm nothing now." During the war his religion had consoled him, more perhaps as a memory of innocent and good people than as any personal faith in a saving deity. In the years of idleness it had slowly faded as indeed almost everything had faded in those years. He had given up his country for a God in whom he no longer believed. But no, he would never have had the guts to go back. Yet he had thought about Russia so much in that camp, lying on his bed through interminable summer afternoons, feeling hungry and smelling the pines and the creosote, and had imagined himself surrounded again by his own language and his own people.

"The picture, the icon. Did you have that with you all the time?"

"Not all the time, no. It was my mother's. After she died some friends of ours in Prague took it, that lawyer's family. Then after the war they traced me through the Red Cross and brought it to me in the camp. It's the only thing that was *there* and is *here*."

It was odd to think that it had hung in his mother's bedroom in that house in St Petersburg. His mother's bedroom was dark, full of wavery hanging curtains, laces and nets. It was stuffy and smelt of eau de Cologne. It was even stranger to think the icon had made that journey than to think that he himself had. Perhaps because he had grown old and the icon had not.

"It's lovely. It must be worth an awful lot."

"It is. I was always thinking someone would steal it in the camp. I think they might have done only they were a bit afraid of it, superstitious about it. I keep my room locked here—there are always sneak thieves about in this part of London. I meant to say to you to always lock up carefully. It might frighten a thief even here though. It's supposed to be a miraculous icon. It belonged to a church before it came into our family, and they say it used to be carried on a procession once a year round the town, and while it was out it made all kinds of things happen, people suddenly confessed their crimes or became reconciled with their enemies."

"Has it done any miracles for you?"

"No. But then I deserve no miracles. I have lost my faith." He had lost his country and he had lost his faith. The great dark glittering enclosed interior of the Russian church had been a home, a house for him, for so many years of his childhood and his youth. A bearded Russian God had listened in that darkness to his supplications and his prayers, chided his failings, forgiven his trespasses, loved him. Very slowly it had come to him that after all the building was empty. The vast presence was simply some trick of the gloom. There was nothing but the darkness. And now he had a son who could not conceive of God.

"I love the icon," he said. "I burn incense for it. It's like feeding it. It's more than a symbol." Yet what could it be but a symbol? He was a sentimental superstitious man. He loved the icon because it had been his mother's and had lived with them in Petersburg. Perhaps it somehow satisfied his defeated sense of property. He loved it too as a blank image of goodness from which all personality had been withdrawn.

"And you came to England?"

"In the end, yes."

"And then—?"

"Nothing special then. I worked in various jobs. And here I am now talking to Pattie." How had the years passed? Well, they had passed. Sometimes in memory the time seemed telescoped and it seemed that it was Hitler who had knocked on the gates of St Petersburg. His manhood had been somehow casually taken from him. Fifteen years in camps, the whole middle of his life. More than that, indeed, since he had never really stopped living in a camp. In England he had moved on from one shanty and nissen hut to another. He was living in a camp even now. He had made his corner. That was all.

"I wish I could work in one of those places," said Pattie.

"You mean a refugee camp? Why?"

"It would be real—one would be near to real misery—helping people—"

"Nothing's more unreal for the people who live there. Camp life is a dream, Pattie. It's all right for the welfare workers. Oh, I've seen so many of them, so cheerful, so pleased with themselves! Nothing makes people feel happier and freer than seeing other people suffering and shut in! Well, they were good enough people those welfare workers, you mustn't think me a cynic. But between their self-satisfaction and our dream somehow the reality was lost. Perhaps God saw it. Only a saint could be in the truth there."

"Well, I should like to be a saint, then."

Eugene laughed. "All the world's a camp, Pattie, so you'll have your chance. There are good corners and bad corners, but it's just a transit camp in the end."

"So you do believe in an after life?"

"No, no. I just mean nothing matters all that much. We are not here for long."

His words sounded into a silence in the brightly lit room. Pattie twisted her hands a little and then as the silence continued she got up. "I must get back to my work. I've stayed far too long. And I shouldn't have made you talk about those things."

"No, it's done me good. One must talk about things and not hide them. Next time you will tell me about you."

"There's nothing to tell about me," said Pattie. She brushed the crumbs off her skirt.

"Why, there must be. Everyone has had their adventures. Oh, I'm so glad! You've eaten three cakes!"

"I oughtn't to have. I'm much too fat. I keep meaning to go on a diet."

"Please don't! You've a wonderful shape. I like you just exactly the way you are."

"Really?"

"Yes, really. You should be thankful. One day you'll be thin and you'll wish you weren't. A thin woman is a reminder of death." He recalled poor Tanya, thinned to the bone, looking at him with accusing dying eyes. She was a wisp in his memory, denuded of substance. He had not been too kind to her. He had resented her pregnancy, resented her illness. And she had become so thin, so thin.

"I must go now."

"You'll come again, won't you, like this?"

"Well, yes, I'd love to."

"And look—when the fog lifts—let me take you to see the sea."

"The sea—oh, could you?"

"Nothing easier. And promise you won't go with someone else first!"

"There's no one else who—Oh, I'd love to go with you to see the sea, *love* to!"

"Eugene."

"Eugene."

"Then that's fixed."

She smiled at him now out of her floating hair.

After she had gone, Eugene stood for a while looking up at the Father and the Son and the Holy Ghost. No, he had not been too kind to Tanya. Then a moment later he started thinking about how he would take Pattie to see the sea.

# Chapter Six

MURIEL closed the front door of the Rectory softly behind her. The intensely cold air invaded her head and she sneezed. She still had that confounded cold. The fog, like a hushed lifted finger, imposed quietness. With her nose deep in her handkerchief she began to walk along the pavement and immediately the Rectory was lost to sight and she was walking on a roadway through the middle of emptiness. She could see the frozen earth, whipped up into little crests, for a short way on her own side of the road. The other side of the road was invisible. The sound of a fog horn resounded in the thick air and seemed to move round her in a circle. She moved silently in the middle of a dying echo of sound.

After a while she stopped walking and listened. Nothing. The close thick dome of fog shut in her little ball of shadowy visibility and the hazy air stroked her cheek with a cold damp touch. The woollen scarf which she had drawn over her head was already quite wet. She pushed her handkerchief back into her pocket and breathed vigorously, pushing little streamers of vapour out in front of her face. She stood there wide-eyed, listening, waiting. The fog excited her.

She had spent that morning trying to write about it. She had added a number of stanzas to her philosophical poem and the fog had somehow got in. Curling, creeping, moving and yet still, always receding and yet always present, everywhere and yet no-where, imposing silence, imposing breathless anxious attention, it seemed to symbolize everything which at this time she feared. Fear had come into the poem and she had been surprised at it. Was she afraid? What was she afraid of? There was no place for fear. She had shaken her sleeping-tablets in their little blue bottle. Now as she stood there on the pavement with a fast-beating heart the emotion seemed more like love than fear. But can love be love of a dark nothing?

She moved on slowly, her feet, sticking to the damp frosty pavement, making a very slight sound. She had decided that she would soon read some of her poem to Elizabeth, only Elizabeth had not rung that morning. Muriel was pleased with the poem. Perhaps it was the poem itself that had transmuted that strange fear into the equally strange love which made her now so thrilled and restless. She shivered, swinging her gloved hands, feeling herself all warm and fiercely alive, bundled inside her clothes. She breathed the cold foggy air with delight. Then suddenly she stopped again.

Upon the waste land to her left, and now quite near to her, just emerging from the wall of fog, there was something upright. It was so still that she thought it must be a post. And yet it had the look of a human being. Only now did she realize how odd it was that there was absolutely nobody about. Next moment it seemed even odder, and frightening, that there was a person standing there in the fog before her, standing perfectly still, standing as she herself had stood, waiting perhaps and listening. It was certainly a person, a man, and he was facing towards her. Muriel hesitated and moved cautiously on another step. Then she saw that the man was Leo Peshkov.

It was as impossible for them not to greet each other as if they had met in the deepest jungle.

"Hello," said Muriel.

"Hello. Isn't the fog wonderful?"

"That was just what I was thinking," she said. "I'm enjoying it terribly."

"I've been standing here for ages hoping to frighten somebody. I hope I frightened you?"

"You certainly did! Isn't it very odd that there's nobody about?"

"Not specially. There's nothing down here except warehouses, And anyway being Sunday—"

"Oh, it's Sunday, is it. I hadn't realized."

"Call yourself a parson's daughter and not know it's Sunday!"

Muriel thought the young man rather pert. She said a little coldly, "Well, good day. I'm just going down to the river."

"You'll never find the river that way."

"I expect I'll manage. Goodbye."

"Look, I'll show you the way to the river. Honestly you won't find it otherwise. There are just little alleys in between the warehouses and you have to know them. Do you mind walking across all this muck?"

"But the river *must* be this way. If I go straight on—"

"The river's all round us here. We're on a sort of peninsula, it loops round. This is the quickest way, come on."

The boy moved away as he spoke and was vanishing into the fog. Rather exasperated, Muriel stepped off the pavement and followed him. She had been in a mood for being alone.

The earth of the building site, which had seemed fairly level, was covered with hummocks and slippery cups of ice. The surface of the earth was frozen but brittle and there was mud beneath.

"Wait a minute, don't go so fast."

"Sorry. I expect your high heels—Oh I see you're wearing what they call sensible shoes. You can take my arm if you like."

"I'm all right. Is it far?"

"Only a step. It's rather exciting, this sort of wilderness, isn't it. I'll be very sorry when they build on it. There's a super view of St Paul's and lots of other churches. You'll see when the fog lifts."

It was strange to Muriel to think that they were surrounded by invisible domes and towers and spires. She had ceased to think that she was in a city at all.

"Here's the pavement again, we're almost there."

A blank wall suddenly towered up in the fog and there was another darkness near. Muriel felt herself enclosed.

"This is one of those alleys I told you about. It gets narrower and there are some steps. Watch out, it's rather slimy. Hang on to the wall if you can."

Muriel touched the wall with her gloved hand. Great cakes and scabs of semi-vegetable matter fell into the slimy stuff at her feet. She could feel it getting inside her shoes. She cautiously descended some steps holding on to a chain slung against the wall. There was a space of pavement and a lampost. Then some more steps and suddenly water.

"Well, there it is," said Leo. "Not that you can see much of it at the moment. But you wanted it and there it is."

Here the fog seemed lighter in colour and slightly less dense as if it dreamed that somewhere the sun shone. Muriel could see fifteen to twenty yards of swift flowing water, a dark luminous amber, which was whisking along with it a strewing of woody fragments and long weeds resembling hair. Again very near a fog horn sounded and Muriel felt the same emotion of which she could not say whether it was fear or love. The steps descended into the water. She went to the bottom step and then turned to look up at Leo.

He was leaning against the wall at the top of the steps. He was dressed in a short shabby black overcoat with its collar well turned up around a striped woollen scarf, and his close-cropped hair, darkened by the damp air, looked like a sleek leather cap. He had the bright provisional look of a diving duck or a water sprite which has just that minute broken the surface. Muriel, appraising him for a moment as if he belonged to the world of art, noted the satisfying roundness of his head. What made him so beautiful? Perhaps the coolness of those very wide-apart eyes.

To cover up what had become too long a stare she said, "Is there a bridge near here? Can one get across?"

"My good woman, there aren't any bridges here. We're down in dockland. It's easy to see you're a country mouse."

Muriel reflected for a moment. She could not let this one pass.

Yet if she picked it up she was inviting something approaching a relationship.

She said, "If you and I are going to see anything of each other with any sort of pleasure, on my part at any rate, you will have to mend your manners quite considerably."

A look of poised cunning satisfaction replaced the bland mask and then faded into it again. Leo came down a step or two towards her, but still not close. "Shall I kneel down and apologize?"

A moment before Muriel had attributed his jauntiness to a natural "I'm as good as you" attitude of a servant's son. Now she realized that he had wanted exactly what he had got, something which made them familiars, accomplices. She had fallen into a trap.

She said coldly, "Don't be silly. I just don't care for your being quite so familiar. Now I think we should go back. I'm sorry to have to ask you to guide me again, but I should certainly get lost by myself."

"Oh, don't go yet," he said. "Please. It's rather wonderful here."

It was rather wonderful, and Muriel in fact felt no urge to move. The enclosed solitariness of the place made the spot significant in an almost religious way. The intense cold did not numb but heightened consciousness. Muriel turned back to the silent hurrying river. It smelt of rotten vegetables and somehow too, and very purely, of water.

"You're at some sort of technical college?" she said to Leo, not looking at him. He had now come to stand close beside her.

"Yes. I hate it though. I'm not good enough at maths. There's a chap there just down from Cambridge who puts us through it. I can't keep up. Were you good at maths?"

"Not bad. But I imagine school maths are different."

"Well, yes they are. I can't cope with this stuff at all, it's the whole way of thinking that's beyond me. It hurts my mind all the time. He keeps saying he's being exact about something and I just can't see that he is. Oh, I can't explain. I think I'm going to chuck it and take a job."

"Won't your father be disappointed?"

"My father? What the hell do I care what my father thinks?"

"Why, aren't you fond of him?"

"Fond of him? Haven't you read your Freud, girl? Sorry, I'm not supposed to talk like that, am I. You know all boys hate their fathers. Just like all girls are in love with them."

Muriel laughed. "I'm not in love with mine. But I'm sure your father is proud of you, getting yourself a grant and all that."

"He doesn't care. He's got plenty of money. He's a writer, really, or thinks he is. He just does that portering job for fun. When he's tired of it he'll move on. He's just an eccentric."

"Really."

"He pretends he's a poor Russian refugee, but he isn't Russian at all, he's German. A banking family from the Baltic, you know. Been in England all his life. Pots of money."

"Oh. Well, well. What about your mother?"

"My mother's a wonderful person, you must meet her. She's English of course. They separated years ago and she's married again. She married a baronet in the north of England. I quite often go there. They're awfully grand people. I'm in love with my mother."

"Really. How interesting.'

"My mother is a great beauty and fearfully extravagant. We're a family of eccentrics, I'm afraid. Do you know what my father's passion is?"

"What?"

"Gambling. All Russians are gamblers, you know."

"I thought you said he wasn't Russian.'

"Well, those Baltic Germans model themselves on Russians. He adores roulette. Just as well he can afford it. He goes to Monte Carlo, then he has an attack of conscience and does penance by taking some beastly obscure job. He's doing penance at the moment. He'll break out again quite soon."

"I see. I trust he makes you a generous allowance."

"Not a bean. That's because he hates me. He wishes I'd been a girl. All fathers hate their sons. They're afraid of them. The young sapling threatens the aged tree and all that. It's an old story."

"Too bad. How old are you, Leo?"

"I'm twenty. May I call you Muriel?"

"Yes, I suppose so."

"May I ask you how old you are, Muriel?"

"Yes. I'm thirty-four." It occurred to Muriel the next moment she could have said forty-four and been believed.

"I expect you must be terribly experienced."

"What about?"

"Sex, of course. What else is there to be experienced about?"

"Oh yes, I've had plenty of experience."

"I suppose you're heterosexual? So many girls aren't these days."

"I'm fairly normal."

"Nobody's *normal*, nobody worth meeting, that is. What kind of fellows do you fancy?"

"I prefer older men. I mean, a good deal older than myself."

"Pity. Not that I was going to offer my services. That would be what you call impertinent. Anyway I've got a girl friend. Well, no, I haven't. I've ditched her."

"I'm not all that interested in sex," said Muriel. "I've been around. One does get tired." Leo's pertness together with the extreme cold infected her with a sort of light-headed insouciance. She was quite moved by the vision of herself as a weary experienced middle-aged woman. She wished she had claimed to be at least forty.

"Girls get tired. Men don't. I'm dying to experiment, but I can't find anybody witty enough. As it is, it's just the same old thing over and over and over again. You wouldn't believe how easy the birds are at my college. You just look at them and they roll on their backs.'

"So you *are* bored already."

"Oh no, not really. I suppose at my age biology prevents boredom. But it is rather dull. They haven't anything inside their minds, and I do think sex is talk too, don't you? I couldn't argue with them like I could argue with you. They're flabby. And it's all so casual, there's no drama, no mystery, no tension. They've been had before, they'll be had again. They just walk through one's bed as if it were a railway station."

"I imagine you walk through their beds in much the same way."

"Well, yes, I do, I suppose. But I don't want that. Do you know that I've never had a virgin?"

"Tough luck. I suppose they're hard to come by these days."

"That's the trouble. I wish I'd lived in the days when girls were secluded."

"Secluded?"

"Yes, cloistered, shut up, just never seen. Girls are too easy these days. I want to find a girl that's hard, protected by her family, a girl that's hidden in a country house, a girl one isn't allowed to see, kept behind screens and curtains and locked doors."

"I dare say she'd be just as empty-headed when you got at her."

"No, no. She'd be wonderful, pure. And think of the excitement. Like in Japan. Just catching a glimpse of somebody's sleeve or smelling their perfume. Or scheming for weeks to look through a cranny and see a girl's hair."

"Not so nice for the girls," said Muriel. It occurred to her with amusement that Leo still did not know of Elizabeth's existence. She detached a lump of frozen matter from the wall and tossed it into the ring of amber water.

"I'm not interested in their welfare. Besides, any girl of spirit would enjoy it. Imagine the intriguing there'd be. All the endless planning to get a letter through, and waiting at windows at night, and bribing the servants and all the danger! I'm just fed up with ordinary women. That's why I've never really been in love. I think I could only love a virgin, a girl who had been kept away from everybody, absolutely shut up and hidden and sort of reserved. She'd be a sort of sleeping beauty and I'd have the task of setting her free and I'd be the first man that she ever saw."

" 'How beauteous mankind is! Oh brave new world, That has such people in it!' "

"What?"

"Never mind. You've given yourself a difficult programme."

"Impossible. I shall have to turn homosexual."

"Leo."

"Yes."

"Why did you tell me all those lies about your father?"

"Oh dear. How did you know they were lies?"

"Because I asked him a lot of questions about his life and he told me what was obviously the truth."

"Of course. You're the sort of person who's good at finding things out. You're sharp. I'm afraid of you.'

"But did you really expect me to believe all that stuff?"

"I don't know. Yes, I think so. I just lied for practice, really. Artistry."

"Artistry?"

"Yes, I'm an aesthetic type. I have no morals. You don't believe in God and all that crap, do you?"

"No", said Muriel. "Though that's not the same as having no morals."

"It is, you know. I'm one of the problems of the age. I'm a lone wolf, a bit like what's-his-name, that chap in Dostoevsky. I want to train myself in immorality, really get these old conventions out of my system, so whenever I have a chance to tell a lie I do so. Values are only relative anyway, there are no absolute values. And life's so short. And there's the Bomb. And any day you may wake up to find yourself getting lumpy and hey presto it's cancer."

"I know. What do you want out of life, Leo?"

"I want to be famous and powerful and rich. That's what everybody really wants, only they haven't the nerve to say so. Moral people are just retarded. They haven't got wise to themselves."

"You could be right," said Muriel.

"You agree, oh, goody! Let's be juvenile delinquents together. At least it's a social role."

"Only I just don't think it's worth while to try to be what you call immoral. I think the conventions go deeper than you imagine."

"You mean I'm acting out of morality by other means? What an awful thought."

"It's possible. What else do you do by way of immorality practice?"

"Well, I'm just going to demonstrate."

"What?"

"I want you to lend me some money."

Muriel laughed. "So that you could try your hand at not paying it back, I suppose!" She turned to look at him. His face was pink and wet with the fog. The leather cap of darkened hair made him resemble a racing driver or a young gladiator. "I haven't any money," she said. "How much do you want?"

"Seventy-five pounds."

"I can't help you. I haven't a sou."

"Too bad. It was worth trying, wasn't it? You might have been filthy rich."

"What do you want it for?"

"It's something to do with a girl. You know."

"Hmmm. Well, you'd better steal something. That would be worthily immoral."

"Do you know, I think I will. I've been feeling for some time now that I must perform an *act*. I think I've never really performed an act. Have you?"

"Lots. I think we'd better go now," The conversation, which

74

had amused and exhilarated Muriel, had now become depressing. Perhaps the air had grown darker.

"Do you know, I think you're a marvel. You're somebody very special. You're a free woman, free, like a man. I'll be your cavalier. You'll set me tasks. Like knights and ladies. I'm sorry I told you those lies."

"Never mind. Only don't practise on me in future."

"I say, don't you think you ought to punish me for the lies?"

"Possibly. What method do you suggest?"

"I don't know. I must pay a forfeit."

Muriel, who had started up the steps, turned again to the hurrying water. It was now a slightly purplish grey. "You must make a sacrifice to the Thames."

"Oh, splendid! What shall I sacrifice?"

"Anything you have with you which you value."

"I know. My college scarf. I'm rather fond of it really. It will symbolize the lovely new life without mathematics."

He stepped down, tearing the scarf from his neck, and with a big gesture threw it curling out over the water. It fell noiselessly, darkened, and before it could sink was tugged away into the circle of fog.

It happened so quickly that Muriel gave a gasp of distress. It was a violence, like drowning something. She got to the top of the steps.

"Wait a moment, Muriel," Leo was beside her.

"What is it?"

"Muriel. You told a lie too."

"What lie?"

"You're never thirty-four, my dear."

She laughed, leaning her head back against the gritty wall. "All right. I'm not thirty-four. I won't tell you how old I am. Leave it that I'm older than you."

"An older woman. That's it. But look, don't you think you should pay a forfeit too?"

"Maybe. What is my forfeit?"

"Kiss me."

Before she could move he had placed his hands on each side of her and was already closing his eyes. They stayed there motionless mouth to mouth. Muriel's eyes closed too.

# Chapter Seven

MARCUS FISHER had decided that things had gone far enough and should be allowed to go no farther. He had now called at the Rectory no less than six times and been turned away on each occasion by the inscrutable Pattie. Telephone calls simply evoked Pattie again, evasively adamant. His letters to Carel and Elizabeth remained without answers. He sat in his room at Earls Court, watching the window become totally dark at three o'clock in the afternoon, and found that he could no longer work. If his own telephone ever rang it was always Norah.

Marcus's book, provisionally entitled *Morality in a World without God*, had got away to a good start before Christmas. He had hoped to be able to continue to write fast. He had plenty of material, it was simply a matter of putting it in order. He had decided to discard his historical introduction and to mention no names of earlier thinkers. Let his critics assign him to a tradition and a school. He would speak simply, with the sole authority of his own voice, and his crystalline densely textured argument need not be flawed by references to others, though at the close he might modestly admit to being, after all, just a Platonist.

His purpose was no less than what he proposed to call the demythologizing of morals. Compared with this the demythologizing of religion, upon which the theologians were so cheerfully and thoughtlessly engaged, was a matter of comparatively little moment. Deprived of myth, religion might die, but morals must be made to live. A religion without God, evolving so relentlessly out of the theological logic of the centuries, represented nothing in itself but the half-conscious realization that the era of superstition was over. It was its too possible consequence, a morality without Good, which was the really serious danger. Marcus's intention was to rescue the idea of an Absolute in morals by showing it to be implied in the unavoidable human activity of moral evaluation at its most unsophisticated level, and in doing this to eschew both theological metaphor and the crudities of the existentialism which was the nemesis of academic philosophy.

He had completed a first chapter entitled *The Metaphysics of Metaphor* in which he argued that the idea of a spiritual world as something separate, magnetic and authoritative need not be regarded as a metaphysical concept. A rough draft of a section explaining the role of Beauty as a revelation of the spiritual had been set aside, and would probably appear as the climax of the work. Marcus was currently engaged on a chapter called *Some Fundamental Types of Value Judgment*, and found himself quite unable to make progress. He had put off the decision about whether to introduce the idea of the Synthetic A Priori as such, and was now paralysed by it. He had lost his grasp. His theories no longer radiated an energy of their own, they had been overcome by a superior power. He could think about nothing but Carel and Elizabeth. Imaginary conversations with Carel drifted like ectoplasm in the closed-in room. And the image of Elizabeth, her new face of a woman veiled in pale floating hair, followed Marcus to his bed and hung above his sleep.

After several days of this torment Marcus was resolved that he must end it by somehow getting inside the Rectory and confronting his brother. He very much wanted to see Elizabeth too. He had begun to be extremely troubled by the idea that she might have felt herself neglected by him. Why had he ever stopped writing to her? There were so many things he could quite easily have done to show her he still remembered her. It was especially unjust, since he had really thought about her a great deal. Why had it never occurred to him to send her some flowers? Should he perhaps do so now? He had idiotically allowed her to become a stranger, and now from within the hazy luminous globe of her peculiar seclusion she both attracted and menaced him.

On the last two occasions of visiting the Rectory he had, after his failure at the front door which he had grown to expect, walked round the house, looking at the lighted windows and speculating about which room was which. He had even tried a back door, which turned out to be locked. This exercise had occasioned feelings of guilt and fear which Marcus had unflinchingly enjoyed. He said nothing to Norah about these investigations. Norah had her own plan of campaign and had invited the Bishop, together with Marcus, to dinner at the beginning of the following week. The topic for discussion was to be "what to do about that man". Norah was in danger of becoming irrational on the subject of Carel. Of course, poor Norah had her own troubles where the Rectory was concerned. Marcus knew that she had written several letters to Muriel and had received only one short evasive reply which ignored Norah's plea for an early meeting. Norah blamed Carel for this. "He makes everyone round him as mad as he is," she had said, and did not now moderate her language. She had been used to call Carel "neurotic". Fortified lately by further "stories" from the other parish, she had moved on to calling him "unbalanced", "psychotic" and "a thoroughly evil man". He ought to be removed from his post. There was after all a responsibility to the community. The Bishop must be made to realize. Marcus had pooh-poohed these enthusiasms, but later had grown pensive. Some ray from Carel had fallen even upon himself.

Following some instinct, Marcus had all along concealed from Norah the degree of his distress about his brother. She would certainly not approve of what he had come to call his "expedition" and was best left in ignorance of it. It would seem to her melo-dramatic, ill-advised, and lacking in what Norah valued above all else, straightforwardness. Marcus reflected with a little satisfaction on how impenetrably unstraightforward he felt about everything to do with Carel. Moreover, given that the venture was unpre-dictable, he was better off without witnesses to what might simply prove an exercise in making himself ridiculous. He was in a mood for avoiding Norah in any case. She was becoming embarrassingly eager about her plan for having him as her upstairs lodger, and appeared to have switched from regarding it as a possibility to regarding it as a certainty, only whose details remained to be fixed. Marcus could not recall having said anything to occasion this change.

What Marcus proposed to do was simply to get inside the Rectory somehow, preferably by a back door or window, but if necessary by forcing Pattie, and to introduce himself into his brother's presence. As the need to see Carel grew greater and greater in his mind the obstacles grew smaller and smaller. He would certainly enter the Rectory. He thought he knew his brother well enough to hope that once he was actually there Carel would subject him to nothing worse than calm irony, would perhaps enact surprise. Why so much fuss over so little? He was just on the point of replying to his letter. Why this extraordinary agitation, my dear Marcus? Why indeed? Then he would see Elizabeth. And then all would be well. A great peace would descend and a great light would shine like the light of a lost childhood. Or would something unimaginably different happen?

Marcus was glad of the fog that evening. It was after eight o'clock and there was no one about as he walked along the pavement through the building site. Moving as softly as he could, he heard his steps resound a little, as if the sound were curling back about his feet, not able to get away through the thick air. In the heart of the extreme cold he apprehended the warmth of his body with an exhilaration which made him feel dazed and drunken. He had decided to pause as soon as he saw the lights of the Rectory and stand quite still to collect his wits and to make his breathing more normal, for he was beginning already to gasp a little with emotion. It was not unpleasant. He must be getting near now. But as he strained his eyes to discern the lighted windows his left hand came sharply into contact with something. It was the Rectory wall. Marcus had come right up to it without noticing it. The house was in total darkness.

Marcus touched the wall, and his fingers slid over the sharp corner of it, feeling the brick on one side and the flat cement on the other, and he shuddered. He felt like someone who has walked into an ambush. He held on to the house and felt a menacing heart beat inside it. It rose above him, seemed to lean over him, and vanished into the fog. He held onto the house, but helplessly, as one might for a moment hold onto a much stronger opponent. Why were there no lights? They couldn't all have gone out. If there was one thing that was certain about that household it was that they kept indoors. It was almost as if they had been expecting him. He imagined some appalling colloquy within as they waited, listening. Marcus began to move along the sheer cement face of the house, slithering now upon frozen earth. The iron-hard bumpy ground hurt his feet. The face of the house sweated with cold. He moved along it like an insect, touching it with his hands and his knees and the toes of his shoes. There must be some simple explanation. Doubtless the lights were on on the other side of the house. They were all together perhaps in the dining-room or the kitchen. Then quite suddenly the wall gave way in front of him.

Marcus stood perfectly still. There was a greater blackness. There was a door which the pressure of his hand had already opened. There came to him again the sense of a trap. He could not recall having seen this door, and for a moment he wondered whether he had not in the darkness come to some quite different house. He pushed the door a little further and a strong familiar smell which he could not for the moment identify mingled with the foggy air. Marcus hesitated. Then he thrust his head forward and took a step. The next instant he had fallen headlong in through the doorway.

The difference of level was in fact little more than a foot, but it seemed to Marcus like a sudden descent into a deep pit. The door swung to behind him leaving him in total blackness, lying full length upon an uneven surface. It was like a sudden attack, and for a moment Marcus lay quite still in sheer shock and fright, not even quite sure that he had not been pushed or struck from behind. Then he began to be dreadfully afraid of suffocating. He tried to sit up, gasping for breath. There was a strange noise which seemed to come from underneath him. He was probably not inside the Rectory at all, but had fallen into some sewer or underground working where terrible fumes would take his consciousness from him. He managed to get into a sitting position and tried more deliberately to calm himself. He breathed slowly and evenly and as he did so he recognized the strange smell. It was the reassuring smell of coal. He had fallen into the Rectory coal hole.

Greatly relieved, Marcus began to shift himself cautiously about upon the slope of coal. His shoulder was extremely sore from the impact and one leg seemed to be absent. He rubbed his limbs and gradually reassembled his body round about him. The sheer darkness was now beginning to appal him and he fumbled in his pocket for some matches. It had also occurred to him that if this were indeed the coal hole then there must be a way from it into the interior of the Rectory. He struck a match and held it up.

He had seemed to be in an enormous black void as large as an amphitheatre. Now the walls almost crushed him by their closeness and the ceiling descended to touch his head as he sat awkwardly upon the slope of coal. He seemed monstrously large in the little cellar. He saw his black hand trembling in the light and the corner of the wall, banded with triangular cobwebs, all shivering slightly. His hand trembled and the flickering light went out, but he had seen the other door. It was just before him, inches away, set two feet up in the wall. A moment later Marcus was entering the Rectory on his hands and knees.

Here too it was pitch dark. He rose stiffly to his feet and began to grope until he touched a wall. He stood listening, and then began to shuffle forward as quietly as he could, one hand on the wall and the other held out in front of him. His breathing seemed to be making a great deal of noise in the expectant stillness of the dark. His forward hand touched something, recoiled, and touched again. He felt the panel of a door, drew his fingers down it until he found the handle, and very slowly opened the door into another black space. He moved a step or two and began to search for his matches again. Then he heard voices suddenly quite near to him.

A voice he recognized as Pattie's said, "It's no use phoning the Electricity Board again."

Another voice, he thought it must be Muriel's, said, "Why not? You didn't make enough fuss the last time."

"*You* telephone then! It isn't just us. The whole area's blacked out. It's no use making a fuss."

"Why the hell you didn't have enough ordinary common sense to buy some candles—"

"All *right*, all *right*."

"Pattie," Marcus said, or rather tried to say. His voice quavered so much that all he produced was a little raucous cry. At the same moment he struck a match and immediately dropped it. The match went out.

There was silence in the space in front of him. Then Pattie's voice in an alarmed whisper said, "There's someone there."

"Well, we'll soon find out who it is."

A match flared a little distance away. Marcus gestured towards the light. He wanted to be known.

"Ooh! It's a black man. He's waving his arms."

"Don't be a fool, Pattie. My God, it's Uncle Marcus."

As the match went out Marcus dimly saw figures near to him. He took a step forward. A new voice murmured, footsteps receded. Then there was a rustling of heavy stuff and something displaced the darkness beside him. A hand brushed against him, sought his sleeve, and closed firmly over his wrist.

"Marcus."

"Carel."

It was like the apprehension of a criminal, but Marcus submitted to it with the most profound relief. Guilt and fear passed away from him completely.

"Come upstairs, Marcus. You find us in a strange moment."

The hand tugged his wrist and Marcus followed, stumbled at a stair, and began to mount. The stuff of the cassock impeded him, touching his knees and thighs at each step, and a memory, perhaps of being so led by his mother, dazed him for a moment. When he reached the top of the stairs he found that he had closed his eyes. He was led in through a doorway and a door closed behind him. His wrist was released.

"Will the lights come on soon?" said Marcus. His voice was querulous like the voice of a child.

"Yes, they'll come on soon."

It seemed to Marcus that he had been in the dark for hours. The darkness in the room was velvety without any vestige of light. Marcus fumbled it like cobwebs from in front of his face.

"Oh Carel, I'm so glad to see you."

"Rather an odd remark in the circumstances."

"Carel, what's that terribly strange noise?"

"It's the underground trains."

"You should have let me see you."

"You smell rather agreeably of coal, which I suppose explains how you got in."

"I'm terribly sorry, Carel, terribly sorry—"

"You have done me no harm, my dear Marcus. I am only afraid that you may have ruined your clothes."

"Oh, hang my clothes. Please, why didn't you let me see you?"

"We have little to say to each other."

"It *can't* be like that, it *can't* be," said Marcus. The darkness oppressed him terribly. Now it seemed to be running through his head. He closed his eyes tight to keep it out. "You are my brother," he said, like the utterance of a charm or a vow.

"A somewhat conventional idea."

"It's not an idea, it's a fact!" Marcus's eyes blinked as if they were weeping black tears. He reached out an invisible hand, touching nothing, and nearly fell over. "Don't speak like that, Carel. I must see you and I must see Elizabeth."

"Elizabeth is a sick girl. She does not receive visitors."

"I'm not a visitor. I'm her guardian."

"You have never succeeded in doing anything for Elizabeth. You have scarcely written her a letter for years. You are not her guardian."

"I am, I am!" cried Marcus. The cry seemed like a futile assertion of his own existence.

"You would only upset her. She lives in her mind, far away."

"What on earth do you mean? Do you mean she's become— strange—unbalanced—or something?"

"What quaint language you use. No, no. She is just not in your world."

"But I've got to satisfy myself—"

"Are you not becoming a trifle impertinent?" There was a laugh and a soft heavy-skirted movement. Marcus recoiled.

"I'm sorry, Carel. I'm very confused I'm afraid. I do wish the lights would come on. It's so odd talking in the dark like this. I don't feel quite myself. Carel, where *are* you? Haven't you got a torch or a candle or something? I can't find my matches." Marcus groped. He needed to know where Carel was, he needed to touch him. Carel's voice seemed to wander in the dark.

"Keep still or you will knock something over. In a minute I am going to take you out to the door."

"Don't torture me like this. You'll see me tomorrow, won't you?"

"Please don't keep trying to see me, Marcus. I am not in your world either. It is only by some metaphysical mistake that we can apprehend each other at all."

"Carel, how can you be so *unkind*, so *unchristian*."

"Come, come. I don't think we need descend to that."

"You haven't stopped believing in God, have you, Carel? That at least—"

"You are the one who knows that in this age no intelligent person really believes in God. I am told you are writing a book about it."

"But it's not true, is it, Carel, about you, all the things they say—"

"I don't know what they say."

"That you don't believe any more but you go on—"

"If there is no God there is all the more need for a priest."

"But, Carel, it would be wrong, awful—"

"If there is no one there no one is going to mind."

"You're not serious. It's all part of this—torture—and the lights going out and—Carel, I just don't understand. They say such odd things about you. If you've lost your faith surely you— But, no, you're just laughing at me."

"I think you are the believer in God, Marcus. You certainly seem to believe in the possibility of blasphemy."

"But surely you *ought* to—"

"Come. No tribunal dreamt of by you could really concern itself with me. Now I shall take you out."

"I don't believe a word you say."

"All the more reason for you to go."

"No, no, no!"

Marcus felt a physical turmoil all about him as if the darkness were seething and boiling. He reeled, suddenly unable, after such a long blindness, to keep his balance. "Carel, where are you? Sorry, but I must touch you for a moment. Could you give me your hand? Carel, I'm here. I'm reaching out my hand."

Marcus moved forward, reaching out in front of him in the dark. He touched something cool and fleshy which came to meet him, he clasped it and then uttered a loud cry. Something dropped heavily to the floor. The skirt of the cassock brushed by and Carel laughed.

"What was it?" said Marcus in an incoherent mutter.

"Just a carrot. Flesh of my flesh."

"I think I'd better go," said Marcus.

"Good. This way." A firm hand upon his shoulder propelled him from behind.

As Marcus emerged on to the landing it confusedly occurred to him that he might call out Elizabeth's name. But the darkness daunted him. A cry in that thick obscurity would have been something dreadful. He passed down the stairs and stood submissively while the door was opened. The foggy air opened a cold shaft of space.

"I'll come tomorrow," he said, and found that he was whispering.

"No, don't. Goodbye." A light push propelled him out of the door.

Marcus took a step or two on the icy pavement. He heard the door being bolted behind him. Then his legs gave way and he fell over rather slowly, kneeling and then sitting upon the pavement. As he sat there he saw all the lights go on inside the house.

# *Chapter Eight*

"EXCUSE me, it's Anthea. Anthea Barlow from the pastorate. You remember me. I wonder if—"

"I remember you, Mrs Barlow. If you want the Rector I'm afraid you're unlucky again. He's not seeing any visitors."

"Oh dear. You see I actually—"

"I'm sorry."

Pattie was thoroughly unhappy. She did not like being in London. The fog and the solitude oppressed her terribly. She had now found her way to the shops, but it was a long and tiring journey, and coming back across the building site she always felt nervous. Once she had seen a man standing very still upon the earth near the pavement and had found herself quite unable to walk past him. After a moment or two she had realized that it was Leo Peshkov who had suddenly laughed and vanished away, leaping and waving his arms, into the fog. She found the young man disagreeable and the incident frightened her.

She was also finding her task as doorkeeper an increasing strain. At the other parish people had understood Carel's eccentricities. Here it was often difficult to know what to say. Carel had told her to turn everyone away. The effort was becoming really exhausting. As Carel decreed that the door should not be answered in her absence, she often came back from shopping to find several people hopefully waiting outside. Marcus Fisher had kept on calling, and Mrs Barlow called every day, and there were others who seemed to expect to see the Rector, including a man from some committee who was very disinclined to take no for an answer, especially after he had had it three times. However, Pattie did not complain.

Pattie's anxieties about Carel, which never became anything clear or definite, were growing more intense. At the other parish

88

Carel had been protected by a carapace of custom. He was "that strange Rector" and people were even rather proud of his peculiarities. Here he seemed both more alarming in himself and more utterly unprotected. He stood out, huge and monstrous, from his surroundings, as if he were the only just perceptible inhabitant of some other dimension. He scarcely seemed to be *in* the Rectory at all. And in guarding his door Pattie sometimes felt as if she were shielding a creature which would be automatically attacked by the ordinary people who rang the doorbell should they ever get to know of his existence, crushed in scandalized horror: unless the apparition of Carel should perhaps on the contrary maim or destroy his enemies.

Pattie knew that these were scarcely sensible thoughts. But as she had no defence for herself against the perpetual hostility of the world, so she had no defence for him. The menace came straight through. She was also, on her own account, going through a time of being frightened of him. He was very moody and frequently harsh with her. He had been extremely angry with her for not having locked the door of the coal hole, and so having let in Marcus Fisher, who still appeared to Pattie in memory as a huge Negro. After scolding her, Carel had shaken her and pushed her away from him. Pattie wept for long afterwards in her own room about this. She felt rejected, as if her whole person must have repelled him. It was true that she had not had a bath since she arrived at the new Rectory. The bathroom, which was in the part of the house not served by the central-heating system, was very cold.

Pattie continued to indulge her daydreams of going away and starting life all over again, but they lacked seriousness. They hovered like faintly illuminated strip cartoons at the back of her mind, performing some automatic soothing function as Pattie cleaned the house. A certain amount of new material had been added to these phantom pictures by Eugene Peshkov's stories of his life in the various camps. Pattie pictured herself as a selfless welfare worker, giving her life a meaning by her devotion to those who suffered. Anonymity had been forced upon her. She would make anonymity her glory and her crown. She had of course attended to Eugene's rather cynical remarks about the self-satisfaction of the welfare workers. Must one, really to help the sufferer, suffer oneself? A purely good person would do so automatically just like Jesus Christ did. Eugene had said one would have to be a saint. Well, Pattie might be a saint. How did she know that she was not since she had never tried? Yet wasn't it a desire simply for happiness, for a happiness without guilt which she could enjoy, which made her dream these dreams at all? It was all very confusing.

There was perhaps another reason why Pattie's visions of sanctity were less than urgent. Eugene Peshkov was beginning to occupy a place in her life and in her mind. Pattie had walked straight into a friendship with Eugene like someone walking through an enormous open doorway. She was just surprised to find herself inside. "Getting to know somebody" was usually for Pattie a very difficult task involving a lot of anxiety and effort on her part and which never really emerged from a sort of confusion. In fact, apart from Carel, she had never properly got to know anyone. But she had become completely at ease with Eugene almost straight away. That a sort of complicity of fellow-servants had helped here did not trouble her in the least. She was only sorry that she had not forestalled his calling her "Pattie" and made him call her "Patricia". But then she was not yet worthy to be called "Patricia".

There was a kind of wonderful confidence and completeness in Eugene which attracted everything in Pattie that was tattered and bedraggled. He was so "full of himself". Something glowed out of him, some light perhaps from his very earliest childhood, which seemed everything that Pattie needed and had always lacked. Also he seemed to her an innocent person and this warmed her heart in an almost mysterious way. Pattie coveted his innocence, scarcely knowing what this meant, she rubbed herself dog-like against it. Eugene represented the good clean simple world out of which she had irrevocably slipped. Also she loved his sufferings and envied him their significance. "Hitler", "Prague", these were names which gave sense to what one had suffered. Of course, at the time there had been no sense. But it was a consolation to be able to understand afterwards that something with a name had happened to one. When she had tried to tell Eugene about her own childhood she had failed to make a story. It was all little senseless pieces. His life had its meaning all the way through. The meaning of her life was hidden in the future, in the time when she would become Patricia.

Of course, she had said nothing to Eugene about her relations with Carel. This troubled her very much and in fact prevented her new friendship from sufficing to make her happy. Some very lively and very central part of her responded to Eugene. But all round this, like old thick vegetation, there remained the unintelligible tangle of her involvement with Carel. This was the stuff of which she was made, she was this huge matted thing. Indeed, in some terrible inescapable way she was Carel. The Pattie who was Eugene's friend was just a tiny hopeful puppet inside the real Pattie. Could she ever tell this to Eugene? She thought that she could not.

As Pattie looked down now into the bright eager face of Anthea Barlow she was thinking about Eugene's suggestion that he should take her to see the sea. Would Carel mind? It was extraordinary that such a question could even arise. But still it seemed to her, in a quite separate and special way, a pure and joyful thing that she should some day go with Eugene to see the sea.

"I'm sorry, Mrs Barlow," she said again, and began to close the door.

"I ventured to send him a little note by the post."

"I'm afraid he won't have read it."

"Well, may I come inside just for a second? There's a little something I'd like to leave."

Mrs Barlow had somehow got past Pattie into the hall. Worried, Pattie hesitated and then closed the door. She cast a quick look behind her towards the stairs. The hall was bleak and dim in the light of a single naked electric-light bulb which hung down in its centre, distributing a sort of quasi-luminosity which made things shifty and insubstantial. The furniture was uneasy in the cold watery light. Wicker chairs, a table with bamboo legs, a modern imitation oak chest, stood purposelessly about. Pattie stood in the space and looked at Anthea Barlow. She knew that Anthea Barlow was her enemy.

"Do you mind if I slip my coat off? It's just to feel the benefit, you know, when I go out again. Really, I think it's colder than ever. It's just starting to snow. I find snow so exciting, don't you?"

Pattie now saw that Mrs Barlow's curly black fur coat was covered all over with minute white crystals, as if some very fine lace had been drawn over it. The heavy coat flopped on the back of one of the chairs and from there to the floor. Pattie let it lie.

"What did you want to leave? I'm afraid I'm rather busy."

"Just these snowdrops. A little gift for the Rector. I've ventured to write a scrap of a note to go with them. Aren't they darlings?"

"Mmm," said Pattie.

Mrs Barlow, solid now in a black woollen dress with a diamond-looking clasp shaped like a basket of flowers, had produced a small paper bundle from the recesses of her person. The points of snow upon her fur hat, melted now, were like little glass beads. She handed over the bundle to Pattie. The letter had been pinned to the rustling paper. Peering in as one peers at a baby, Pattie saw the flowers, crisp as white icing or peppermint. They gave off a faint fragrance.

"So sweet, aren't they. February Fair Maids, folklore calls them. They're supposed to bloom on February the second, that's Candlemas Day of course, in honour of Our Lady's purification."

"They're pretty," said Pattie grudgingly.

"These ones have come early, they just couldn't wait! I expect they're from the Scilly Isles. Most of those early flowers are. Little sillies, I always call them!"

"Well, thank you, Mrs Barlow and now—"

"Oh, please let me stay just one more minute. I really won't keep you. There's so much I want to ask. You know this appeal about restoring the church—"

"I don't."

"Oh, I see. I imagined Father Carel would have talked to you about it."

"The Rector has said nothing about it." Pattie resented the familiarity of the title.

"Well, perhaps it's not the sort of thing he'd tell you. Anyway there's this plan to launch a big appeal to restore the church and the idea is that Father Carel is to go to America to appeal for funds—"

"I'm afraid I know nothing about it, Mrs Barlow. And now I really must ask you—" Pattie was afraid that Carel would be very angry with her for having let this troublesome woman into the house. She had an almost superstitious fear that he might come out on to the landing and be seen by the intruder.

"But it's very important. There's this committee meeting tomorrow and that's why I really did want a little word with Father Carel. You don't think—?"

"I'm sorry."

"Is he *ill?*"

"No, he's not ill," said Pattie. She did not like the change of tone. Mrs Barlow was a determined woman and not by any means such a fool as she looked.

"But I mean, well, is he perhaps feeling a little overburdened? We all find life a little too much for us sometimes, don't we? We get a little off our balance, a little depressed, a little—"

"The Rector is perfectly well," said Pattie.

"I'd be so glad to have a chat with him. A sympathetic outsider with a little experience—I might even be able to help. And in fact I'm—"

"Sorry, no," said Pattie.

"I do wish there was anything, *anything* that I could do."

"I'm very busy," said Pattie.

"Well, we are all busy, especially we women. I do wish you'd let me help. Helping people is what I'm for. For instance, I'd be awfully pleased to take Elizabeth out for a run in my car, when the weather's a little better, that is."

"*Elizabeth?*" said Pattie. She stared at Mrs Barlow's rather large and crazily enthusiastic face, damp and flushed a lobster red now with the comparative warmth of the house. "Elizabeth? How do you know anything about Miss Elizabeth?" As she spoke she apprehended Elizabeth, in a way that was familiar to her, as if she were a guilty secret. Often it happened that people did not know of Elizabeth's existence at all. Carel said it was better so. Even Eugene did not yet know that there was another girl in the house. Pattie had been inhibited from telling him partly because "Elizabeth" was also the name of his lost sister.

"Oh well, parish gossip, you know. You can't keep anything private in this parish. A lot of regular old chattermaggers we are, I'm afraid!"

"But it isn't a real parish. There aren't any people. I can't think how—"

"Elizabeth must feel a little dull sometimes. It's so hard on a young girl. I'd be so glad to come and talk to her."

"I think you'd better go, Mrs Barlow."

"Of course, she's got you and Muriel. Quite a family. You must all be very devoted to Father Carel. I know *you* are, Pattie. I may call you Pattie, mayn't I? After all we've met quite a number of times now. You've been with Father Carel a long time, haven't you?"

"Here's your coat," said Pattie. She thrust the damp furry bundle on to Mrs Barlow's black woollen bosom and opened the door wide. The almost total darkness of the afternoon loomed coldly in, and a few very small snowflakes came twisting and turning onto the doormat.

Anthea Barlow sighed and put on her coat. "Ah well. I'm rather a madcap, I'm afraid. You'll get used to me. People do."

She looked at Pattie and then smiled appealingly, holding out a hand sideways in a way which invites, not a formal handshake, but the warm spontaneous clasp of friend with friend. Pattie ignored the hand.

"I shall come again," murmured Anthea Barlow.

She went out into the darkness and a just audible movement of snowflakes covered her departing form. Pattie shut the door and bolted it. Then she listened and heard with relief from upstairs the distant strains of the Nutcracker Suite.

She took the paper off the snowdrops and dropped it, together with Mrs Barlow's note, into a wastepaper basket. She had no intention of troubling Carel with Mrs Barlow's importunities. She decided that she would give the snowdrops to Eugene. She looked at them. A clear line of the purest palest green was drawn round the scolloped rim of each drooping white cup. The flowers had a sudden presence, an authority. Pattie looked down at them with surprise. She saw them as *flowers*. They made, in the continuum of dark days, a pause, a gap as it were, through which she saw so much more than the springtime. Calling the lapséd soul, and weeping in the evening dew, that might control the starry pole and fallen, fallen light renew.

Holding the snowdrops lightly against her overall she moved to the window. A complicated frost picture was forming on the inside of the pane. She scratched it with her finger, making a round hole in the sugary frost, and looked through. The snow, just visible in the dusky yellow dark, was falling thickly now, the flakes turning slightly as they fell, composing together a huge rotating pattern too complex for the eye, which seemed to extend itself persuasively and enter the body with a sighing hypnotic caress. The whole world was very quietly spiralling and shifting. Pattie stood dazed and looked out at the snow for a long time.

Suddenly behind her in the house she heard a loud cry and the sound of opening doors and running feet. Someone was urgently calling out her name.

She turned quickly back to see Eugene, who had rushed into the hall, huge and distracted, his arms waving.

"Oh, Pattie, Pattie, it's gone!"

"What's gone?"

"My icon. Somebody's stolen it. I left the door unlocked. Somebody's stolen it away!"

"Oh dear, oh dear," said Pattie. She opened her arms to him. He came straight to her and she hugged him. The snowdrops were crushed between them. Somewhere up above a head and shoulders moved in the dark. She smelt the perfume of the snowdrops crushed upon Eugene's breast. She went on hugging him and saying "Oh dear, oh dear, oh dear."

# Chapter Nine

THE treacle tart was brown and crisp on top, golden and succulent and granular once the surface had yielded to the spoon. The Bishop covered his portion evenly with cream and delicately licked a finger. "One must not exaggerate," he said.

Marcus stared gloomily at the tart. It was his favourite pudding. Only today he was without appetite.

Since his visit to Carel he had been in an extremely disturbed state. He had imagined that his boldness would procure him some automatic liberation, the switching on of some immediate calm. He had even imagined, with a naïvety which came straight out of his childhood, that Carel was reserving for him, like an enormous treat, some quite special reassurance. What had come to him from that darkened encounter was a more fearful because more unintelligible agitation. He could not but regard it as significant that there had been no light. His desire now simply to see Carel's face had become obsessively connected with a fear that he should find his brother disfigured or monstrously changed. Carel and Elizabeth haunted his dreams, huge obscure figures whose doings he could not afterwards remember. Hitherto he had at least been able to think of them separately. Now in some compulsive way which he could not quite understand he thought of them together, and the new connection, the new pattern had somehow the effect of a *perpetuum mobile*. Marcus could not perceive the principle of this machine which so jerked him to and fro, but he felt it had something to do with Carel's remark that Elizabeth "lived in her mind".

Marcus did not know what was intended by the remark, but it did not occur to him to believe, or even conjecture, that Elizabeth was in fact out of her mind. What did come to him afterwards, obscure and disturbing as a large unpleasant-looking object rising through deep water, was the idea that Carel was out of his. Marcus

97

had never before for a second, however much he had heard it reiterated by Norah, entertained the view that his brother was insane. If it was not madness then there was only one other thing which it could be.

These reflections were entirely new to Marcus, and he was amazed at how far he had come, or how far he had been rather as it were shot, through the violence of his meeting with Carel. Yet he could, he felt, have confronted rationally any possibility, any conjecture, concerning insanity or concerning that which was worse, if it had involved Carel alone. It was the addition of Elizabeth to the situation which made it tormentingly problematic and constituted the distressful machine which now gave him no rest. He needed desperately to see Elizabeth. Her image burnt in his mind, a steely dazzling point of pure innocence. It was not that he at all coherently thought of her as menaced. What he felt was very much more like some sort of monstrous jealousy.

He regretted having spoken of his experience to Norah. He had recounted simply the facts of the conversation and had made no attempt to render the atmosphere, nor had he, for some reason, brought himself to tell her that it had all taken place in the dark. But even this much he ought not to have told. He ought to have kept it all covered up and let its chemistry work within him in secret. On this subject Norah could utter only blasphemies. And utter them she did crowingly, understanding everything at the crudest level and frankly exulting at having acquired some more, and she imagined conclusive ,"evidence" for her case.

"I trust I am *not* exaggerating, Bishop," Norah was saying.

The Bishop had small hands and feet and a clean boyish face. It annoyed Marcus to hear Norah calling him "Bishop". He himself had started calling him "Sir" and had then realized with irritation that the Bishop was probably younger than he was. Marcus was at the age when he was still scandalized to find a younger person in a position of authority.

"As I see it," Norah went on, "it's a matter of responsibility to the public, to say nothing of the Church itself. It's highly dangerous for an unbalanced man to have that sort of power. Anything could happen. There must be ecclesiastical machinery for at least investigating a case of this sort."

"Well, well, who is to say in these days who is mad and who is sane? Let him who is without neurosis cast the first stone! What an absolutely delicious treacle tart. I find so few people are prepared to take trouble with puddings these days."

"You ask who is to say," said Norah. She was beginning to get a little cross with the Bishop. "I answer that I am prepared to say. Tolerance can go too far and in my view nowadays usually does. A spade must be called a spade. We are confronted here by a man who is both mad and wicked."

"Can he actually be both?" said Marcus. He had not so far managed to get himself into the conversation.

"I should certainly call Carel an *eccentric*," said the Bishop. "The Anglican Church has been noted for its eccentrics. In the eighteenth century—"

"We are not, thank heavens," said Norah, "living in the eighteenth century."

It disturbed Marcus that the Bishop referred to his brother as "Carel" although it appeared that they had only met twice.

"I shouldn't worry too much, Miss Shadox-Brown. As the psalmist says, 'verily every man at his best state is altogether vanity.' Otherwise rendered, it'll all come out in the wash! No thanks, no more tart. I have rather wolfed mine, haven't I. I'd love some of that delicious crumbly cheese."

"Well, I think *something* ought to be done," said Norah. She slid the cheeseboard briskly up to the Bishop's plate. "Naturally we thought we'd consult you first. But Marcus will have to take some steps about Elizabeth. After all he *is* her guardian and he must be allowed to see her. I am certainly going to take legal advice."

"I don't think we should be too hasty," said Marcus. He was

99

annoyed and distressed and almost frightened by a vision of Norah, lawyers, even police, interfering in something as intensely private as what his relation with Carel and Elizabeth had now become. He regretted not having utterly discouraged Norah from the start.

"I agree with Marcus," said the Bishop. "It's easy to make an ill-considered fuss. Not so easy to pick up the pieces afterwards. Do you mind if I help myself to some more of that superb claret?"

Oh, so I'm Marcus now, am I, thought Marcus. The Bishop was a fast worker. It was a professional facility.

"My point would be that the fuss would not be ill-considered," said Norah. "And I'm very surprised that you aren't more interested in what Carel said to Marcus about having lost his faith." This had already been recounted verbatim.

"Belief is such a personal matter, especially in these days," said the Bishop vaguely.

"He may have been pulling my leg," said Marcus.

"You know quite well he wasn't," said Norah. "He was being downright cynical. A priest, calmly announcing that he doesn't believe in God!"

"Well, if I may say so without frivolity, it rather depends on the tone that is used! I understand you are writing a book on the subject, Marcus?"

"Not exactly, sir," said Marcus. He felt like a schoolboy being interrogated and noted with annoyance his conditioned reactions. "I'm not writing about God. I'm writing about morality. Though I am going to devote a chapter to the ontological argument."

"Excellent, excellent. The only sound argument in the whole of theology, in my humble view, only don't quote me! I'm so glad. We need all the help we can get."

"But I'm not a Christian," said Marcus.

"Well, you know, the dividing lines are not by any means as clear as they used to be. Passion, Kierkegaard said, didn't he, passion. That's the necessary thing. We must remember that the

Holy Spirit bloweth where it listeth. It's not the gale, it's the windless calm that is Godless. 'Where's the bloody horse?' if you follow me!"

"But there's still a difference between believing in God and not believing in God," said Norah.

"Oh, certainly. But perhaps this difference is not quite what we once thought it was. We must think of this time as an inter-regnum—"

"Whatever Carel believes," said Marcus, "he certainly believes it with passion."

"Precisely. I would myself conjecture that your brother is a profoundly religious man," said the Bishop.

"Oh, rubbish!" said Norah.

"But what is it that he believes?" said Marcus. "That still matters, doesn't it?"

"Well, yes and no," said the Bishop. He was scraping the cheese out of his ring with a delicate finger nail.

"What about Jesus Christ?" said Norah.

The Bishop frowned slightly. "As I was saying, we have to consider this time as an interregnum. It is a time when, as one might put it, mankind is growing up. The particular historical nature of Christianity poses intellectual problems which are also spiritual problems. Much of the symbolism of theology which was an aid to understanding in earlier and simpler times is, in this scientific age, simply a barrier to belief. It has become something positively misleading. Our symbolism must change. This after all is nothing new, it is a necessity which the Church has always understood. God lives and works in history. The outward mythology changes, the inward truth remains the same."

"You haven't exactly answered my question," said Norah, "but never mind. I think if you're going to ditch Jesus you ought to say so in plain terms. The religion *is* the myth."

"No mystic has ever thought so," said the Bishop, "and whom can we better believe? 'Meek darkness be thy mirror'. Those who have come nearest to God have spoken of blackness, even of emptiness. Symbolism falls away. There is a profound truth here. Obedience to God must be an obedience without trimmings, an obedience, in a sense, for nothing."

"I'd rather say he doesn't exist and be done with it," said Norah. "But are we all supposed to become mystics then?"

"It is a time of trial," said the Bishop. "Many are called but few are chosen. The Church will have to endure a very painful transformation. And things will become worse yet before they are better. We shall sorely need our faith. But the Lord will turn again the captivity of Zion."

"That's as may be," said Norah. "I think myself this scientific age needs to hear more about morality and less about the Lord."

The Bishop smiled. "I am not speaking of course about a person," he said. "A person could be dispensed with. Indeed must be dispensed with. What we have to experience is not the destruction but the purification of our beliefs. The human spirit has certain deep needs. Do not misunderstand me when I say that morality is not enough. It was the mistake of the Enlightenment to imagine that God could be characterized simply as the guarantor of the moral order. But our need for God is something which transcends morality. The slightest acquaintance with modern psychology shows us that this is not a slogan but a fact. We are less naïve than we were about goodness. We are less naïve than we were about sanctity. What measures man as a spiritual being is not his conventional goodness and badness but the genuineness of his hunger for God. How does Jehovah answer Job? 'Where wast thou when I laid the foundations of the earth?' is not an argument which concerns morality."

"Well, I've always thought it a very bad argument," said Norah. "Goodness is good conduct and we all know what that is. I think you people are playing with fire. Coffee?"

The turn of the conversation had upset Marcus. He did not like to hear the Bishop talking like this, he was almost shocked by it.

It occurred to him now how much it mattered to him that all that business should still go on in the old way. He did not believe in the redeeming blood of Jesus, he did not believe in the Father and the Son and the Holy Ghost, but he wanted other people to believe. He wanted the old structure to continue there beside him, near by, something he could occasionally reach out and touch with his hand. But now it seemed that behind the scenes it was all being unobtrusively dismantled. That they should be deciding that God was not a person, that they should be quietly demoting Jesus Christ, this made him feel almost frightened.

Norah was saying something, offering him a coffee-cup. A ship's siren was booming on the river, somewhere outside in the foggy dark. The warm well-lighted well-curtained room seemed suddenly to be spinning with the immobile motion of a top. Marcus gripped the table. "But suppose," he said to the Bishop, "suppose the truth about human life were just something terrible, something appalling which one would be destroyed by contemplating? You've taken away all the guarantees."

The Bishop laughed. "That's where faith comes in."

"The supposition is meaningless," said Norah. "Here, take your coffee."

# Chapter Ten

MURIEL finished reading, tossed the last sheet down, and looked at Elizabeth. She had read out some twenty stanzas and had found herself extraordinarily moved by her own poem. Towards the end her voice had quite faltered with emotion.

They were sitting on the floor on either side of the fire in Elizabeth's room. The chaise-longue, against which Elizabeth was leaning her back, faced the fireplace and boxed them snugly in. Muriel, who was sitting up against the Chinese screen, switched off the reading-lamp behind her. The blazing fire sufficiently lit the room, casting quick splashes of golden light on to Elizabeth's face and making fugitive shadows rush to the corners of the ceiling. The curtains were pulled though it was still afternoon.

There was a silence. Then Elizabeth said, "It's rather *obscure* isn't it?"

"I don't think it's obscure. It's not half as obscure as most modern stuff."

"Have you made a plan of the whole thing?"

"No, I told you. It just grows."

"Wouldn't it be a good idea to know where you're going?"

"I'd rather not."

"I wonder if you *are* in love with somebody."

"I'm not in love! I've told you that too."

Muriel desperately wanted Elizabeth to tell her that the poem was good. That was all that she wanted to hear. Now with a dull half-conscious obstinacy which Muriel felt and saw as clearly as if it were a physical emanation Elizabeth was preparing to say anything and everything about the poem except that.

"Oh, it doesn't matter!" said Muriel. She got up abruptly,

crumpled the scattered sheets together in her hand and threw them over the back of the chaise-longue. Then she said, "Sorry, Elizabeth."

Elizabeth seemed not to have noticed. She sat staring into the fire, her eyes huge with some kind of private puzzlement. She shifted restlessly, undulating her body, caressing her legs. A long sigh turned into a yawn. Then she said "Ye-e-es" half under her breath. Muriel looked down at her with exasperation. She hated these times when Elizabeth was "switched off". It seemed to her that they came more often now. A sort of apathetic coldness, a vagueness, would drift over her cousin like a cloud. Her limbs would creep and twitch, her eyes fail to focus, and her will be present only as an animal determination to evade contact, to deny satisfaction. All that remained undimmed then was her beauty, which glowed with the soft chill of a wax effigy. There was still something dreadfully fascinating about this artificial deadened Elizabeth.

Was the poem any good, Muriel wondered. Could one really tell with one's own stuff? She was well aware of that golden glow of ideal intention which, for the artist, covers so often the achieved reality of his own art so that it is hard to see the contours of what he has done amid the shimmering lights of what he might have done. Sometimes she felt that her work was good, and felt, what was perhaps even more important, that she was on the road, that she had got a technique and knew how to improve. She was no longer a scribbler down of random inspirations. She knew now how to work, steadily and for hours on end, like a carpenter or a shoemaker. She could dissolve and reassemble her best felicities without a craven fear of spoiling them. She could even a little compel and invite those dark regions out of which the images drifted like miraculous kites. She felt all this at times. At other times, and for no special reason, it was all dust and ashes. She had a versifying facility but there was nothing solid there upon which she could rest a lever to lift herself up into the free air of real poetry, though she should work till doomsday. It would all end in nothing.

Muriel had been amused and then annoyed by Elizabeth's insistence earlier in the day that Muriel must be in love. This was something in fact which Elizabeth said at regular intervals, interpreting as symptoms some trifling vagueness or some ephemeral euphoria on her cousin's part. Muriel was always touched on these occasions by a sense that Elizabeth exclaimed so much about it because she constantly feared that it might happen. Muriel provided the reassurance that was wanted, and the subject was dropped. This time, however, Elizabeth was being more than usually hard to convince. "Who, after all, could I possibly be in love with?" Muriel had asked her. Elizabeth had looked enigmatic and had later interrupted the reading of the poem to point out that Muriel's verses were a further piece of evidence.

Muriel had reflected a good deal afterwards about her curious encounter with Leo Peshkov. Since the scene by the river she had seen little of him, she thought he had been away, neither had sought the other's company. The scene itself had amused her, even excited her by a harsh bizarre quality, a touch of an oddness, which she felt missing from her life; but about the boy she felt detached to the point of coldness. His physical youthfulness repelled her and she found his pertness and his affected cynicism unattractive. Muriel had in her constitution a kind of dignity which demanded slow approaches, reticences, subtlety. With a younger person too it was essential that she should be in control. She could not altogether forgive Leo for having surprised her, though she laughed a little about it as well. She was prepared to be "amused" by Leo and to admire his beauty as she might have admired an animal or a work of art. But on the whole she found him "juvenile" and there was nothing about him which touched her heart.

When Elizabeth had started this latest "you're in love" campaign the image that had in fact quite suddenly surged up, startling Muriel for a moment, had been that of Eugene Peshkov. Of course

Muriel was not in love, least of all with a broken-down janitor, old enough to be her father, with whom she had only talked a few times. Yet some warmth of which the source was Eugene did for her pervade the house. Some plainness about him, some absolute simplicity attracted her. He seemed to represent that world of thoughtless affections and free happy laughter and dogs passing by in the street from which she felt herself to be totally separated. Sometimes she thought, but hopelessly, that it might be just this separation which damned her poetry. Whatever the barrier was, Eugene was on the other side of it, an emblem of something which Muriel wanted but which her nature forbade her to have. But also simply as himself he moved her, she liked his drooping moustaches, his old-fashioned politeness, the curious way he bowed to her, his big bland kindly face and his extremely dirty corduroy trousers. He was an utterly harmless and friendly presence, like a Russian house spirit, or Domovoi, whose picture she had once seen in a book of mythology. Muriel was moved too by his history, she felt whole-heartedly sorry for him, and she had been especially upset by the recent theft of his precious icon. She was beginning to want to touch him, to stroke him consolingly. But of course this did not amount to being in love, it was just that the prospect of getting to know him was a pleasant one. Once or twice seeking him out in his room she had been inordinately irritated to find Pattie there.

Beyond Elizabeth's dreaming head, eyes closed now, alternately darkened and made to shine like a shaft of goldened aluminium, was a vase of flowers, chrysanthemums, which had been sent to Elizabeth by Uncle Marcus. The girls had composed a number of thank-you notes, each wittier than the last, but none had been sent yet. Elizabeth particularly disliked chrysanthemums. They would have to see Uncle Marcus sooner or later, Muriel supposed. Elizabeth was indifferent. Muriel had not spoken to her father about this or indeed about anything else for some days. She was aware that he was seeing nobody. Callers, determined or even desperate ones, including the wailful Mrs Barlow, were all turned away. Letters were unanswered and in fact unread. Muriel was vaguely uneasy, but she had seen her father in such moods before. She herself would have to form a policy soon about Uncle Marcus and Shadox. Of course there was no question of their seeing Elizabeth until Carel permitted. Muriel would have to see them though, placate them perhaps. There was no hurry. She was always a bit fussed at the thought of meeting Shadox. She disliked, but also a little feared, that dreadfully robust common sense. There was the faint but ever-persistent possibility that Shadox might be right.

As Muriel stood looking down at Elizabeth's still spellbound head she leaned back a little against the angle of the wall where it turned into the alcove where the bed was. Her hand groping behind her touched the place where the two partitions joined and she felt the crack in the wallpaper, the place from which in the linen room one might peep through into Elizabeth's room, into her room and into the further darker subaqueous cave of the French mirror. Muriel removed her hand guiltily. She thought immediately of Elizabeth's corset and for a second she seemed to see it, to see her cousin X-rayed, hollowed out, a skeletal maiden of steel with a metal head. The vision excited her strangely. She banished it the next moment and began to think about Elizabeth's illness. There was so much fatalism now in her thoughts. Did she really believe that Elizabeth would ever be well or able to lead a normal life?

They had all become so used to shielding Elizabeth, to keeping her with them as a sort of hidden treasure. Was there something odd and unnatural about it? It occurred to Muriel that what made the whole régime seem simple and ordinary was Elizabeth's own attitude to it, her co-operation, her even gay co-operation, in what, with another twist, might have seemed an imprisonment. Yet had this too, lately, imperceptibly, changed? Perhaps Elizabeth, with growing up, had become more fully conscious of her plight, of an awful separation from life. Perhaps she had soberly judged by now that she would never be cured, never be healthy and free. This might account for the increasing apathy, the slight withdrawal of warmth, which afflicted Muriel and made her feel for the first time and on her own account a sort of claustrophobia, a sense of being shut in somewhere with her cousin. Elizabeth had for so long played the gay child, the sunshine of the house. It startled Muriel to find herself, as she now regarded the drowsing entranced head, seeing something different, something even a little alarming. La Belle Dame sans Merci.

Of course this was nonsense. Her imagination was becoming morbid. The interminable fog was making them all a bit nervy. Still it was true that Elizabeth was living an absurdly isolated life. She ought to meet more people, she ought to meet young men. She ought not to be immured to the point at which communication became difficult. Should they not, before it was too late, break out? Muriel was surprised to find how strongly she took to this metaphor. What exactly was there to break out of? What was she afraid of here which made her dream vaguely of an escape, a rescue, a shock which might dissolve barriers and bring to something which seemed dark and cramped the sudden light of change?

Muriel shook herself and began to pick up the scattered papers from the floor. She said quietly to Elizabeth, "My dear."

"Mmm?"

"I must go and shop for us, otherwise we'll have to have eggs again. I'll be about an hour, in case you thought of ringing."

'Mmmm."

"I'll take the plates away. Sorry they got left."

"I hadn't noticed them."

"Can I get you anything special?"

"No thank you, sweetheart."

"I'll bring you a little present."

"You're sweet."

"The fire should be all right till I get back. Don't try to lift that coal-scuttle yourself."

"I wonder if it's still snowing."

"I think it's stopped."

"I wish it would snow properly. I feel it would drive the fog away. I haven't been able to look out of my window since we arrived."

"I know, darling. Soon will. Oughtn't you to write to Uncle Marcus?"

"Maybe. Shove over my cigars, would you."

"What will you do while I'm away?"

"Jigsaw. Nothing. More likely nothing."

"I won't be long. Don't smoke too much."

The eyes were closed again as Muriel moved to the door. She went out quietly. Outside the linen room she paused. What was Elizabeth like when she was alone? For a second Muriel visualized some extraordinary change which might come over her cousin as soon as the door was shut upon her. Some metamorphosis from passivity into activity, from calm into despair. Suppose she were to creep in and look through the crack? She hurried herself on. Spying was a meanness she could not stoop to. But it was not just that. She would be afraid to look.

Muriel dumped the lunch plates in the upstairs pantry and went to her own room, where it was extremely cold, and put on her overcoat. She locked the room after her, a precaution she used since the recent theft, though the only things which she feared to lose were her poems and her bottle of sleeping-pills which she imagined nobody would want to steal. She came down the stairs to the strains of the Eighteen Twelve Overture. A softly closing door cut them off. The image of Elizabeth faded. Muriel decided that she would just go and ask Eugene Peshkov if she could buy him anything at the shops. She had asked him this several times. He always said no, but it was a pretext for seeing him and Muriel regretted that since the dreadful loss of his icon she had not had an opportunity to condole with him properly. Also she wanted, just now, a reassurance, the reassurance of Eugene's presence in the house.

The annexe with the boiler room was reached through a windowless corridor beyond the kitchen where unshaded electric light burnt day and night. A smell of coal and incense pervaded this tunnel. Muriel went through and stopped outside Eugene's door. At once, with a sudden sharp pain, she heard Pattie's voice inside the room.

"Looking for me?"

"No." Muriel did not turn round. She affected to be looking for something in her handbag.

"But you must be," said Leo. "I'd say you were. Won't you walk into my parlour? I've been like Mariana in the Moated Grange just waiting for you to come."

Leo edged round Muriel, touching her very lightly on the shoulder, and went to open the farthest door. He stood on the threshold invitingly. Muriel hesitated and then walked into the room. She could still feel the place on her shoulder where Leo had touched her.

"What are you scowling at?"

"I'm not scowling," she said.

The room, which was very warm, was a high box with walls of brown crumbly cement which made it seem like a space hewn in sandy soil. An uncurtained window above head level was dark. A cream-shaded bulb attached to the ceiling gave a pearly light. Chinese rush matting covered the floor. A low narrow divan bed was covered with a printed Indian coverlet. Three wooden stools stood in a row against the wall. In one corner a trim one-deep pile of books reached up to the level of the window. A plain oak chest with an embroidered cushion on it stood behind the door. Two Japanese prints of galloping horses were stuck on to the wall above the bed. There was nothing else in the room except a chess board upon the floor. There was no table.

Muriel was slightly surprised by the room. "You're neat."

"I'm practising to change my sex."

"Where do you do your work?"

"My *what?*"

"I see you play chess."

"I have to pretend to for professional reasons. Do you?"

"Yes, but I'm not much good." In fact Muriel played quite well, but she had never been able to persuade Elizabeth to learn. She decided at once that she would never play with Leo. He might win.

"We must have a game. Won't you sit down? One sits on the floor here. The stools are just symbolic." Leo sat down cross-legged with his back against the bed.

Muriel hesitated again. She wondered if Pattie was through with Eugene yet.

"Tell me one thing truly for once, Leo. Did your father have a title when he was in Russia?"

"A title? Good heavens no. I didn't imagine you were one of those people who think all émigré Russians have titles."

"A pity," said Muriel. "He has such dignity. He ought to have been a prince."

"What about me? Couldn't I be a prince too?"

"You—!"

"All right. I'm a democrat. A materialist. A scientist. A post-atomic man."

"I see your books are all science fiction. Haven't you any serious books?"

"In pawn. Sit down, you serious girl. Or are you afraid to?"

Muriel sat down against the wall with her legs tucked under her and stared at Leo who stared at her. Leo was dressed in jeans and a white high-necked Irish sweater. He looked formidably spare and neat, like his room. Muriel studied his face. He had a short faintly freckled nose, rather full lips, and eyes of an extremely light luminous grey. His reddish-gold hair, thick but cut very short, growing well down on to his neck, was as glossy as healthy fur.

"You're quite good-looking," said Muriel.

"Are you going to reward me for it?"

"Why should you be rewarded? You seem to live in a world of rewards and punishments."

"You owe me something,"

"Why?"

"Because you deny me yourself."

"As you have no claim on me I owe you nothing if I keep myself."

"Then reward me just for being beautiful. I have so few pleasures."

"I have nothing else to give."

"A solitary girl has infinite gifts. A secret rose tossed from a window, a perfumed handkerchief that flutters down, as if by accident—Ah, those were the days."

Muriel recalled again the curious fact that Leo was evidently still unaware of Elizabeth's existence.

"What do you want to be given?"

"Well, I'm a modest boy. A virgin most of all. But if you haven't one handy I'll settle for one of your shoes. Not the sensible variety if possible. Did you know I was a fetishist?"

A strange idea had come into Muriel's head. Supposing she were to introduce this beautiful animal to Elizabeth? The idea, even before it had announced itself clearly, was significant and exciting. Elizabeth was asleep, spellbound. Why not awaken her with a shock, with this shock?

The next moment Muriel told herself it was impossible, idiotic, dangerous. Carel would never agree to Elizabeth's seeing Leo. Leo was much too, the word occurred to her, real, too grossly, too discordantly real. Carel only approved of very dim and effaced young men as visitors for Elizabeth, and he was unlikely in his present mood to sanction any visitors at all. Besides, could Elizabeth stand such a shock without being seriously upset? She was so used now to the absolutely familiar routine, the muted and harmonious ceremony of slow movements and low voices.

But was that not just the trouble? The closed system which encircled her like a dance in slow motion was exactly what had made her sleepy. It was what had made her sleepy and what had made Muriel feel of late that she was stifling, that she was herself a captive. They had held their breath for Elizabeth long enough. It was time for something noisy and unexpected, for something a little unpredictable and entirely new. Leo was noisy, unexpected, unpredictable and new. Muriel's imagination juxtaposed them. The image was pleasurable.

"Fresh air," said Muriel.

"What?"

"Sorry, I was thinking aloud."

Would her father be very angry? Well, did it matter if her father was very angry? Was it not time that something was done in the house which had not been minutely scrutinized and authorized in the slow darkness of Carel's mind, so that it seemed at last that they were all just the shadows of his thoughts? Elizabeth had not seen a single presentable young man since she had grown up. O brave new world!

Of course it would shake Elizabeth, and she might even resent something so sudden. But why should not Elizabeth be shaken, shaken out of that menacing drowsiness? A shake, a shock, would do them all good. It would be something invigorating, exciting. With Leo as her delightful tool Muriel would move to the attack. Why did it now seem so like a sweet warfare? Well, she would make war upon her cousin. And here in a way Leo's lack of seriousness made him the ideal implement. Leo would further the game, but there could be no complications, no infections, no muddle. Nothing dangerous could happen. With Leo she would procure Elizabeth an experience. She would procure herself an experience.

"You say you've ditched your girl friend?"

"Absolutely. I'm for sale."

"Supposing I were to tell you," said Muriel, speaking slowly, "of a beautiful and solitary virgin hidden away in a dark house?"

"I'd say you were having me on."

"You don't know about my cousin Elizabeth?"

"Your what?"

"I'm not the only girl in the Rectory. There is another girl here, younger and more beautiful. My cousin."

"You mean here, within these walls, now?"

"Yes."

Leo stood up. He looked startled, almost frightened. "Another girl. *Really?*"

"Yes, really, Leo."

"This is a joke."

"No it isn't."

"But why haven't I seen her?"

"She's been a bit ill. Nothing serious, a rather tiresome back. She keeps to her room at present." The corset. Should she tell Leo about the corset? The idea of telling him was curiously exciting.

"But why is she hidden away? Why is she kept a secret?"

"She's not kept a secret. It was pure accident you didn't know about her."

"That odd bell I've sometimes heard ringing. Was that her?"

"Yes."

"A girl with a bell. How old is she?"

"Nineteen."

"And is she really beautiful?"

"Very beautiful."

"And a virgin?"

"Yes. In fact she's hardly met any men at all."

"Does she know about me?"

"Yes." It was a half truth.

Leo had resumed his normal face. "Lead me to her!"

"Not so fast," said Muriel. "You must take certain vows first of all."

"I'll vow anything."

"First you must promise to be guided by me and to obey me absolutely. Elizabeth has led a very solitary life. She must be treated very gently and ceremoniously."

"What does ceremoniously mean? That I can't even kiss her?"

"She and I will decide that. You'll find her very different from the little nitwits at your college."

"You're not going to be there all the time, are you?"

Muriel had not even reflected about this. Now the idea of being there all the time seemed rather pleasant. Of course nothing was really going to *happen*. "No, of course not. Not if you behave well."

"I hope I won't have to behave too well."

"But you promise to obey me?"

"Yes, all right, I promise."

"Good. Now the second thing. You must have no ties or other complications of any kind. Elizabeth deserves your complete attention, otherwise it's not on. What about that business you asked me for money for? Was that true, by the way?"

"Oh that. That's all over. I fixed it. The little job's been done. The girl is free. She's got another boy already."

"Where did you get the money from?" said Muriel.

Leo stared at her and then made a grimace and abruptly turned away. He moved into the corner of the room and inclined his forehead to the wall.

"Go on, Leo."

"Shall I confess?"

"Yes, confess. I'm unshockable."

"Will you keep it dark?"

"Maybe."

"Well, you know that old religious picture my poppa was so keen on? I took it and sold it."

"Good God!" said Muriel. She pulled herself to her knees and stood up.

"Naughty, was it?"

"How could you have been so utterly rotten!"

Leo twisted his head round. "I thought you were unshockable. Anyway you yourself suggested I should steal something."

"I didn't mean it. And to steal that, to steal from your own father, to take away something he loved so much—"

"The Roman Catholic Church says children can't steal from their parents. It's a matter of concepts."

"You know quite well it's stealing."

"Well, then, fathers are just the ones to steal from. I explained to you last time about fathers."

"Does he know you took it?"

"No, of course not. What would be the point of telling him? He'd just be peevish."

"I think it's the meanest, rottenest thing I've ever heard of."

"I thought you were outside all those old conventions. You aren't being very clear-headed, are you, my dear?"

"Don't talk rubbish. How much did you get for it?"

"Just what I needed. Seventy-five pounds."

"And they just gave it to you? It's probably worth far more."

"I told you I was a modest boy."

"You must get it back," said Muriel. "You must get it back even if you have to steal it back."

Leo pulled himself out of the corner and sat down on the bed. "Now you're really muddling me."

"You sold it to a shop?"

"Yes, a classy antique shop in Shepherd's Market."

"I hope to God they haven't got rid of it already. You *must* get it back. Leo, how *could* you!"

"Quite easily, old dear. I told you I needed a great big liberating act. That was it. Down with fathers."

"You don't mean it. You know you've acted rottenly. You can't jump out of morality as easily as that."

"Can't I, Muriel? Have you ever heard of quasars?"

"What?"

"Quasars. They're a kind of star. Never mind. Just you cast an eye on the universe and then talk to me about morality. Suppose we're all being directed from somewhere else by remote control? Suppose we're just frogspawn in somebody's pond?"

"Well, and suppose we're not. You don't mean any of this rubbish. You're ashamed. You must be."

Leo stared up at Muriel with a blank bland expression. "I may be prepared to enact shame. Will that do?"

"You must go to your father and tell him."

"Prodigal son act?"

"You must say you're sorry. You must *be* sorry. And you must get that icon back somehow, *get it back*."

"I shall have other things to do. I'm just going to meet your virginal cousin."

"Oh no, you're not."

"You promised!"

"I didn't. It was a very bad idea. Oh God, I'm so *confused*." Muriel put her hands to her face as if to find tears which she suddenly heard in her voice.

"Please. Look, if I confess to my dad and if I get the bloody icon back will you let me have your cousin?"

"Well, if you do those things I might let you meet her. Otherwise not. And that's definite."

"A quest! A quest! It's on. I'll take my chance. I'll even take my chance on your estimate of her beauty."

"Leo, Leo, I just don't understand you. How *could* you have deliberately hurt your father so much."

"Quasars, Muriel, quasars, quasars, quasars!"

# Chapter Eleven

"WELL, I must go," said Pattie. "I've been here for *ages*. I don't know when I've talked so much to anybody. You must think I'm a regular chatterbox. But I never talk usually."

"Don't go, Pattie."

"I must."

"When will you come again?"

"Soon. After all, I'm in the house, aren't I?"

Eugene held out his hand to Pattie. He had now established a ritual of hand-shake greetings. It was a way of touching her. He enclosed her hand and his fingers momentarily caressed her wrist. He let her go reluctantly and she whisked out of the door with a wave and a smile.

Eugene fussed a little about his room. He stacked up the cups and saucers and brushed the cake crumbs off the furry green table-cloth. Pattie had eaten four cakes. He watered the potted plant. He had taken to watering it rather too often since the icon had gone. He noticed that the leaves were turning yellow. Then he sat down on a chair and looked up at the empty space where the icon had been.

Where was it now? It was odd to think that it was *somewhere*. He would have preferred to think it had ceased to exist. He seemed to see it suffering, yearning, calling out vainly for him in a little voice, weeping miraculous tears. Of course this was idiotic, it was childish. The thing was only a bit of wood. He must have some sense of proportion, some sense of scale about his loss. He had tried to prompt Pattie into telling him so, but she was far too sympathetic to understand his cues. It was no good expecting brisk and bracing talk from Pattie. He would have to tell himself that it was only an old picture, after all. He had had real losses and survived them. Why this ridiculous grief now? He was better off without the thing. Perhaps he had prized it too much. It was his last real possession and it had shielded him from the knowledge that he had lost everything.

Yes, he thought, that was it. A sense of possession, a sense of being clothed, which he ought long ago to have surrendered had remained to him because of the icon. That object had seemed to concentrate, to keep with him somehow symbolically, all that he had lost, his dear ones, the years of his life, Russia. So long as he had it these things did not seem utterly gone. Yet should he not have known it, then and all along, that he was a man who had lost everything? There was nothing reserved or kept. What he had loved and valued had ceased entirely to be. What feebleness in him had deferred the message till now? Let it go, let it go. Now he was a stripped man and the better for knowing it. So he told himself; but he could not yet really think in this way. The icon had travelled so far and so long with his family, like a dear good animal. He kept grieving about it, pitying it, pitying himself and wanting consolation.

Pattie had supplied some of this. Her exclamations of distress were constantly renewed on his behalf as with raised hands she bewailed his loss. He had talked to her incoherently about the icon and had gone on to tell her more about his family, about his mother, about his sister. He had said things which he had thought could not be said or told any more. This bound Pattie to him. Some of his substance had passed into her. Of course she could not understand. She could not be an ageing Russian émigré with Europe in the bowels. But she knew about deprivation, and she looked at him with her dark reddish eyes all round and moist with concern and she smiled and nodded out of her drift of black hair and leaned sighing towards him as if so much sympathy was a physical pain.

He had tried to make her talk about herself, and she had told him a little about her early childhood. But she had said she had forgotten herself as a child and that as an adult she had had no history. She said once, "I haven't begun to exist yet." I will make you exist, Eugene had said to himself confidently. He had begun to want to touch Pattie. He did touch her, not only in handshakes, but in fugitive secretive ways, acting as if he were unaware of himself, tapping her arm as he told a tale, stroking her shoulder when he offered her some tea. He had plans for touching her hair. These touches made a sort of physical pattern in the room, a tantalizing incomplete Pattie, magnetically present and inviting. Inviting too he sometimes felt were her urgent eyes, blood-red in their corners, dark red somehow even in their blackness, passionate in their mute confused questioning of him. The idea came to him that he was falling a bit in love with Pattie, and when he thought this he calmed himself at once by a repetition of the things she so often repeated herself: I'm here, I'm in the house, I'll be back soon. There was plenty of time for him to get to know Pattie Meanwhile she was necessarily, consolingly, easily there.

"Oh, hello." Leo had put his head round the door.

"Come in, come in." Leo's visits were rare. Eugene jumped up. He felt physically awkward in the presence of his son as if some electrical discharge had disabled and diminished him. He jerked himself away past the bed and dangled against the wall.

"I've been trying to see you for ages. I thought that female would never stop yapping."

"I wish you wouldn't talk in that ugly way," said Eugene automatically, wearily. He had said this to Leo so often.

"Well, it doesn't hurt her, does it? All right, sorry. Won't you sit down? You look so odd over there in the corner."

Eugene sat down. He contemplated his tall slim son with a surprise that never diminished, a surprise at seeing him so grown-up, so large, so handsome, so impertinent. With the surprise came timidity and the muddled pain of an inexpressible love. Always they blundered at each other, there was no technique of contact, no way of taking hold. On Leo's face Eugene read the equivalent of his own amaze: a look of uncertain apprehensive boldness. They were present to each other in the room as unintelligible, unmanageable objects. Eugene hunched himself.

"What is it?"

"I've got something to tell you. 'Confess' I suppose is the word."

"What?"

"It's about that old thing."

"What thing?"

"That icon thing."

"Oh. Has it been found?" Eugene forgot his physical distress. His body filled out again.

"Not exactly. But I know where it is. At least I think I do."

"Where, where?"

"Not so fast," said Leo. "It's a long story. Do you mind if I get on to the bed?" He crawled into the lower bunk and crouched there on his knees, peering out.

"Where is it, what's happened to it?"

"Well, you *see*, I took it, in a manner of speaking."

"*You* took it?"

"Yes. I needed some money, so I took it and sold it. I imagine it's still in the shop I sold it to."

Eugene was silent. He felt an immediate and intense pain of humiliation. He could not look at Leo, it was as if he himself were ashamed. He stared at the floor. Leo had taken the icon and sold it. It was not the clean loss that he had imagined and tried to make terms with. It was something muddled and ugly and personal, something twisted back into him, something that disgraced him. He drooped his head and continued to be silent.

"Well, aren't you going to be angry with me?"

With an effort Eugene looked at the crouching boy. He felt no anger, only the shame and discomfiture of someone who has allowed himself to be hopelessly hurt and worsted. He felt the old shame of the years in the labour camp present like stripes upon his body. He said at last, "Get off that bed and let me see you properly."

Leo got up promptly and stood before his father, bringing his heels together with a little jump. His long mouth turned involuntarily upward at the corners, almost like a caricature of a happy person. His pale freckled face was attentive and expectant.

"Why did you do that, what did you want the money for?"

"Well, you *see*, I know it's rather awful, but I suppose I'd better tell you, I embezzled some college funds. It was the kitty of a club I was treasurer of. I spent the money on all sorts of things, frittered it as you might say. And then I had to account for it."

Eugene had a sense of being cornered which he had often had before. Leo was enacting a scene and forcing him to enact a scene too. Was there no way out of this, no means by which they could talk simply and directly to each other, no appeal or cry which could break through that so familiar flow of patter? He looked down at Leo's pointed shoes. Anger might help, but he could not feel anger, only a miserable hangdog sense of defeat. He was a man derided by his son who could do nothing.

"It was a wrong thing to do." The words as he uttered them seemed to Eugene totally meaningless. One might as well have said them to Hitler or a hurricane.

"I know, but I had to have the money." Leo's tone was explanatory and eager. "Otherwise I'd have been disgraced."

"You are disgraced. Oh well, it doesn't matter now." Eugene wanted Leo to go away. He wanted the thing to stop hurting him in *this* way.

"Good heavens, you can't say *that*. Of course it matters. Anyway, I'm going to get it back for you."

"I don't see how you can. If you've spent the money. Anyhow, I don't want it back. I can live without it."

"You mustn't let me off like this!"

"I'm not letting you off. I just don't want to talk about it any more. It doesn't matter."

"Oh, please don't be so sort of quiet. You ought to be furious with me. You ought to box my ears."

"I can hardly start now," said Eugene. He looked up, frowning like a dazzled man, into the pale eager face. He added, "Now please go away."

"But I haven't said I'm sorry."

"You aren't sorry."

"Well, it's just a state of mind, you know. There's nothing to it."

"It's enough that you've stolen my icon," said Eugene. "I don't want to listen to your half-crazy chatter too. I don't understand you. I never have."

"That's better. You're getting cross. It'll do you good. Perhaps it'll do me good. Look, I *am* sorry, you know. It wasn't one of my better ideas. But I *will* get it back. I expect I'll just have to steal it again."

"If you steal it," said Eugene. "I'll hand you over to the police."

He rose to his feet. He felt quite suddenly the release of anger. It came as a relief, a sense of contact. It was if he had taken a grip upon Leo at last.

"But you want the thing, don't you?"

"Not any more. You've spoilt it. You've spoilt everything. And you've done it quite deliberately. You sicken and offend me. I've tried to bring you up properly and you're a liar and a thief."

"Well, maybe I didn't have much of a chance."

"What do you mean?"

"I've never lived in a real house. How can I have any sense of property?"

"I did the best I could for you, I did everything for your sake," said Eugene. The plaintive tone came naturally, then anger again. How could he be so taunted?

"We've just camped out all our life. You've never wanted to *do* anything."

"I've worked as I can, and I've supported you. I'm still supporting you."

"No you aren't. And you haven't even tried to be English."

"I couldn't try. Anyway why should I try? I'm Russian. So are you."

"No I'm not. I'm not anything. I can never make you understand it's all meaningless to me, it's *nothing*." The playful tension had gone from Leo's face. His mouth drooped, his eyes were screwed up, he looked like a threatened almost tearful child.

"You can't deny what you are."

"I'm not that. I hate it all. I hated that bloody icon too. You've made a little Russia all round you. You're living in a dream world. All you ever really wanted was a bolt hole."

"Stop shouting at me!"

"I'm not shouting. And you've forgiven the Soviet Union."

"I haven't forgiven the Soviet Union. Well perhaps I have. I can't alter history. Why should I hate my country?"

"It isn't your country. You haven't got a country. And you've made me not have one either. God, I wish I were American!"

"That's the most dreadful thing I've ever heard you say. And keep your voice down. They'll hear you in the Rectory."

"What do I care if they hear me in the Rectory? Let them hear. We're as good as they are, aren't we? You with your "Miss Muriel" and your "please sir", like a bloody slave."

"Stop speaking to me like that, and get out of this room. You've never respected me. You've never loved me as you ought to."

"Why should I love you? You're my fucking father."

"Please, please, please," said Muriel, who had just come in the door.

Leo immediately turned his back and put his hands up to his face. Eugene stared at her stonily, still rigid with his fury. He was intensely upset at the intrusion and extremely angry that Muriel had overheard.

"I'm very sorry," said Muriel. "I did knock, but you were both talking so loudly you couldn't hear."

There was a pause. Eugene looked at the wall. He felt disgust with himself disgust with Leo, disgust with everything. His body relaxed into hopelessness. Leo had composed his face and turned now to look at Muriel. He looked at her blankly and dully as if waiting for guidance. Muriel was gazing at him with fastidious distaste.

"You oughtn't to speak to your father like that," said Muriel. "I think you're loathsome."

Leo looked at her still for a moment as if he were very tired and could scarcely understand her. Then he smiled. "A reptile. Is that it?"

"Oh, get out!" said Muriel.

Leo half turned towards his father, but without looking at him, made a quick gesture as of throwing something away, and then left the room closing the door sharply behind him.

Muriel dropped her eyes before Eugene. She was dressed in her tweed overcoat upon which pinpoints of snow still glittered here and there. There was a sugary white ridge upon each shoulder. Under her arm she was clutching a small brown-paper parcel. Eugene looked at her short hair, damp and darkened and stringy at the ends, and at her thin clever face, and he hated her English alienness, her absolutely unconscious superiority, and the fact that she had dared to order his son out of the room. His scene with Leo should have run its course. Perhaps he and Leo understood each other after all. He had felt it just now as Leo went away. Even the anger and the shouting had been a connection, like an embrace, something which brought them closer together. They might have worked out a meaning between them. Now the impertinent intervention of this girl, and what she had witnessed, had made it all jagged and ugly, simply shameful for them both. He breathed deeply with misery and resentment.

"I'm terribly sorry to butt in," said Muriel, looking at him at last. She seemed a little breathless. "But I just couldn't listen to him saying those things." She seemed very embarrassed, but her gaze was intrusive, almost aggressive.

Well, why didn't you go away, thought Eugene. He said, "Yes."

"I'm awfully sorry," said Muriel.

Eugene was silent. He could not forgive her for what she had overheard.

"I hope you don't mind," Muriel went on, "Mr Peshkov—Eugene—may I? I hope you—don't mind—" She dropped her eyes again and began to fumble with the brown paper parcel she had been carrying.

"What is it?" said Eugene.

"Please forgive me," said Muriel. "I've brought you a little present. A Russian present. I was so terribly sorry about your icon. I know this can't be a substitute. But I thought it was very pretty, and I thought it might, well, cheer you up a bit. I do hope you like it."

The wrappings fell to the floor and Muriel held out something small and brightly coloured towards Eugene. He took it automatically and stared at it. It was a painted Russian box of the familiar traditional kind. The figures of Russlan and Ludmilla stood out in glossy red and blue against a very black background.

Eugene looked at it with anguish and puzzlement. It reminded him of something, something dreadful; and for a moment it was as if some awful shaft of memory were about to open wide. Where had he seen just this before, very very long ago? The veiled memory was dreadfully present with some content of unutterable pain and loss. But it did not declare itself. He continued to stare at the box. Then tears came up into his eyes and overflowed. He tried to check them, to conceal them with his hand. He bowed his head over the box, weeping. He could not stop the tears and he still could not remember.

# Chapter Twelve

"THOSE who thought to rescue the idea of Good by attaching it to the concept of will intended chiefly to prevent the corruption of that sovereign value by any necessary connection with specific and 'too too human' faculties or institutions. Since a good conceived of as absolutely authoritative was deemed an insult to human freedom, the solution in terms of action was tempting. If goodness resided in a movement or in a pointing finger its very mobility would preserve it from degeneration. I have already argued that such a theory commits the fallacy it professes to avoid by proving to be but the covert praise of a certain type of personality. Will, choice and action are also the names of the ambiguously human. I come now to a more serious and thought-provoking objection. If the idea of Good is severed from the idea of perfection it is emasculated and any theory which tolerates this severance, however high-minded it profesess to be, is in the end a vulgar relativism. If the idea of Good is not severed from the idea of perfection it is impossible to avoid the problem of 'the transcendent'. Thus the 'authority' of goodness returns, and must return, to the picture in an even more puzzling form."

Marcus surveyed his latest paragraph, the opening of chapter five, soberly and, he trusted, objectively. There was a prophetic tone in what he wrote which he had at first attempted to eliminate. He had conceived of the book as something very cool and hard, composed of a series of extremely simple propositions. But his prose, as it were expropriating his thought, was increasingly producing a kind of stuff which was distinctly rhetorical and persuasive. The temperature was rising. Perhaps this was inevitable. The sheer complexity of the argument could not but produce, as it were by friction, a certain heat. Could philosophy really be passionless? Should it be? Marcus, with a profounder satisfaction, answered no. But it was important to be crystal clear. He did not intend his book only for the philosophers. He had his responsibilities to the age. *Le Pascal de nos jours*. He smiled.

Marcus had returned to his book as to a definite consolation. Its growth reassured him. There was daily more of it and more of him. He rose upon it like a ship on a lifting tide. Yet he had been upset and threatened and his confidence was far from whole. He had been shaken, in some way that he could not fully understand, by his encounter with the Bishop. In his distress about Carel he had vaguely hoped for something from the Bishop. He would have welcomed a chance to talk about his brother in simple, even in crude terms. He had expected the Bishop to represent a sort of ecclesiastical version of Norah's common sense. He had expected something brisk and jovial and confidentially down-to-earth. That was what Bishops were like, indeed what they were for. And the Bishop had seemed to know this too, since he had in a way feigned just such a persona. But what had actually been said was something alarming, not what it should be, as if the lines of a play had been subtly altered. Some kind of reassurance which Marcus had wanted about Carel, about the whole situation, had simply not been forthcoming. Behind the Bishop's tolerant psychological small-talk, behind his worldly aphorisms, there opened a black scene, as if the walls had rolled away to reveal the trough of the heavens, dark, seething with matter, riddled with void, and without any intelligible principle of organization. Marcus felt a surprised relief on returning to his book to find that the arguments seemed as sound as ever.

Marcus was not sure what verdict on Carel he had wanted from the Bishop. It seemed a treachery to wish for an adverse one. Yet it would certainly have helped to have at least a simple one. Of course the Bishop would have had to be discreet. But there are ways of discreetly placing people and reassuring other people. Marcus would have liked to have been included in some kind of committee decision, some gesture of the solidarity of the sane. He realized, slightly shocked at himself and at the same time aggrieved, that what he had wanted was an assurance that Carel was an unfortunate, a sick man, a psychological case of some fairly familiar kind. For if he was not that what was he?

Something upon which Marcus had relied had been removed and now there was nothing to stop what he feared becoming larger and nearer. Yet what did he fear? Carel did not threaten him personally, Carel was scarcely aware that he existed. Why did this dark figure seem always to loom beside him? Marcus knew that he must go again to see his brother, and he tried to put this idea to himself with simplicity, as a rational plan; but there was still that same whiff of dread. He feared that something senseless would happen, he feared to hear Carel laugh, to see Carel move in a way that would reveal that black seething universe again, reveal it perhaps suddenly close at hand, like an ants' nest, like a smear of insects' eggs upon the tip of the finger.

He had sent flowers to Elizabeth and she had not replied. First he was hurt, then he was frightened. He did not want his picture of Elizabeth to be transformed too. Already he could feel it changing mysteriously as if some positive malignant force were acting upon him, upon her. Elizabeth turned and turned, a figure in a dark veil becoming a cocoon of darkness. He could no longer visualize her face. Some cloud had drifted across her image. There was danger. But was it danger for him or for her? He decided daily that he must dispel these absurd fancies by going to visit her, walking straight up to her room if necessary. They could hardly keep him out by force. Or could they? Anything was beginning to seem possible. Marcus brooded, and extremely bizarre and disturbing imagery pursued him to the far threshold of sleep and on into the turbulence of dream.

It had been another day of fog, and foggy smells mingled with the odour of tobacco. Warm in the room, even the fog smelt familiar and friendly. It was late evening now, after ten o'clock, and Marcus had put his manuscript aside. A clutch of letters concerning school matters had still to be answered before he retired. It was proving impossible to keep entirely clear of school. He must decide about the appeal for the new chemistry building. That couldn't be left until the summer. He put the letters out in order of importance, stirred a cup of hot milk and yeast extract, and listened to the purr of his gas fire and the murmur of traffic in the Earls Court Road. The curtains were drawn and a single lamp revealed the business-like littered table and the very large glass-fronted bookcase superscribed *Manners Makyth Man* which had belonged to Marcus's father. The engravings of Rome and the two chocolate-brown cloisonné vases on the mantelshelf were also family pieces. Partly indifferent to his surroundings, partly uncertain of his taste, Marcus had acquired few things for himself. In fact, although he had lived in the flat during school holidays for several years now, the place still had a certain air of the provisional and the temporary. This suited Marcus, who liked to think of himself as an austere man. He enjoyed the plainness of the little flat, and he liked the area and the village life of Earls Court. He was used to it. Why on earth had he agreed to move into Norah's top flat, where there would be endless fuss about cushions and curtains? He appeared to have agreed.

There was a loud buzzing noise close behind him and Marcus jumped. For a moment he clutched at his heart. What was the matter with him? He had been affrighted simply by his own door bell. Yet who could it be at this hour of the night? Marcus rarely had late visitors.

His flat was on the first floor. He opened his door and turned on the landing light and ran down the stairs. Still in some agitation he fumbled at the door and opened it.

A muffled figure with an upturned coat collar stood in the night haze outside. For a moment, for no good reason, Marcus thought it was Carel. Then he saw that it was Leo Peshkov.

"Oh!" said Marcus, as if he had been struck. Recovering himself he said, "Good evening, Leo. What can I do for you?"

Leo had a woollen scarf over his head. He parted his coat collar and spoke through the aperture, his hands beneath his chin. "Could I come in and talk to you for a minute?"

"A bit late, isn't it?"

"All right, I'll come back tomorrow."

"Come in, come in."

The icy foggy air drifted with them up the stairs. Marcus's room was perceptibly colder.

Marcus turned more lamps on. He was agitated and pleased that Leo had come. He began to debate whether or not to give the boy whisky. "Take your coat off. Yes, sit there."

Leo, who was looking round him with interest, had been in the room once before, on an occasion Marcus preferred not to recall. Marcus, making an unsuccessful appeal to the boy, had felt himself patronized. The memory stiffened Marcus now. He determined to make a display of his detachment. He sat down opposite to Leo on the other side of the fireplace. Now they were both in low leather armchairs, their feet extended towards the golden panel of the fire. Leo's face, usually so pale, was pink and still pinched with cold, his nose glowing and his eyes watering. His features composed in Marcus's gaze and he shook himself into presence. "Ouf!"

The cold night had already made a bond between them. "Cold out?"

"Bitter."

"Snowing?"

"Not now. It's nice in here. I'm afraid I've got a cold coming on, do you mind? You know how you feel it when you come in into the warm."

"Have some—hot milk?"

"No, thanks."

"Whisky?"

"No. Better wait. You may be kicking me downstairs in a minute."

"Come, come, what's this about?"

"Shall I be terribly brief and direct?" Leo wiped the moisture from his face with a handkerchief, crumpled the handkerchief, and leaned against it as against a pillow. The attitude had an unconscious coyness. He smiled a tired intelligent smile which Marcus remembered. He was a very good-looking boy.

"Yes, please."

"Well, I want some money."

"I don't think you can be quite as brief as that," said Marcus. "You'll have to tell my why. And I warn you the answer's almost certainly no." He smiled and curtailed the smile.

"Well, I thought I'd be put through it. Where shall I start? You won't approve."

"Never mind. Go on."

"But I do mind. Let me see. Well, the start I suppose is that I'm engaged to be married."

"Really," said Marcus. He was aware of being disagreeably surprised.

"Yes. Well now, my fiancée's old man is mad keen that we should buy a flat, in fact a particular flat he had his eye on, and he was prepared to put up some money so that we could get a mortgage provided I put up some too."

"So you want me to lend you some?" said Marcus.

"No, no, not so fast. You don't come in for some time yet. About seventy-five pounds the old man said. He regarded it as a sort of test of me. I'd just got to get it from somewhere or else."

"And did you?"

"Yes. And you'll never guess how."

"How?"

"You won't like this bit."

"Go on, go on."

"You know that family icon, that religious picture with the three angels my old father doted on? I took it and sold it."

Marcus vaguely remembered the icon. "Your father let you do this?"

"No, I just took it. You might say in a manner of speaking that I stole it."

Leo was leaning forward now and was studying Marcus with a fascinated almost delighted expectancy. With a baffled sense of being experimented on Marcus controlled his face. There was something familiar and somehow deadly about the situation. Leo knew him too well. Marcus was not unduly concerned about Eugene's icon but he was very concerned to make the right impression on Leo. He decided to say coolly "Proceed."

"My pa was terribly upset."

"I dare say. So you got the money."

"So I got the money. I sold the thing for seventy-five pounds. But then the silliest thing happened. You'll think me an awful fool."

"Never mind what I think you. What happened?"

"You see this girl. Her name's Sally. She has a brother. His name's Len. And Len knows a lot of racing people. And—you'll think me an awful fool—"

"Get on with it."

"Well, Len talked me into putting the money on a horse he said was a certainty and the horse didn't win."

"Too bad," said Marcus. "Now I suppose you want me to lend you seventy-five pounds so that you can get in with Sally's father. I think you're going to be unlucky."

Marcus still spoke coolly. He could feel Leo watching his face with cat-like attention. Marcus automatically lifted a hand and hid behind it, feigning to shield himself from the fire. His interviews with Leo had always had an almost technical ease and precision of pattern. He felt now in the tension between them, in Leo's bright expectation, the machine-like force of the familiar system. But on this occasion somehow everything must be made to be different, the pattern must be broken. It occurred to Marcus that it was just the pattern which had always prevented him from really reaching, really knowing Leo. Marcus removed his hand and gave the boy a cold almost inquisitive stare. Yes, everything could be made different. He stiffened his face.

"Oh no, no," said Leo. He had allowed a pause. "I'm surprised that you think *that*. I'm prepared to bear the consequences of my actions. I'll take my chance with Sally's pa. But I don't see why my father should suffer."

"You deliberately made him suffer."

"I know I did. Don't you think it possible I might regret it, that I might feel ashamed?"

"Ashamed?" said Marcus. "You?" Then he suddenly began to laugh. He stood up and went to the table and laughed heartily over his manuscript. He felt liberated into the warmth and light of the room, able to wave his arms, able to move. He said to Leo, "Have some whisky." He began to get it out of the cupboard. By the time he was handing over the glass Leo was still looking disconcerted. Marcus felt so pleased he had almost forgotten the story.

"You don't think much of me, do you?" said Leo.

"Not much," said Marcus. "But go on telling me what you want."

"Well, I won't insist on feeling ashamed," said Leo. He was in control again and slightly smiling. "How does one know what one feels? It's all subjective anyway. Never mind my motives. I don't know what they are myself. I want to get the icon back."

"So you want me to lend you seventy-five pounds."

"It's not so simple I'm afraid," said Leo. He stood up and sipped his whisky. They faced each other, leaning against opposite ends of the mantelpiece. "It would cost you a bit more than that."

"You mean—"

"Yes. I went back to the shop to see if it was still there and it was in the window marked three hundred pounds."

"I see," said Marcus. "So you have proved to be a fool as well as a knave."

"I have proved to be a fool as well as a knave. I'm sorry."

"What I can't see," said Marcus, "is why you come running to me with this unsavoury story."

There was a silence, during which Marcus regretted the question. Leo lowered his eyes and then said softly, "I'm sure you know why."

Marcus's exhilaration had vanished. They were back at cat and mouse. Marcus said hastily, "I'm certainly not going to help you." But as he said it he felt with a kind of panic that of course he certainly was and that Leo knew it too.

Leo smiled down at the brass fender and then became solemn again. As if he had not heard Marcus he went on. "I'm sorry that you exclude the possibility that I might feel shame. I'm not as bad as you think me. But let's talk about acts not motives. I wouldn't ask you this favour just on my own behalf. I simply must get that icon back. My old papa is heartbroken." He smiled again.

"Your father really cares very much about the thing?"

"It's his most treasured possession. He's completely crushed. He's aged ten years."

"Well, don't smile about it," said Marcus. He felt the old familiar helpless irritation taking charge of him. He wanted to hit Leo. "Really I think you're the most completely selfish and cold-blooded young person it's ever been my misfortune to meet."

"I'm sorry," said Leo, scarcely audibly. He lifted a cautious wistful face and then drooped his head.

"You certainly ought to regret what you've done and I hope you do. You've always imagined that you could just give up morals, but it's not so easy. You're not as free as you think."

"I'm finding this out," said Leo in the same whispering voice.

"Oh, confound you!" said Marcus. This was not how it was supposed to be. All this had happened before many times. He added, "I'm not interested in your muddles and I'm not going to help you out, and that's that."

Leo surveyed Marcus cautiously. Marcus turned his back and fiddled with the letters on the table. There was a silence. Then he heard Leo say, "In that case I'd better go. I'm sorry to have bothered you."

Marcus turned. Leo was picking up his overcoat. Marcus took the coat out of his hand. Leo stared at Marcus and his face filled out with serenity, it glowed. He said "Aah—" Marcus threw the coat on to the floor.

"What's the address of the shop?" said Marcus.

"Here, it's on this paper, I've written it down."

"I'll go and see the shopman," said Marcus. "I promise nothing. Now get out."

Leo picked up his coat and scarf and put them on. He looked at Marcus now with the same serene beam, radiating not gratitude so much as a gentle solicitous pity. Then with a deliberation which was almost that of curiosity he reached out and touched Marcus on the shoulder. It was a tentative tap, not like a caress. Marcus caught Leo's retreating wrist, squeezed it violently, and threw it from him. For a moment they faced each other, staring. Then Marcus moved back, putting the table between them. "Get out."

The door closed. Marcus sat down, breathing heavily. He drank some whisky. He felt excited and disgusted. A little later he began to laugh. He went to bed and dreamed of Carel.

# Chapter Thirteen

"**M**URIEL."

"Yes."

"Could I speak to you for a minute."

Muriel came slowly back up the stairs. Her father had spoken through the half-open door and it seemed to be dark inside the room. The Pathetic Symphony, loud enough a few minutes ago to reach her in her own room, had now been turned down to a husky whisper.

Muriel pushed the door cautiously as if she expected some obstruction behind it and edged into the room. Although it was morning and slightly less foggy than usual, Carel still had his curtains drawn. The room was both cold and stuffy and Muriel conjectured that her father had been up all night. A single angle-poise lamp shed light upon a book open upon his desk. Carel, invisible for a moment, materialized out of the black horsehair sofa. He moved to the desk and sat, pulling the lamp upward, and the room lightened a little.

"Shut the door. What time is it?"

"About ten."

"Sit down, please."

Muriel sat down uneasily, facing him across the desk.

"Have you found employment yet, Muriel?"

"Not yet."

"I trust you will."

"I will."

"How is Elizabeth this morning? I heard her bell ringing."

"She seems much as usual."

"I want to talk to you about Elizabeth."

Muriel stared across at her father's handsome curiously stiff face. One side of it was revealed by the lamp, one blue eye illumined, the other side was dark. It was a face too much in repose, a face such as one might find in a remote mountain cave, belonging to osme inaccessible indifferent hermit of an unknown faith, of a faith beyond faiths. Muriel shivered. A familiar feeling of depression, fear and thrill came to her from her father like an odour.

Muriel had awakened that morning in distress. She recalled with misgivings her interview with Leo and the curious bargain she had apparently made with him. The idea of introducing that irresponsible animal into the orderly and enclosed world of Elizabeth now seemed to her not ill-considered so much as senseless. She saw now more clearly that what had appealed to her in Leo and made her see him as perhaps "good for" Elizabeth, as even somehow "good for" herself, was precisely that moral, or rather immoral, friskiness, that cheerful willingness to behave badly which had had such an ugly issue in the unspeakable theft and in the scene with Eugene which she had overheard. She had thought of Leo as potent, as a sort of pure elemental force. It had been indeed some sense of the "purity" of that force which had led her so readily to conceive of him as an instrument. A creature so simple-heartedly egoistic could not be a menace. This was not the kind of thing which Muriel feared. It was the kind of thing which she flattered herself she could control. Yet now she felt both shocked and muddled, disgusted by Leo's behaviour and yet unable resolutely to judge him, as if she herself had already become in some way his accomplice.

She found relief in an intense pity for Eugene, a pity potentiated by her failure to condemn his son. She left the house in extreme agitation to do her shopping, and was arrested and excited when, passing down Ludgate Hill, she had seen the Russian box for sale. She had never really noticed this sort of object before, and the way this one had so vividly attracted her attention could not but seem significant. She ran all the way back to the Rectory. She had expected Eugene to be pleased with the box and her thought of him, but she had not expected him to be overcome. His tears of gratitude startled Muriel and made her momentarily very happy. She had been right, and he had been glad that she cared. Later she regretted that she had allowed herself to become embarrassed and had left him too quickly. She ought to have stayed, she ought to have put her arms around him, she could almost at that moment have kissed him. Tossing on her bed that night she imagined kissing him and groaned into her pillow.

Now Muriel felt guilty in front of her father in the half-dark room. She had always felt guilt before him. She felt it now because of Leo but especially because of Eugene. She was beginning to love Eugene. Muriel held on to the edge of the dark.

"What is it, Muriel?"

"Nothing. What did you want to tell me?"

"It's about Elizabeth. I am rather seriously worried about her."

Muriel concentrated her attention. The lamp cast a circle of light in a wide arc over the desk. The other side of the circle fell somehow to the floor and was scattered. If only there was light outside the room, light which could be let in. Muriel felt her father's eyes upon her like a steady pressure upon her face. She stared at the clear-cut arc of light. "She seems all right to me. She hasn't been complaining of any new pains."

"I am not referring to her physical condition."

Muriel felt a point of sleepiness in her mind like a little cloud. It buzzed. More like a swarm of bees perhaps coming nearer, nearer. She rocked herself a little in her chair, scraping one ankle against the other.

"Elizabeth's all right. I can't think what's worrying you."

"Have you not observed a degree of apathy?"

Muriel had observed this. But it had no significance. She said hastily, "No. Yes. The move tired her, that's all. And this beastly weather."

"I think that is not all. You should be more observant of your cousin. She has become incapable of reading."

"Well she's read a little——" It was true that Elizabeth had read practically nothing since their arrival in London. She had spent most of her time either fiddling with the jigsaw puzzle or sitting looking into the fire. But Elizabeth had had such moods before. It was inevitable in a girl so cloistered. It was surely nothing of importance.

"She has come to live much more in her mind. Everyday reality means less to her. Do you not see this?"

"No," said Muriel with an effort. She lifted her eyes to meet her father's gaze. His eyes though steady seemed to shift a little with some sort of regular motion. Muriel felt as if her own eyeball had become an enormous area over which Carel's gaze was systematically ranging. I must deny everything, Muriel said to herself, scarcely knowing what she meant. I must deny everything.

"She is trying to leave us," said Carel softly. He laid his hands flat upon the desk in front of him, the fingers neatly together.

"I don't know what you mean," said Muriel. "If you're suggesting that Elizabeth is becoming a bit unbalanced or something then I just don't agree. She's perfectly well." Her voice sounded harsh and raucous in the room, breaking through some tissue of murmurous noise which she became aware of as the Pathetic Symphony still whispering on.

"She is trying to leave us," said Carel. "A difficult time lies ahead for you and for me. If it is impossible to keep her here we must as far as it is possible go with her." He spoke yet more softly and with deliberation, pressing down his hands on the desk and leaning slightly forward.

"I really don't understand you," said Muriel. She felt drowsy, stifled, frightened. She formed vaguely the idea of something which she needed. Perhaps it was air, perhaps it was light, perhaps it was courage. She formed in her mind the word "courage". She must deny everything.

"You understand very well, very well Muriel," said Carel. "You have always understood about Elizabeth."

"You know I'm very fond of Elizabeth—" said Muriel.

"We are both very fond of Elizabeth. We have always taken great care of Elizabeth. She is our treasured possession. Our joint possession."

Muriel felt, I must resist this. She was being taken into some kind of plot, enlisted in some unspeakable alliance. She was being told that she had always been in some kind of plot, some kind of alliance. It was not true. Or was it true? "No, no," she said, "no."

"Come, come, Muriel, what are you denying? We have always looked after Elizabeth together. We shall go on doing so. It is very simple."

"I think she's perfectly all right," said Muriel. She found that her hands were still gripping the desk, her fingers pointed toward Carel's fingers. She removed her hands and clasped them tensely together.

"Of course she's all right, Muriel, and she's going to go on being all right. Only we must take more care of her, extra-special care of her. We must protect her from shocks. She must be allowed her thoughts, her dreams. There must be no shocks and no intrusions. These could have the gravest consequences."

The Pathetic Symphony came to its murmurous climax and the gramophone switched itself off. In the alarming silence Muriel said loudly, "I don't agree. I think she needs to see more people. She's just a bit bored. It would do her good to see some new people. All this loneliness makes her sleepy."

"Sleepy," said Carel. "Precisely."

There was a pause. Muriel seemed to hear some sort of murmuring beginning again in the silence. Perhaps it was her thoughts, her thoughts which Carel had so uncannily been able to read.

Carel went on. "It is dangerous to awaken a sleep-walker."

"Elizabeth isn't a sleep-walker," said Muriel. "She's just a girl with a bad back who gets a bit lonely and depressed." Yet the image of the sleep-walker was terribly apt. "Courage," Muriel said to herself again, and then wondered if she had said the word aloud.

"The gravest consequences," said Carel. "Elizabeth is a dreamer who weaves a web. That web is her life and her happiness. It is our duty, yours and mine, to assist and protect her, to weave ourselves into the web, to be with her and to bear her company as far as we can. This is a difficult task and one which can only be achieved in an atmosphere of complete quietness and peace." His voice sank to a whisper.

"Naturally I shall try—" said Muriel.

"There must be nothing to startle her, no sudden movements, no upsetting of the familiar routine which you have set up and maintained so admirably round about her. She could not have wished, I could not have wished, for a more zealous nurse. You have done very well. But increased care and increased vigilance is necessary now. We must be more gentle with her than ever. I want your assurance, Muriel, that you will observe this vigil with me."

"I still think—" said Muriel.

"Elizabeth is increasingly unable to sustain shocks of any kind. I want your assurance, I want your promise, that you will protect her as faithfully as you have always protected her."

"Of course—" said Muriel.

"You will see to it that she is not intruded upon or troubled? Do you promise that?"

"Well, yes—"

"That is good. I shall rely upon you. We have a precious possession which we must guard together."

Muriel was silent. She felt she ought to protest, to deny, to cry out, to call out Elizabeth's name, to summon some distant boisterous gods into this too deadly quiet place. But she could not speak.

"We understand each other," said Carel. There was a tone of dismissal.

Muriel stood up. She tried to say something, but now Carel had stood up too. A desire to get quickly out of the room took her as far as the door. She looked back into the darkness. How tall he was. She got herself out through the door and half closed it.

*Frère Jacques, Frère Jacques, dormez-vous?* The Pathetic Symphony began again from the beginning.

Muriel stood at the bottom of the stairs. The house had huddled itself again about the scarcely audible music. She wanted air and motion, running, flight, anything rather than this stillness. She could not think about Carel or about the strange bond which he had seemed to make between them. The existence of her father weighed on her bodily, oppressing her like matter not like thought. She felt loaded and brought to her knees by Carel. If this burden could only slip off her, if some merciful gravity could only release her from it. But the dark image descending had already brought into view its illumined counterpart. Eugene. Of course all the time she had been with her father she had been thinking about Eugene. Only that had preserved her from the pressure of that gaze. She had uttered Eugene's name to herself, perhaps she had uttered it aloud. I will go to him now, she thought, and I will tell him everything. I will lay my head against him. All will be well.

She was light now. The weight had gone. Her limbs trembled with lightness like a leaf touched by the breeze. She moved through the kitchen and on towards his door. Her body leaned towards him, she was falling, falling. She reached his door and stopped dead. There was a voice within. Pattie's voice.

Muriel stood there, half stooping with the force of her going. Her face began to wrinkle up and she covered it with her hand.

"You again," said Leo behind her. "Come inside."

Muriel turned slowly. She got herself through the door of Leo's room. Then she began to cry.

"Deary deary deary me," said Leo. "Sit down. Here on the bed. Have my hank, it's quite clean."

Muriel took the handkerchief and mopped her eyes. She gave

a very long exhausted sigh, staring with unfocused gaze at Leo's feet. The source of tears, touched for an instant, had dried again. Muriel had few tears.

Leo knelt beside her and put an arm round her shoulder. Then he squeezed her rather clumsily with both arms and drew away, squatting before her on the floor. "What is it? Tell Uncle Leo."

"It's nothing," said Muriel in a cold tired voice. "I just got into a—terribly irrational state. I'm all right now."

"No you're not. I can see. Do tell."

"It's too complicated. You wouldn't understand."

"Well, stay and talk to me anyway. Talk about anything. I'm good for you, you know."

Perhaps he was right. She stared at the touchable fur-like hair and the pale grey eyes, luminous with solicitude and laughter. He was a being who did not tolerate nightmare. "All right. You tell me some things. Have you got that icon back?"

Leo stood up. "No I haven't, but I will, I certainly will. Look, let's really talk to each other, shall we? I'm tired of all this fighting and joking. You must make me be serious. You can if you try. Will you try?"

She looked up at him. "I can't do anything with you."

"Because you think so badly of me? You do think badly of me, don't you?"

"I don't know," said Muriel. "It doesn't matter. I think so badly of myself."

"It's not play."

"I know it's not play."

"About the icon. I will get it back. And if you don't mind I won't tell you how. But I'm not proud of myself. I've just done something which even I—"

"You haven't been stealing again?"

"No. Worse. But I won't tell you that. There's something else I want to tell you, though it's less important. Symbolic really. Why should you care?"

"What are you talking about?"

"When I told you why I sold the icon I wasn't telling you the truth. In fact I told one lie to you, another one to my father and another to—well, a third party who's got involved."

"I gathered you wanted money for an operation for a girl."

"Well, it wasn't quite that. What I mean by 'quite' was that—Well, you see there *was* this operation, only that was some time ago, months ago, and the girl really has gone off with someone else. It's not her. You see, the point is I borrowed money at the time for the operation. I borrowed it, well, from an older woman who was, well, sympathetic."

"I see. So now—"

"This had consequences," said Leo. "I don't mean anything sensational, I mean I didn't have to go to bed with her to get the money. It's not like that at all. She's awfully correct. But she's so—we've had to become intimate friends, if you see what I mean. She's so friendly and sympathetic and wants to know about me and help me. I feel like a wasp stuck in the jam. And while I owed her the money—"

"You couldn't very well ditch her."

"Yes. Though I wouldn't put it quite like that. After all she isn't my girl friend. I just wanted to get away and I couldn't."

"You were prepared to use her but not to face what you call the consequences?"

"I suppose it comes to that. Not very nice is it? Though I was pretty desperate at the time. The fact is I can't stand her. And I feel all the time I'm half lying to her, well more than half. And while the bloody money's still at stake—"

"I suppose she doesn't *want* the money?"

"No. She keeps telling me I can have it as a present. But I can't. That's not morals, it's psychology."

"Often the same thing. I see the difficulty."

"You do believe all this, don't you?" said Leo. "I've told you a lot of things which aren't true. This is true."

"I believe this," said Muriel. She did. "Have you paid her the money now?"

"Well, no," said Leo. "That's the point. At least this is what, in a way, you are doing for me, or I am doing for you. I didn't expect this."

"I don't understand you."

"I'd made a plan for keeping the money to pay the debt and getting this third party to buy back the icon for me, but I can't do it."

"What's stopping you. Surely not the demon of morality this time?"

"Yes, I suppose so. I've always imagined that I could just give up morals, but it's not so easy. I'm not as free as I think."

"It was true that you got seventy-five pounds for the icon?"

"That was true. Well, I'm going to hand it over today to the person who—well, the person who's going to get the icon back for me."

"And from whom you'd concealed that you still had the money?"

"Precisely. He'll have to pay a little bit more than that for the thing I'm afraid. But it's a gesture."

"Which you'll accompany with some other suitable falsehood?"

Leo stared at her and then laughed. "Yes! I'll hand it over anyway. Oh God! Are you pleased with me, Muriel?"

"But you're still in the fix with your sympathetic older woman."

"Yes. I can't think about that now. I'll find some way out. Look, my dear, you did mean it, didn't you, about your cousin?"

Muriel looked away from him. An apparition rose before her, a stifling darkness which buzzed in the corner of the room like a tower of bees. She turned quickly back to Leo. "Yes."

"Do understand," said Leo, "that I'm not an utter fool. I act the fool a lot of the time, but I won't be out of order here. I do want to meet your cousin, just meet her, whatever happens next and even if nothing happens. Of course I've thought about her endlessly since you told me. I can't help being romantic about her. But if you'll let me meet her I'll be good. I swear I'll be orderly and do whatever you say."

"Yes," said Muriel.

"Won't you tell me a little more about her? What's she like?"

Muriel set her teeth. She could feel that source of tears in her again, like something vibrating far away. She stood up. "Not now. Some other time. Now I must go."

"I've said something wrong."

"No, you haven't."

"Don't be cross with me, Muriel."

"I'm not cross."

"Don't be unhappy."

Getting to the door, Muriel seemed to stumble against Leo. He put his arms round her in the same awkward way and she held on to him fiercely for a moment. As she went out she could hear Pattie's voice still speaking in Eugene's room.

A few minutes later Muriel was quietly letting herself out of the front door. It was very silent outside. The fog was a little less dense and the air was filled with snow. Huge soft white flakes gyrated noiselessly round her, seeming to touch the ground and rise again to flit through the air in a design which just baffled the eye. The flakes came so thickly they seemed to pack the atmosphere with dense stifling furry cold. Muriel beat them away from in front of her face and then went on with head lowered. The thick snow squeaked under her boots. A bundled-up figure materialized and passed her, going in the direction of the Rectory. It looked like Mrs Barlow.

Muriel walked swiftly, not looking where she was going, trying to think. At least her ability to think seemed to have come back to her. She had been subjected to a strong pressure. Carel had used authority, and though he had uttered no specific threats it was an authority with a menace in it. Yet what could he threaten her with? Muriel felt she was in danger of losing touch with reality. She had had no time to reflect between seeing Carel and seeing Leo; yet she had instinctively clung to her plan of somehow using Leo. She was frightened of Carel, she was frightened of disobeying Carel. But she was even more frightened of something else, of an isolation, a paralysis of the will, the metamorphosis of the world into something small and sleepy and enclosed, the interior of an egg. She felt as if Carel had tried to recruit her for some diabolical plot, or rather to hypnotize her into a sense of its inevitability. She had needed the roughness, even the absurdity, of Leo to persuade her again of her own existence as a rational independent creature.

Yet why did she suddenly think of it all as a diabolical plot? If it was a plot it was one with which she had herself long co-operated. She had never challenged the view that Elizabeth was ill and needed to be protected from the shocks of the world. She herself had been Elizabeth's chief protector from those shocks. She herself had made, and made with deliberate care, the bower in which Elizabeth now seemed so alarmingly drowsy and entranced. It had all seemed necessary. Doctors had come and gone and shaken their heads and warned against exertion and recommended complete rest. Elizabeth was an invalid and was leading the life of an invalid. What was mysterious about that?

Why can't I think of it all more simply, thought Muriel. Perhaps it was inevitable that Elizabeth should lead a rather quiet life. But it was not inevitable that she should see so few people. Carel had somehow jumbled everything together. It just needed a little sorting out. It wasn't such an all-or-nothing business. Why shouldn't Muriel just go to her father in a firm straightforward way and say to him that she thought Elizabeth needed more company and why shouldn't she meet young Leo Peshkov for a start? It wasn't a monstrous suggestion. Why then did she so immediately feel that it was?

Certainly what she ought to do was to try to explain the whole thing to Eugene. He was there, he was wise, and the idea of thus "involving" him was at once consoling. But would he approve of the idea of Leo being introduced to Elizabeth? Well, why on earth shouldn't he? It was only to Muriel herself that the plan appeared like a violent action, like the sudden breaking of a mirror. To a rational outsider the idea would seem quite ordinary. Though to make the outsider really understand would it not be necessary to infect him a little with her own more lurid vision of the scene? Yet could she? Would not these fires pale then and seem quite unreal? *Were* they not quite unreal? I must talk to Eugene, Muriel said to herself. But her image of talking to Eugene was of being held very closely and tightly in Eugene's arms.

"Muriel!"

Muriel shied, slipped, and nearly fell off the pavement. A figure was standing near her in the brownish-white flurry of the snow. Where am I? was Muriel's first thought. She had walked at random and now someone was calling her by her name.

"Muriel—"

Muriel recognized Norah Shadox-Brown. "Oh, hello—"

"My dear girl, what luck to run into you. I was just going down to call. That brown demon on the door always says you're out. I was going to call her a liar this time, so it's just as well I met you!"

"Oh, yes—" said Muriel. She felt so cut off from Shadox, so listlessly unable to conceive of her, it seemed hardly worth replying.

"Muriel, I want to have a serious talk with you."

"It doesn't matter," said Muriel. She wondered how she could get away from Shadox, but she had no strength to invent a lie.

"What did you say? Look, there's no point in standing about in the snow. You're looking perished with cold. You're not in a hurry, are you? It's not far to my house. We can walk it in five minutes. A brisk walk will warm us up. No talking on the way! Come along then, quick march!"

Norah thrust her arm through Muriel's and began to urge her

along the road. Their boots sank into the deepening snow. Snow-flakes like cold wool drifted into their panting mouths. Speech would have been impossible in any case.

Muriel struggled feebly for a moment. Then she quietly, gasping to herself, resented the pressure of Norah's arm on hers, of Norah's thigh against hers. Then she became indifferent and allowed herself to be hauled along. She even shut her eyes and fell into a sort of trance.

"Here we are. Up the stairs. I'm up on top. No one lives down below. But of course you've been here before."

Muriel had been there once before, on an occasion she preferred not to remember, when Shadox had been trying to persuade her to go to the university.

The sudden warmth of the sitting-room was almost painful. Her thawing feet ached and a fiery touch seemed to outline her face. Automatically Muriel took off her coat and her scarf and laid them on a chair. With some difficulty she took off her gloves. Her hands were stiff and white with cold. She thrust one under her arm and compressed the stiffness, expecting to hear it crack. Her hands were becoming five-fingered patterns of pain. Muriel realized that those tears were going to start again. She felt their glow in her eyes. Whatever happened she must not cry in front of Shadox. She went to the window and coughed gruffly into her handkerchief.

"What a day!" said Norah. "Sit down, Muriel. I think we both need some liquid refreshment! I'll just make us some coffee. Excuse me for a moment."

Muriel continued to stand, smoothing her face all over with the handkerchief, and watching the steady descent of the snow. The snow filled the air, not seeming any more like separate flakes, but like a huge fleecy white blanket which was being gently waved to and fro just outside the window. The door opened again and the coffee-tray clinked down on to the table.

"You look like a refugee, my child! Do sit down and tell me

how you are. You ought to have answered my last letter, oughtn't you. It would have been polite!"

"I'm sorry," said Muriel. She came back towards the fire and sat down. "I've been—so depressed since I came to London." She oughtn't to have said that. It was just what Shadox wanted her to say.

Norah was silent for a minute or two studying Muriel. Then she said, "I think you'd better tell me all about it."

Muriel looked round Shadox's sitting-room. It was just as she remembered it. A coal fire blazed in the grate and cast sparks of light on to the big brass-handled fire-irons. The mantelpiece was covered with white china cups with elegant flower decorations upon their spotless gleaming sides. White wooden bookshelves filled the two recesses. Norah's books, with all their paper covers still upon them, seemed as neat and clean and colourful as her china. The flowery chintz upon the chairs had faded to pleasant powdery hues. Excellent modern reproductions of recent French masters hung upon the walls. The wallpaper was spotty with very small roses. Muriel breathed it in with what she was amazed to find was a sense of relief.

She looked at Shadox. Shadox hadn't changed either. Shadox never changed. She had looked just like that all the years Muriel had known her. The glittering silvery-grey straight hair framing the lined kindly face, a uniform colour of light biscuity brown. The strong mouth and shrewd confident eyes. Shadox had once represented everything which Muriel despised. Her kindness had seemed sloppy and intrusive, her confidence a blind reliance upon musty values. Now Muriel, giddy suddenly with a sense of having become infinitely older, apprehended Norah as being marvellously, perhaps savingly, innocent.

"I'm a bit worried about my father and my cousin," said Muriel.

"I'm not surprised. Your father is a difficult man. And Elizabeth has a particularly tiresome sort of illness. Here, have some coffee. Tell me how it is."

"It's hard to say," said Muriel. "I confess it's getting me down. Of course, Elizabeth *is* ill, she can't really go anywhere and she's not supposed to lift things and so on. But I feel my father rather exaggerates it. He tends to keep her a bit too cooped up, and he's so touchy about her having visitors. I think Elizabeth ought to see more people."

"I entirely agree. I've always taken that view myself. Of course, your father is rather neurotic, isn't he. He's the sort of man who dislikes visitors of any description. I imagine he hates having strangers in the house."

"Yes, he does," said Muriel. It had not occurred to her that there might be this simple explanation of Carel's reluctance to let anyone visit Elizabeth.

"I've known lots of people like that. It's particularly unfortunate in parents who inflict their misanthropy on their children! Of course one has to use tact. How is the child herself? Morale fairly high?"

"Not bad. I'm amazed how cheerfully she puts up with it on the whole. Only she's got rather sort of tired and apathetic lately."

"It's a wretched time of year and I expect it's an anticlimax after the move. Naturally she needs a bit of a change, a diversion. Of course, what she needs most of all is men friends."

"I thought of introducing her to Leo Peshkov," said Muriel. She said this with a sense of uttering some extraordinary blasphemy in a concealed form. It was like saying swear words in a foreign language.

"Excellent idea," said Norah. "He's on the spot, isn't he. A rather disappointing young man. Not much spunk. But he's quite nice and you couldn't want anything more harmless."

"I doubt if my father will think so," said Muriel.

"Why in heaven's name should your father object? If you ask me he's a neurotic, selfish, isolated, self-obsessed person. It's a very familiar type among men. I hope you don't mind my saying so, Muriel, but a spade is a spade. You must just be firm with your father. You're still a bit afraid of him, aren't you?"

"Yes—" said Muriel. She looked into the dazzling fire and dug her fingers into the corners of her eyes.

"How old are you, Muriel my child?"

"Twenty-four."

"Well, isn't it about time you stopped being afraid of your father?"

"Yes—" said Muriel.

It was all perfectly simple after all, there were no nightmares. Elizabeth was a bit lonely. Naturally she needed a change, a diversion. Carel was tiresomely neurotic. He hated visitors. But Elizabeth must see some young people. Leo Peshkov was quite nice, perfectly harmless. Muriel must just be firm with Carel. Carel was a selfish, isolated, self-obsessed person. It was a familiar type among men. Muriel must simply be firm with him. Muriel was twenty-four and it was about time she stopped being afraid of her father. It was all quite simple and quite ordinary.

"Don't cry, Muriel," said Shadox. "There's nothing dreadful. It'll all come right. Drink up your coffee. It'll all come right, my dear child."

# Chapter Fourteen

EUGENE PESHKOV woke up to the knowledge that something very odd indeed had occurred. He lay drowsily with eyes half-closed in the cavern of his lower bunk wondering what it was. It was something odd, disturbing and wonderful. Whatever could it be? He rolled over and propped himself up on an elbow, rubbing his eyes. Then he realized that the sun was shining into the room.

The room was bleached by the sunshine and lightened and enlarged by it as if it had been lifted up and opened out into an expanse of air. The sky to be seen through the high window was clear and pale and so quivering with radiance that it could scarcely be seen as blue, an azure as brilliant as a diamond. There was too a certain familiar quality in the light, a certain tinkling glittering pallor, which made Eugene's whole body vibrate with a consciousness almost too piercingly physical to be called memory. He leapt out of bed and put on his dressing-gown. Then putting a chair against the wall and mounting upon it he looked out of the window.

The fog had been rolled away and the sun shone out of a sky of icy sizzling blue on to a vast expanse of deep untrodden snow. The building site had become a huge snowfield beyond which was revealed a great horizon of snow-touched domes and spires, twinkling in the intense crystal light.

The emotion which had metamorphosed Eugene's body now located itself violently in his stomach and he got down in haste. The first thing on which his dazzled eyes could focus was the painted Russian box. He still could not remember what it was associated with the box which so much afflicted him. Some very similar box must have played a part in his childhood. He supposed it might be something to do with his mother or his sister. He put his hand on the box and felt its glossiness, hoping that touch might tell, but nothing came except some ray of unnamable anguish adding itself to the disturbance occasioned by the snowy light. Eugene dressed quickly. He had slept late. He could hear Pattie moving things in the kitchen, he could hear her singing. Even inside the house sounds rang with a difference, higher, as if they flew higher in the air, thinner, purer, like crystal echoes of the snow. This too in all his sinews he knew, he knew.

Eugene had gone to bed the night before in a state of misery. The loss of the icon had been simply painful, a blow. But the revelation of his son's iniquity had been a shock of a different kind, something which forced him to become not just a victim but an actor, and an absurd and stupid one. He realized now how much he depended on quietness and order and passivity for his well-being and for the dulling of what he still knew of man's inhumanity to man. Was his stoicism just a resigned forgetfulness after all? He could tolerate what was simple and could be endured passively, as he endured now in passive retrospect the catastrophe of his life. But Leo's action was a personal attack which jabbed his personality and brought back the ugly particulars of the past. Those things too, at that time, had hurt and humiliated in this way. And then there had been the distasteful intrusion of Miss Muriel, what she had witnessed and what she had said. Eugene's security was shaken, his indispensable dignity, his sense of decorum, everything which protected him utterly from the casual monkey race of the English and made him their superior. He felt menaced and diminished.

However, that had been yesterday before the great manifestation of the sun and the snow. Now Eugene felt disturbed and excited, distinctly better. He regarded himself in his shaving-mirror. Since Pattie's arrival he shaved every day. He stroked his moustaches which curved stiffly, thick on the lip and tapering to two wiry points below. They were a rusty brown, the colour his hair had once been. His hair, a peppery grey, still grew in a wavy tonsure round his bald spot, luxuriant enough to conceal it except when the wind was blowing from a certain direction. He examined the hair in front. Perhaps it was getting a little thin. He coughed in a sympathetic way at his mirror image and then hurried out of his room and into the kitchen.

"Oh, Pattie, look. Isn't it wonderful?"

"Wonderful! Everything's different."

"Let's go out quick. You've taken his breakfast up, haven't you?" For some reason Eugene could not name the Rector.

"Yes, Wouldn't you like an egg?"

"No, no, not today. Let's go out. Get your coat."

"I don't know if I ought to—"

"Come on. I'll show you the river. I'll show you the snow."

A few minutes later they were walking on the snow with long shadows behind them. The snow on the building site was untrodden, crisp and frosty on the top, so that their boots broke the crust with a brittle sound. The low bright sun slanted across the snow making little blue wave-like shadows on its surface, and making the snow crystals here and there shine so brightly that Pattie kept stopping with an exclamation, hardly able to believe that there were not jewels strewn about her feet. The air hummed with brightness and Eugene's body ached with memory.

He was wearing his old trench coat, a garment so stiff and hard that it was like putting on a mould of clay. Pattie wore her grey coat of rather rabbity fur and a red woollen scarf round her head. Her black hair, beginning now to be a little frizzy, made a dark frill about her round brown astonished face. She walked a little gingerly, as if hesitating to break the dry crust of the frozen snow which the sun now made to look golden as if it were baking. She turned often to look back at their footprints. The snow below the surface was woollier, bluer. She stared at Eugene with spellbound exhilaration and surprise. Eugene laughed too. The vapour from his breath, freezing upon his moustache, had made it stiffen with a pleasant tickling feeling. He felt a little giddy with the light and the opened hugeness of the past. He put an arm round Pattie's shoulder. "The sun suits you. It's funny, but I keep thinking you've never seen snow before."

"I feel as if I've never seen snow before."

"Of course this isn't real snow."

"It *is* real," said Pattie.

After a moment Eugene said, "Yes, you're right." He felt crazy and happy. He kept his arm on her shoulder, guiding her.

"Where's the river? I haven't even seen it."

"I'll show you. I'll show you the river. I'll show you the sea."

They had come into a street where the snow was trodden a little and where wavy ridges of white patterned the blackish red of brick walls. A few people passed, bundled up in coats and scarves, with a strained dazed smiling look upon their faces. Eugene and Pattie came round a corner past a little public house and out of the shadow of the street on to a quay where the curve of the huge river lay before them, full to the brim and moving fast, a steely bluey grey covered in scaly golden flecks, and beyond it the sky line again of towers and domes and spires, all pale and clear against a sky of light blue, like a blue stone polished until it glittered.

"Oh!" said Pattie.

They stood a while watching the water move. They had the quayside to themselves.

"It's so fast."

"The tide is running."

"And so huge."

"It's near the sea."

"Which way is the sea?"

"That way. We'll go there soon."

Eugene leaned on the granite wall of the quay. The snow, dry and almost warm, lightly powdered the sleeves of his coat. He took off his glove and felt with pleasure the bite of the air upon his hand. He scooped the snow a little and fingered the dry hard ridges of the granite. The huge echoing light, the dense feel of the stone, the hastening movement of the wide river, the glittering arc of buildings low upon the horizon, dazed and transported him. He felt himself the centre of some pure transparent system, infinitely spinning, infinitely still. There was no place in this limpid universe where darkness could hide. He said, "Pattie, I feel so full of joy, I hardly know where I am."

He took a handful of snow. It was light, almost substanceless. He turned to Pattie. She was looking at him, dazed too, smiling. The cold made dark red fires glow in the brown of her cheeks. With her hair confined by the scarf her face looked round and plump, sweetly childish, wholesome like fruit. Eugene lifted his handful of snow up to the curve of her cheek and felt the warmth of her with his snowy hand. A little whiteness dusted on to her glowing skin. She was brown and warm and laughing beside him.

"Ouf! It's going down my neck!"

"Take your glove off," he said. "You must feel the snow. It's not cold really. There." He took her ungloved hand in his. He wanted to see her brownness against the white. He sank their joined hands slowly into the snowy coping of the granite wall.

"Oh, it *is* cold!"

"It's lovely."

"It's like cold sugar."

"Oh, Pattie, I feel so strange and good. Are you warm enough? I wish I could get you inside my coat like a little cat!"

"I'd purr!"

"Let me warm you." He put an arm awkwardly round her. His overcoat stood up between them like a board. He fumbled his coat a little open and tried to draw Pattie nearer. Her hand, which he was still holding, he tucked in under his arm, leaving it to claw a hold upon the material of his jacket. Shifting the pressure from her shoulder and edging back the collar of his coat with his chin he tried to get a grip on her waist and move her nearer in between the flaps of the coat. He held on to the slippery bunchy fur, pulling at it. It was a gauche embrace. They stood face to face, two rotund bundles of clothing, unable to get close enough, excluding each other. Pattie stared past him, her cheek wet where the snow had melted on it. He felt the cold air assault his body. Then Pattie somehow moved and sidled, and got herself inside the overcoat. He felt her warmth and the weight of her leaning body. With a little grunt she pushed her face into his shoulder. The scarf fell back revealing a drift of curling blue-black hair. Eugene's hand moved to caress it. He said, "I love you, Pattie."

She said, muffled in his coat, "I love you too."

Eugene gave a groan and tried to get his arm right round the fur coat. They shifted, dislodging the snow from the granite wall into their boots. Pattie let go of the back of his jacket and leaned upon him more heavily. She pressed on him like a falling pillar and he felt her warmth from his chest to his knees. He braced himself against her, his hands flat on her shoulders, immobilized and blind. Some time passed. Then with a reflex movement like a slow spring her head gradually lifted and his face inclined upon hers, bone feeling for bone. He kissed the curve of her cheek where he had laid his snowy hand, and began to look for her lips. When he found them some more time passed. With a series of twitches and pressures Pattie began to detach herself.

"Oh dear," she said.

"My dear," said Eugene.

"I'm so sorry," said Pattie.

"What are you being sorry about?"

"I shouldn't have—"

"Why ever not? Come, Pattie, we're not children."

"It's wrong—"

"Well, let's make it right. Pattie, will you marry me?"

"Oh—"

"Don't be upset, my dear. It's just an idea. We'll think about it, shall we? We don't have to hurry each other. Pattie, please—"

"You can't want to marry me," said Pattie, "it's impossible." She had moved away and was standing looking out over the hurrying river. Her ungloved hands, unconsciously cold, clasped and chafed each other.

"Don't look so desolate. Of course I do. Why shouldn't I? I know it's sudden— And I know I'm not much of a—"

"It's not that. You're wonderful to me. Oh, you don't know— But you mustn't want me like that. I'm no good."

"Now, don't be silly—"

"I'm—well, I'm coloured—and I'm—"

"Pattie dearest, don't talk utter nonsense. I might as well tell you that I'm Russian. We are ourselves, two very special people, and we're both exiles and we're both lonely and we've found each other. You've made me so happy and so different since you've been in the house, you must know that. Of course I must seem a hopeless broken-down sort of a case. But I could change things, I'm not a fool. I could earn much more money if I wanted to. We'd live in a proper house—"

"Don't—" said Pattie. She hid her face for a moment. Then she moved, hands in pockets, and bored her head into his shoulder. "I love you, I love you."

"Oh, Pattie, I'm so glad. There, I'm sorry I startled you. Don't worry about anything, there's plenty of time, we'll see. I want to prove to you that I *can* make money—"

"Money doesn't matter."

"Well, think about it, won't you, Pattie. If we do love each other—"

"But you *can't* love me."

"Pattie, stop it." He held her very close, his chin burrowing in the stiff black hair.

Pattie pushed him away again. She put on her gloves and adjusted her scarf. Her face shuddered a little as if her teeth were chattering. She said, "You—you stay here. I'll go back."

"Let me come—"

"No, you stay here. I want you to stay here. Keep it for me little. I can find my way."

"You will think about what I said?"

"Of course I'll think about it. Thank you—thank you—"

She turned now with a sort of awkward dignity and walked away rather slowly, still with the cautious catlike tread. Closing his eyes, Eugene heard the crackle of her footsteps receding. When he looked again she was gone.

He blinked, staring about him. It was as if he had come out of a small room, out of a sealed interior, so much had the scene which had just passed secluded him from his surroundings. The quayside was still deserted, the thick snow upon it marked only with his and Pattie's footprints. He looked along the wide river, breathing deeply, and the giddiness returned, the giddiness it seemed to him of a waltzer; and it was as if he had been dancing over the snow, waltzing so swiftly and so lightly that his feet had never broken the frosty white crust.

Some new sensation had taken residence in his body, new or else very old. He felt it surge upward and he threw his head back like an ecstatic swimmer meeting a wave. He recognized the sensation, it was happiness. Yes, he would marry Pattie, he would live in a real house again.

He gazed at the skyline. The gilded domes and spires twinkled in the sun, a pale whitish gold, blending into the heaped buttresses of the snow. The painted many-pillared façades, blue and terra-cotta under the blurred chequerings of the snow, stretched away diminishing along the endless quays, each window with its tall snowy crest, each capital traced out in arabesques of white. He looked at the long low city upon its huge frozen river. The sun shone for him from a sky of lapis lazuli upon the solemn fortress walls, upon the striped turrets of the Resurrection, upon the vast gilded dome of St Isaacs, upon the rearing bronze of Peter, and upon the slim pure golden finger of the Admiralty spire.

## Chapter Fifteen

"IF dying, as Being-at-an-end, were understood in the sense of an ending of the kind we have discussed, then Dasein would thereby be treated as something present-at-hand or ready-to-hand. In death, Dasein has not been fulfilled nor has it simply disappeared; it has not become finished nor is it wholly at one's disposal as something ready-to-hand. On the contrary, just as Dasein is already its not-yet, and is its not-yet constantly as long as it is, it is already its end too. The ending which we have in view when we speak of death does not signify Dasein's Being-at-an-end, but a Being-towards-the-end of this entity. Death is a way to be, which Dasein takes over as soon as it is. Ending, as Being-towards-the-end, must be clarified ontologically in terms of Dasein's kind of Being. And presumably the possibility of an existent Being of that not-yet which lies before the end will become intelligible only if the character of ending has been determined existentially. The existential clarification of Being-towards-the-end will also give us an adequate basis for defining what can possibly be the meaning of our talk about a totality of Dasein, if indeed this totality is to be constituted by death as the end."

Pattie, who was cleaning Carel's room, read these words in the book which lay open upon his desk. She read them, or rather it was not reading since they meant absolutely nothing to her. The words sounded senseless and awful, like the distant boom of some big catastrophe. Was this what the world was like when people were intellectual and clever enough to see it in its reality? Was this, underneath everything that appeared, what it was really like?

Pattie put down her dustpan and brush and went to the window. A train was rumbling underneath the house. She had still not got used to them. She hitched up her tweed skirt. The fastening had

broken that morning and the safety-pin with which she had
secured it had come undone. It was the afternoon, and the sun
was shining, hazily and reddishly now, between luminous streaks
of cloud. Far off across the snow Pattie could see the black
receding figure of Mrs Barlow whom she had some minutes ago
turned away from the door. The snow-field of the building site
was sugary pink, and the spires of the city beyond, heavily
shadowed on one side and defined on the other in a clear rosy
light, lifted a medley of cubes and cones towards the sky. Pattie
sneezed. Was she getting a cold? Carel hated it when she had a
cold. Perhaps it was just the dust.

Throughout the day Pattie had avoided Eugene. It had not
been difficult, since Eugene through delicacy, perhaps through
sheer happiness, had kept out of her way. Pattie had passed the
time in a mingling of joy and despair so intense that in the end she
scarcely understood which was which. She had not known that
she would love Eugene. But she knew now that she did, and that
she loved him in a quite special way which she had thought to be
impossible to her forever.

Yet also this was not conceivable. She loved Carel and she
could not love anyone else. Even to say this was to say something
too abstract. Into the web of her being which was interwoven with
Carel no alien thing could penetrate, it was too dense, too thick,
too dark in there. She was knitted to Carel by bonds so awful that
it was a frivolity even to call them love. She was Carel.

What then had happened this morning? In the sunlight and the
snow some madness had come, some sudden amazing freedom.
The black years had dropped from her heart, and she had felt
again that free impetuous movement toward another, that human
gesture which makes each one of us most wholly himself. And it
was indeed as if a new self had come to her so that in her out-going
toward Eugene she was complete and there was none of her that
was elsewhere. Out of her dark benumbed being something had
sprung clear and danced. Her joy in Eugene's love, her joy in her

own renewed power to love, had remained with her in purity throughout the day. Yet how could this be?

The innocence which she had prized in Eugene before she knew him well shone round him in glory now. He was a man without shadows. He loved her, simply, truthfully, and offered her a life of innocence. He offered her too, and she had felt it, smelt it, this morning, happiness. Happiness was in Eugene as it is in all blameless people and needed only a touch to make it flow over. It had flowed on to her, it was perhaps what most of all throughout the day had crazed her. She felt that she could be happy with Eugene. She could become his legally wedded wife and wear a golden wedding-ring and live with him innocently. To be married, to be ordinary, to love in innocence.

It was perfectly possible. And yet it was totally impossible. I could not tell Eugene about Carel, she thought, he would shrink from me in horror if he knew. The question of telling did not even arise. Am I still Carel's mistress? Pattie asked herself, and she answered yes. At any moment still, indeed forever, Carel could take her into his bed if he wished. She had no other will but his. Carel was her whole destiny. It was true that she had some-times imagined leaving him, had pictured a redeemed Pattie lead-ing a humble life of service. But this was an idle dream, as she knew now by the contrast between these imaginings and the sharp unmistakable pain of a real possibility. That the real possibility was an impossibility was a contradiction which she would have somehow to learn to live with.

But I love him, said Pattie to herself, as if this simplicity could save her.

"Pattikins."

"Yes." Pattie turned back hastily from the window.

"Haven't you finished yet?"

"Yes, just finished."

"Did you find any traces of those mice?"

"No."

"Odd. I'm sure I saw something."

Guilt wrenched and griped in Pattie's bowels and she felt herself blush, a dusky black blush, as if all the blackness in her blood had risen to accuse her.

"Don't go, Pattie, I want to talk to you."

Carel was wearing dark glasses. The two glossy ovals stared impenetrably, reflecting the pink light, reflecting in little the crowded towers of the city. Remote in the house Elizabeth's bell tinkled a while and then stopped.

"Pattie, would you mind pulling the curtains? I don't like this glare from the snow."

Pattie pulled the curtains.

"More carefully, please. There's still some light showing."

For a moment the room was in total darkness. Then Carel switched on the lamp on his desk. He looked at her with his great dark night eyes, then he took the glasses off and rubbed his face. He began to walk up and down. "Don't go. Just sit somewhere."

The room was very cold. Pattie sat down on a chair against the wall and watched him move. She noticed that he was barefoot under the cassock. The cassock swung with the energy of his steps and as he came near her with each turn it touched her knee with a rough caress. It seemed to Pattie now impossible that Carel should not know of her relations with Eugene, should not know everything that went on inside her mind. His presence subjugated her whole being with a dark swoop, with a pounce of automatic unconscious power. She closed her eyes and something, perhaps her soul, seemed to fall out of her and lie upon the ground underneath those bare marching feet.

"Pattikins."

"Yes."

"I want to talk to you seriously."

"Yes." Pattie put two fingers into her mouth and bit upon them hard.

"Shall we have some music. Could you put on the Nutcracker Suite?"

Pattie went to the gramophone and put the record on with awkward hands. He must know about Eugene.

"Turn it well down. That's right."

Carel continued his marching. Then he went to the window and peered through a slit in the curtain. The pink flamingo sunset slashed the gloom momentarily. "*Frère Jacques, Frère Jacques, dormez-vous?*"

Carel readjusted the curtain and turned back into the semi-darkness. Then, not looking at Pattie, he began rather dreamily to unbutton his cassock. The heavy black stuff parted like a peeling fruit and revealed a triangle of whiteness. Carel began to slip his shoulders out and with a faint sough the black garment fell to the floor in a heap about his feet. He stepped out of it. Underneath it he seemed to be wearing nothing but a shirt. Pattie remembered this routine and she began to tremble.

"Pattie, come here."

"Yes."

Carel sat down in the chair at his desk, turning it sideways. Dressed in the shirt he looked different, slim, young, almost vulnerable, in a way which Pattie could hardly bear.

"There, you shall kneel. I am going to hear your catechism."

Pattie knelt before him. She could not then stop herself from touching his knees. When she touched the bone at the knee and the thin shank of the calf she gave a groan, and bowed her head against him, embracing his legs.

"Come now, Pattie. You've got to listen to me sensibly." He detached her gently from him, and she knelt back, looking up at his face which she could not see very clearly.

"What is your name?"

"Pattie."

"Who gave you that name?"

"You did."

"Yes, I suppose I am indeed your godfather, your father in God. Do you believe in God, Pattie?"

"Yes, I think so."

"And do you love God?"

"Yes."

"And do you believe that God loves you?"

"Yes."

"Rest in that belief. It is for you."

"I will."

"Your faith matters to me, Pattie, it's strange. Are you a Christian?"

"I hope so."

"Do you believe in the doctrine of the redemption?"

"Yes."

"Do you understand the doctrine of the redemption?"

"I don't know. I believe it. I don't know if I understand it."

"You answer well. Will you be crucified for me, Pattie?"

Pattie stared up into the half-shadowed face. Carel's face, usually protected by its curious stiffness, seemed uncovered now, as if a dry crust had been taken off it. His face was naked, moist and fresh, or perhaps it was that the expression was unusually concentrated in the eyes which had grown huge and intent. Carel looked beautiful to Pattie, softened and smoothed and young.

"Yes," she said. "But I don't know what you mean."

"There will be a trial, Pattie, there will be pain."

"I can bear pain."

"Bear it with your eyes fixed upon me."

"I will."

"You might make a miracle for me, who knows."

"I'll do what I can."

"We've been a long way together, haven't we, Pattie beast. You won't ever leave me, will you?"

Pattie was choking now in a flow of emotion. She could hardly speak. "No, of course not."

168

"Whatever I do, whatever I become, you won't leave me?"

"I love you," said Pattie. She gripped his legs again, collapsed at his feet, her head pressing against his knees. She felt her tears brushing against him. He did not now put her away but very gently stroked her hair with a touch she could hardly sense.

"'Woman would like to feel that love can do everything, it is her special superstition.' But perhaps it is not a supersition. Can love do everything, Pattie?"

"I think so, I hope so."

"Be faithful in your love, then."

"I will."

"Pattie, my dark angel, I want to bind you in chains you can never break."

"I am bound."

"I meant to deify you. I wasn't able to. I meant to make you my black goddess, my counter-virgin, my Anti-maria."

"I know I've been no good—"

"You have been infinitely good. You are my sugar-plum fairy. Lucky the man who has the sugar-plum fairy and the swan princess."

"I wish I could have been better—"

"You're a goose, Pattie, a dear, dear coffee-coloured goose. You belong to me, don't you?"

"Yes, yes, yes."

Carel's hands descended to her shoulders and he pressed lightly upon her as he leaned forward out of his chair and came down to the floor, blocking the light. Pattie groaned, relaxing her hold and falling back, wrapped into darkness. She felt his hands fumbling now to undo the front of her blouse.

"Hail, Pattie, full of grace, the Lord is with thee, blessed art thou among women."

# *Chapter Sixteen*

"SUPPOSE she screams?"

"She won't scream."

Muriel and Leo faced each other in Muriel's bedroom. The room was dark and cold. The sun was not shining today. Muriel sat down on the bed. She was feeling sick with apprehension and excitement.

How she had arrived at the firm decision to take Leo to Elizabeth she was not sure. Of course Shadox had counselled it, Shadox had seen it as a perfectly ordinary project. She had come back to it at the end of her conversation, in the course of which she had entreated Muriel to reconsider her decision about going to a university. Shadox had said, "Of course introduce the boy to her and do it now. Everything gets so stuffy and unnatural in your house." But then Shadox didn't know how things were. Or did she a little bit guess? Shadox was not such a fool as she seemed.

Shadox had certainly urged it as an ordinary and indeed obvious project. But of course it was not an ordinary project. It was a strange and significant move in a game the nature of which Muriel herself only half understood and which it now seemed to her that she had been playing for some time. There would be consequences. Muriel was excited and frightened, and although she had attempted to treat of the matter calmly with Leo she had not succeeded. Her mood had infected him and he was now as agitated as she was.

Why had this move, which was to be in effect simply a throwing of things into disorder, come to seem so necessary? When Muriel wondered this she heard again her father's persuasive authoritative voice saying, "We have a precious possession which we must guard together." She heard him say "Elizabeth is a dreamer," she heard him repeat "She is trying to leave us," and she saw Carel's stiff intent face and his smile which looked so much like a grimace of pain.

The need to stir Elizabeth, to wake her, to do something unexpected, simply to see Elizabeth talking to another person had grown in Muriel as something connected with her own self-preservation. Elizabeth's seclusion, the web which Carel said she was weaving, threatened Muriel too. Some process which had been going on for too long, and in which Muriel had herself co-operated, must be arrested. If it were not, Muriel feared, without altogether understanding her fear, that she might find herself somehow at last irreparably shut in with Elizabeth and Carel. For her own sake as well as Elizabeth's there must be raised voices, shouting, opening of windows, and tramp of feet.

There was, besides this, another compulsion. Muriel had allowed herself to become fascinated by the idea of as it were loosing Leo at Elizabeth. There was excitement, of a more agreeable kind, in this too. They were both so good looking! To bring them together, even if this meant no more than juxtaposing them in the same room, would have something of the thrill of mating two rare animals, and Muriel found that her imagination had already busied itself in the matter. Some deep strange love which she had for her cousin had mingled itself with the plan, and it was not surprising that Leo was shivering with anticipation since he saw Muriel similarly afflicted. Muriel was excited, but she was also frightened. She was frightened of Carel, and although she said to herself "There is nothing he can do to me" she knew that there were things he could do. Just as when as a child, although he had never struck her, she had known of terrible punishments. She was frightened too of Elizabeth.

Muriel peered out of her room and listened. There was nothing to be heard except the vibration of a passing train and the familiar sound of Pattie turning Anthea Barlow away from the door. She turned back to Leo.

"I believe I've got a cold," said Leo. "Do you think she'll mind?"

"Damn your cold."

"I'm dead scared. Wouldn't it be a good thing just to warn her?"

"She'd say she wouldn't see you."

"She sounds a most peculiar girl. She's not a bit odd in the head, is she?"

"No, of course not. She's sweet and clever. You'll see."

"Do you think she'll like me?"

"Sure to."

"But what'll she say, what'll we talk about?"

"I don't know," said Muriel. She didn't know. She didn't even know whether Elizabeth mightn't in fact scream. "You won't do anything silly, will you, Leo? I mean you won't jump on her, or anything? She's led a very isolated life."

"Jump on her! I don't think I'll have enough courage to speak to her!"

"Yes, you will, you'll do fine. Just be natural."

"Natural! What a hope!"

"Well, I think we should go along now."

"Muriel, I can't bear it, I'm funking it. Isn't there any other way to do it?"

"No other way."

"And must we go now?"

"Now."

"Give me a minute," said Leo.

He looked at himself in the mirror of Muriel's dressing-table, stroking his furry hair and adjusting the collar of his shirt. He was more carefully, and Muriel thought less becomingly, dressed than usual; or perhaps it was just that his usual jaunty confidence was quenched. He looked a thin nervous scrap of a boy.

"Don't think I'm ungrateful," said Leo. "It's just that I've thought about it so much. I keep saying to myself it's just meeting a girl, but of course it isn't just meeting a girl. And I'm terribly excited. Only just now sheer fright's making me dry up a bit. You know Aristotle says a man dries up even in the middle if he hears someone is stealing his horse—"

"Never mind Aristotle. Come on."

Muriel looked out again. She listened. The house was silent. Across the well of the stairs, Carel's door was closed. She took Leo's hand and squeezed it and led him out into the corridor.

Muriel was trembling. Simply opening the door of Elizabeth's room and going through it with Leo, could that be so difficult and consequential? Was it really a door which led into an altered future? Muriel tried to calm herself. Nothing uncontrollable would happen. Later she would wonder why she had been so nervous.

Elizabeth's room was on the next landing, up a half flight of stairs. Muriel, pulling Leo, had just reached the top of these stairs when she heard footsteps below. Somebody was coming up from the hall. The heavy clumsy tread announced Pattie. Muriel stood for a moment paralysed, seeing what Pattie would see, herself and Leo hand in hand near Elizabeth's door, scandalously, patently guilty. She anticipated Pattie's cries, her shouts for Carel.

Muriel could not bring herself to rush for refuge right on into Elizabeth's room. To burst in, and immediately enjoin silence, that was hardly the way to do it. "Quick," she murmured. She took two long strides along the corridor and threw open the door of the linen room and pushed Leo into the darkness inside. She was inside herself and had quietly closed the door by the time Pattie had rounded the bend of the staircase. She prayed that Pattie was not in quest of linen.

Pattie's heavy footsteps passed the door and then paused further along the landing where there was a cupboard containing the china which was not in general use. Muriel could hear her fiddling about there, chinking things against each other. Leo began to whisper something but she put her hand to his mouth.

Muriel could hear Pattie's movements and now she could also hear Elizabeth's wireless playing softly in the next room, amazingly close by. Her own heart was beating hugely, like some big thing breathing in the house. She was at once very conscious of the thin lighted slit in the wall. With a rumble and a shudder an underground train went by far below them.

Under cover of the train noise Leo whispered, "Who was that?"

"Pattie. She didn't see us. Just wait."

Muriel was beginning to feel an overwhelming desire to look through the slit into Elizabeth's room. Her attention had been concentrated on Elizabeth, like that of a hunter upon a quarry, for so long. To see Elizabeth unseen now seemed the longed-for climax of that attention. For a moment she almost forgot Leo and it was as if what made her breathless with excitement concerned herself alone. She felt reckless and free. But of course with Leo there it was impossible. She must not let Leo know that Elizabeth was in the next room. Leo was temporarily intimidated and subdued, but he was also over-excited and capable of getting suddenly out of hand. Even with a subdued Leo Elizabeth would have enough of a shock. The proximity of Elizabeth during this suspense, the very idea of the spy-hole, might be enough to drive him into wildness.

Then Elizabeth very audibly sighed. The sigh was uncannily close to them. Against her will Muriel found herself staring at Leo in the dark. She could just make out his eyes questioning, motioning toward the wall. Another train passed.

"Is she in there?"

"Yes."

She felt Leo's hand pass like a ring down her arm and clamp on to her wrist. He pressed her hand against his thigh, staring at her. Then he looked a little sideways at the slit in the wall. Muriel could still hear Pattie in the corridor outside.

At the next train Leo said, "We could look through."

"No."

"Please. Looking at girls through screens. Just like in Japan after all. We must."

"No, You said you'd obey me."

The train passed. Muriel stood rigid, very close to Leo in the little dark space, listening to the soft murmur of the wireless and the irregular clink of china. There was a soft shifting flopping sound in the adjoining room and the sigh again. Muriel took deep breaths. She had a dazed sense of her own body as enlarged and strange and then realized that Leo was leaning against her, touching her from shoulder to knee. He released her hand and began to whisper something hot and tickling into her ear. "No," said Muriel, without knowing what he had said. Her own need to look through the spy-hole into Elizabeth's room was now overwhelming. She took hold of Leo's arm, half restraining him, half seeking restraint herself. She felt irresponsible, dangerous. She gripped Leo, and they clung together like two falling angels. "No."

The drone of music filtered through the lighted crack, sleepy, enticing. Muriel got her two hands firmly on to Leo's forearms and her face brushed the soft fur of his head, fragrant of hair and boy. He said very clearly but almost totally inaudibly into her ear, "You brought me here. Don't drive me mad."

"She may be undressed," said Muriel. They were traitor's words. She was losing the struggle with herself.

"Well, you look first and see."

Pattie's movements could still be heard in the corridor. Muriel knew now that she had to look, it had become impossible not to. Was it after all so grave, to steal this illicit glimpse of her cousin? Why was she trembling? Yet she knew that it was grave. Elizabeth was a secret thing whose dignity and separateness was a peril. Elizabeth was taboo. But Muriel was drawn irresistibly now by some concentrated siren ray and she felt awed and afraid as one who faints outside a sibyl's cave.

"You will obey me?"

"Yes, yes, but *look*."

Leo, hot and shivering, seemed glued like a parasite to her side. He was uttering a continuous very soft hissing buzzing sound. Muriel thrust him away and turned her shoulder to him. Now the murmurous strip of light was before her face. It seemed to Muriel that she too was uttering a soft sibilant noise. She knelt quietly with one knee on the floor and leaned upon the shelf, shifting the linen which obscured the lower half of the crack. She thrust her head further forward.

The crack was thin and not easy to see through. Muriel approached until her nose was almost touching the partition wall, and shifted about a little, trying to focus her eyes. At first she could see nothing but darkness and a sharp dazzle of empty light. Then she began to see through into the room beyond.

It was like looking into clear water and it took Muriel a moment to realize that she was looking straight into the big French mirror. Light seemed to fall like a faint concealing veil between her and the mirror. She stared through the arch of the glass trying to fix her gaze upon the dimmer gauzier forms of the reflections which seemed to lie in some reserved and further space beyond the near familiar brightness of her cousin's room. The image of the alcove began to take shape for her and the head of Elizabeth's bed.

Muriel felt a touch on her shoulder. She twitched herself away, trying to recompose the fragile image which was quivering now like water disturbed. She concentrated her vision at last into a small circle of perfect clarity. She saw the end of the chaise-longue close up against its mirror double. Beyond it in the mirror she saw the heaped and tousled bed. She began to see Elizabeth, who was on the bed. She saw, clear and yet unlocated like an apparition, Elizabeth's head, moving, half hidden in a stream of hair, and Elizabeth's bare shoulder. Then there were other movements, other forms, an entwining suddenly of too many arms. And she saw, slowly rising from the embrace, beyond the closed eyes and the streaming hair, white and dreadful, the head and naked torso of her father.

Muriel moved back from her spy-hole. She moved quite slowly, with the strength and precision of a steel machine. She got up to her feet and stood there in the dark room, immobile as a tower rigid, full. Time waited while she slowly, precisely, took complete consciousness of what she had seen. She became aware of Leo, who seemed to have been pawing at her for some while. Another train passed below.

"Let me look now."

"She is naked," said Muriel.

"Let me look."

"No."

"I'm going to."

Leo began to push her out of the way. Muriel pushed back, pressing square against his shoulders. Leo, whispering something, pushed harder. Muriel clasped his waist with one arm and thrust the other across his neck, straining his head back. Her legs entwined with his and he began to overbalance backward across her knee. With an immense crash they fell struggling to the floor. A bright light was turned on in the room.

"I am so sorry," said Marcus Fisher.

Framed in the doorway, with the dusky anxious face of Pattie behind his shoulder, Marcus stood holding a brown paper parcel and a bunch of chrysanthemums. Leo and Muriel, now frantically pushing to come apart from each other, rolled over again upon the floor.

"I am so sorry," Marcus repeated. "I am terribly sorry."

Muriel began to get to her feet.

"I am so sorry," said Marcus. "So stupid of me. I was looking for Elizabeth's room. Of course it must be this one next door." He began to back out.

Muriel saw him move back into the corridor and heard the agitated voice of Pattie saying something. As Marcus moved again, Muriel got herself to the doorway. She took a gasping breath. Holding on to the edge of the door she called out with all the voice she had, loudly and clearly, uttering her father's Christian name for the first time in her life. "Carel! Carel! Carel!"

# Chapter Seventeen

"CAREL! Carel! Carel!"

Marcus Fisher, still stunned by the sudden and unexpected vision of Leo and his niece embracing each other on the floor of what appeared to be a large linen cupboard, was thrown into total confusion by this loud ringing utterance of his brother's name. The inexplicable cry, a cry both of fear and menace, died away and left Marcus paralysed and amazed, standing frozen in the corridor, the flowers trailing from his hand on to the floor.

Something shot past him. Leo reached the top of the stairs and seemed to fly down them in a single bound. His pounding receding feet merged into the subterranean growl of a train. The house shook. The image of Muriel assembled in front of Marcus. She was near to him, facing him and leaning against a closed door. Her face was like an ancient embalmed face, strained and smooth, the lipless mouth opening in a senseless slot. Behind his shoulder Pattie was pouring out a scolding gabble in which he could hear no words. He turned round, shrinking away from the women, and put the flowers down upon a table. He noticed that the top of the table was made of various inlaid marbles, brown and green and white. The light was bad in the corridor. He looked back toward the stairs, expecting to see the tall form of his brother advancing upon him.

The brown-paper parcel which Marcus was still holding under his arm contained the icon of the Trinity represented as angels. He had had to pay three hundred pounds for it at the antique shop. He had never, of course, been in any doubt about his own intentions. As soon as he knew about Leo's curious plight it was evident what his heart had decided for him. He felt about the whole matter a not altogether unpleasant shame. He knew that he should have been sterner with Leo, much more austere and dignified and above all distant, and knew too what weakness it was in him which set this austerity beyond his power. He had been manipulated by the boy, and they were both well aware of it. Yet the very weakness was a pleasure.

Marcus had also been glad, in a quite immediate way, to have a practical occupation, and one which was connected with the inhabitants of the Rectory. He needed desperately to see his brother again, to see the face which had been veiled at their last meeting and which he had dreamed of as disfigured, a demon's face. It was necessary to lay this ghost, to let a mundane and simple reality put such disturbing visions to flight. This was becoming, in the case of Elizabeth, even more urgent. The image of Elizabeth had altered in him in a way quite independent of his rational thoughts. The innocent and sweet girl that he remembered was in danger of becoming in his imagination a Medusa. He must see Elizabeth, the real Elizabeth, soon and arrest in himself a process which seemed to be endowed with an uncanny vitality of its own.

The recovery of the icon provided a simple reason for a visit and even perhaps the authority for an entrance. Marcus had intended to ask for Eugene and to enlist the Peshkovs as helpers before proceeding further. However he had been startled into greater boldness by having the door of the Rectory opened for him pat on his arrival by a departing electrician. As in a dream he walked in. There was no one about. He knew, or thought he knew the position of Elizabeth's room; he had already worked this out in the course of his nightly prowlings round the forbidden house. It was impossible then not to mount the stairs and attempt, with a dreadful quickness, to confront the harmless thing which had begun so absurdly to frighten him.

"Well, Marcus."

Carel had come. Marcus looked at the buttons of the black soutane and then raised his eyes to his brother's face. Carel's face gleamed like enamel, like porcelain, and Marcus realized for the first time how very blue his brother's eyes were, blue with a blue of skies, of flowers. The eyes looked at him through the pale structure of the face. The dark hair was sleek, like feathers of a bird.

"Come, Marcus."

Marcus followed his brother, carried along magnetically in his wake. Muriel and Pattie passed through his field of vision like idle bystanders caught by a camera, and disappeared. He followed Carel closely, almost treading upon the moving he mof the soutane, down some stairs, up some other stairs, and through a doorway. A shaded light shone upon an open book and a glass of milk. A door closed behind him.

"I'm sorry," said Marcus.

There was a silence. Then Carel uttered a low sibilant sound which might have been a laugh.

"It's all right, brother. Sit down, brother."

Marcus found that he had automatically picked up the flowers again from the marble-topped table. He laid them down, together with the brown-paper parcel, upon the desk. He smelt the rather stuffy odour of the brown and yellow chrysanthemums. He sat down upon an upright chair beside the desk.

"Marcus, Marcus, Marcus, I told you to leave us alone."

"I'm sorry. You see I—"

"Think of us as dead."

"But you aren't dead," said Marcus. "Besides Elizabeth—"

"You have no duty to Elizabeth."

"It's not that," said Marcus. He felt crazed and eloquent enough to be exact. "It's not a matter of duty. I'm just getting thoroughly upset about Elizabeth. I keep thinking about her in such an odd way. I've just got to see her. I can't work, I can't do anything."

"What do you mean, thinking about her in an odd way?"

"I don't know, it's ridiculous, I have nightmares about her, as if she'd been changed."

"Mmm."

"So you see I've got to see her just for my own peace of mind."

"Later on perhaps. We'll see. Elizabeth is far from well."

"I'm afraid I don't believe a word you say any more," said Marcus. He felt strangely exhilarated. He peered at Carel, who was standing in front of him now, just outside the direct light of the lamp.

"It doesn't matter." Carel followed the words with a long sigh which turned into a yawn.

"Don't say that. Carel, I want to talk to you properly, please."

"Whatever about, my dear Marcus? Do you want to reminisce about our childhood?"

"No, of course not. I want to talk about you, about what you think and how you are."

"A difficult subject, too difficult for you."

"Are you aware that some people think you're insane?

"Do you?"

"No, of course I don't. But you do behave strangely, seeing nobody and all those things you said to me last time. Is it really true that you've lost your faith?"

"You use such an odd old-fashioned vocabulary. Do you mean do I think there is no God?"

"Yes."

"Well then, yes, I think it. There is no God."

Marcus stared up at the calm tall figure in the half dark. The words had an extraordinary ring of authority. They were words which he himself had always regarded as commonplace. But uttered now they startled him.

"So you weren't pretending last time, you weren't pulling my leg?"

"I wouldn't trouble to jest with you, Marcus, any more than I would trouble to deceive you."

"But Carel, if you really don't believe, you shouldn't go on being a priest. Your vocation—"

"My vocation is to be a priest. If there is no God it is my vocation to be the priest of no God. And now, my dear Marcus—"

"Please, Carel, just a moment, I do wish you'd explain—"

"Be silent for a minute."

Carel had turned and was pacing up and down. Marcus sat hunched and stony still, fascinated.

After a little while Carel said, "Well, perhaps I will talk to you, why not. Last time I gave you the vulgar doctrine. Now shall I tell you how it really is?"

Though he had denied it, Marcus was near again to thinking that his brother was mad. He felt dread of him. Almost involuntarily he said in a low voice, "I'm not sure that I want to hear now."

"Nobody wants to hear, Marcus. It is the most secret thing in the world. And though I may tell you, you will not retain it in your mind because it cannot be borne." Carel was still pacing the room, not with a steady stride but as if wafted rather irregularly to and fro. The cassock rustled and swung, was checked and swung again.

Carel went on, "You cannot imagine how often I have been tempted to announce from the pulpit that there is no God. It would be the most religious statement that could be conceived of. If there were anybody worthy to make it or receive it."

"It's not exactly *new*—"

"Oh yes, people have often uttered the words, but no one has believed them. Perhaps Nietzsche did for a little. Only his egoism of an artist soon obscured the truth. He could not hold it. Perhaps that was what drove him mad. Not the truth itself but his failure to hold it in contemplation."

"I don't see anything so dreadful about it," said Marcus. "Atheism can be a perfectly humane doctrine—"

"It is not as the German theologians imagine, and the rationalists with their milk-and-water modern theism, and those who call themselves atheists and have changed nothing but a few words. Theology has been so long a queen, she thinks she can still rule as a queen in disguise. But all is different now, *toto caelo*. Men will soon begin to feel the consequences, though they will not understand them."

"Do you understand?" Marcus murmured. His hand touched something on the desk and he picked it up. It was a paper dart.

Carel went on, "It is not that all is permitted. To say that was the reaction of a babbling child. No one who had enough spirit to say it ever really believed it anyway. What they wanted was simply a new morality. But the truth itself they did not conceive of, the concept of it alone would have killed them."

"But all the same morality remains——"

"Suppose the truth were awful, suppose it was just a black pit, or like birds huddled in the dust in a dark cupboard? Suppose only evil were real, only it was not evil since it had lost even its name? Who could face this? The philosophers have never even tried. All philosophy has taught a facile optimism, even Plato did so. Philosophers are simply the advance guard of theology. They are certain that Goodness is there in the centre of things radiating its pattern. They are certain that Good is one, single and unitary. They are sure of this, or else they deify society, which is to say the same thing in a different way. Only a few of them really feared Chaos and Old Night, and fewer still ever caught a glimpse—— And if they did perhaps, through some crack, some fissure in the surface, catch sight of *that*, they ran straight back to their desks, they worked harder than ever late into the night to explain that it was not so, to prove that it could not be so. They suffered, they even died for this argument, and called it the truth."

"But do you yourself really believe——?"

"Any interpretation of the world is childish. Why is this not obvious? All philosophy is the prattling of a child. The Jews understood this a little. Theirs is the only religion with any real grimness in it. The author of the Book of Job understood it. Job asks for sense and justice. Jehovah replies that there is none. There is only power and the marvel of power, there is only chance and the terror of chance. And if there is only this there is no God, and the single Good of the philosophers is an illusion and a fake."

"Wait a minute," said Marcus. His voice sounded sudden and harsh and crude in the room, as if Carel's words had not been spoken, but had been noiseless agencies entering the mind by telepathy. "Wait a minute. I wouldn't necessarily disagree with this. But ordinary morality goes on, ordinary decent conduct still makes sense. You speak as if—"

"If there is goodness it must be one," said Carel. "Multiplicity is not paganism, it is the triumph of evil, or rather of what used to be called evil and is now nameless."

"I don't understand you. People may disagree about morals, but we can all use our reason—"

"The disappearance of God does not simply leave a void into which human reason can move. The death of God has set the angels free. And they are terrible."

"The angels—?"

"There are principalities and powers. Angels are the thoughts of God. Now he has been dissolved into his thoughts which are beyond our conception in their nature and their multiplicity and their power. God was at least the name of something which we thought was good. Now even the name has gone and the spiritual world is scattered. There is nothing any more to prevent the magnetism of many spirits."

"But, but," said Marcus, and his voice seemed to be turning into a raucous gabble, "but there *is* goodness, whatever you say, there *is* morality, it's just *there*, it makes a difference, our concern for others—"

Carel laughed softly. "Are there others? Only in the infliction of pain is the effect so contained in the cause as to convince of the existence of others. All altruism feeds the fat ego. This is one of those things which should have been obvious. Only the great delusion kept it from our eyes. No, no, we are creatures of accident, operated by forces we do not understand. What is the most

important fact about you and me, Marcus? That we were conceived by accident. That we could walk into the street and be run
over by a car. Our subjection to chance even more than our
mortality makes us potentially spiritual. Yet it is this too which
makes spirit inaccessible to us. We are clay, Marcus, and nothing
is real for us except the uncanny womb of Being into which we
shall return."

"All right, there have been illusions—but now at least we know
the truth and we can start from there—"

"We do not know the truth because as I told you it is something
that cannot be endured. People will endlessly conceal from themselves that good is only good if one is good for nothing. The
whole history of philosophy, the whole of theology, is this act of
concealment. The old delusion ends, but there will be others of a
different kind, angelic delusions which we cannot now imagine.
One must be good for nothing, without sense or reward, in the
world of Jehovah and Leviathan, and that is why goodness is
impossible for us human beings. It is not only impossible, it is not
even imaginable, we cannot really name it, in our realm it is non-
existent. The concept is empty. This has been said of the concept
of God. It is even more true of the concept of Good. It would be
a consolation, it would be a beatitude, to think that with the death
of God the era of the true spirit begins, while all that went before
was a fake. But this too would be a lie, indeed it is the lie of modern
theology. With or without the illusion of God, goodness is
impossible to us. We have been made too low in the order of
things. God made it impossible that there should be true saints.
But now he is gone we are not set free for sanctity. We are the
prey of the angels."

The house vibrated quietly with soft deep train noise. Marcus
looked down at something which he was holding in his hand. It
was the paper dart which he had crushed into a ball. He realized
that his mouth was open wide for crying like a banished Adam.
He stared up at Carel who was motionless now, staring at the

bookshelves. Carel's eyes were half closed and his face wore a sleepy dreamy expression which was almost voluptuous. I must answer him, thought Marcus, I must answer him. He felt as if some ghastly threatening structure had been materializing in front of him. He said, almost shouting it out, "But you are wrong, there are facts, real things, people love each other, it just is so—"

"One can only love an angel. And that dreadful thing is not love. Those with whom the angels communicate are lost."

"I've changed my mind," said Marcus. "I think you're insane."

"Go, then, go, my innocent brother. Back to your milk-and-water theology. Where wast thou, Marcus, when I laid the foundations of the earth, when the morning stars sang together and all the sons of God shouted for joy?"

Marcus rose. "So you are going to go on being a priest," he said. "You are going to go on with that farce, with all those things inside you?"

"It doesn't matter. When I celebrate mass I am God. *Nil inultum remanebit*. Although there is no judge I shall be punished quite automatically out of the great power of the universe. That will be its last mercy. Meanwhile I endure in the place in which I am. I endure, my Marcus, I wait for it all to finish."

His name, thus spoken as Carel used to speak it in childhood, affected Marcus with a sudden different emotion, warm and weak, a pity more for himself than for his brother. He looked at Carel's face for signs of trouble, signs of despair, but the face was abstracted, faintly smiling, turned away.

Marcus felt that he had been dismissed, perhaps already forgotten. But he could not bear to go like that. He wanted to attract Carel's attention to himself, even if it were in anger. He said, "I brought these flowers for Elizabeth."

Carel turned slowly towards him, looked at him still vaguely, and moved to the desk. He fingered the mop-headed chrysanthemums. "What's in the parcel? Is that for Elizabeth?"

Marcus recalled the icon, and for a moment could not remember why he had it. He said confusedly, "It's that icon, well I suppose you wouldn't know about it, it belongs to Eugene Peshkov—"

"Oh, the Pole."

"He's Russian, actually."

"Can I look?"

Already Carel was pulling off the paper. Under the direct light of the lamp, beside the insipid pallor of the flowers, the solid wooden rectangle glowed golden and blue. The three bronzed angels, weary with humility and failure, sat in their conclave holding their slender rods of office, graceful and remote, bowing their small heads to each other under their huge creamy haloes, floating upon their thrones in an empyrean of milky brightness.

Carel slowly laid it down. He murmured something.

"What?" said Marcus.

"I said 'tall'."

"Tall?"

"They would be so tall."

Marcus looked at Carel. He was still intent on the icon, smiling again, a relaxed happy smile.

Marcus coughed. "It represents the Trinity, of course," he said.

"How can those three be one? As I told you. Please go now, Marcus."

Marcus hesitated. He could think of nothing more to say. The warm weak feeling returned to him and he almost wanted to weep. He said, "I'll see you again."

Carel, looking at the icon, did not reply.

"I'll see you again, Carel."

"Go."

Marcus moved a step or two towards the door. He was incapable of taking the icon out of Carel's hand. He felt again the agony, the impossibility of leaving him so bleakly. He could not leave Carel alone with those thoughts. It must all be unsaid. The spell must be repeated backwards and all must be made as it had been before. He needed suddenly to touch his brother. He came back and, bending a little, closed his hand upon the black skirt of the soutane.

"Don't touch me."

Carel moved quickly, jerking the material out of Marcus's grasp. As Marcus straightened up Carel stepped forward again and for a moment Marcus thought that his brother was about to embrace him. Instead, deliberately, almost carefully, Carel struck him hard across the mouth.

Marcus gasped, his hand going to his face. He felt the flesh hot with shame and hurt. He saw very clearly Carel's metallic features and his china blue eyes fixed upon him with a gaze of thoughtful intensity.

Carel murmured, "You exist, Marcus, just for a moment you exist. Now get out."

The blue eyes closed. Marcus stumbled out of the door.

# Chapter Eighteen

"Funny thing," said Elizabeth, "I've stopped hearing the trains. I never believed I'd get used to them. Have you stopped hearing them too?"

"Yes," said Muriel.

"Jigsaw's nearly finished."

"You've done a lot."

"One does get obsessed near the end. So lazy of me. That fits, doesn't it?"

"Yes, that fits."

"Whatever shall we do when we've finished it?"

They were sitting on the floor in Elizabeth's room with the lamps alight and the curtains drawn. The fire flickered, casting jagged golden reflections into the brownish recesses of the French mirror. Elizabeth's half-smoked cigar glowed in the ash-tray. She sat lazily, one long black trousered leg tucked under her, her back against the chaise-longue and her face to the fire. The points of her strewn hair fell forward on to her shoulders. The front of her striped shirt lolled carelessly open as she fingered a piece of the puzzle. "Only dull old bits of sea left now."

"You've done a lot." Did I say that just now, thought Muriel.

"Mmm. Foggy again, isn't it?"

"Yes."

"I can smell it in here, even with the fire. Has it snowed any more?"

"No."

"Is the snow still there?"

"Lot of it is. It's not so nice now."

Muriel had entered Elizabeth's room with every expectation of an event. Sick with anticipation and fear, she had scarcely been able to get herself as far as the door. She had expected something which, if not exactly an explanation or a judgment, would partake of these and somehow shift a state of mind so terrible that any change must be a relief. What was from moment to moment unendurable was not so much what she had seen. That composite image remained in her consciousness, unassimilated and dreadful, like a mortal illness waiting its hour. What most immediately tormented her was her uncertainty about *them*, the inconclusiveness of her impression that they must know that she had seen, that they must think that she had deliberately spied. The burden was like guilt. Here she needed Elizabeth's help, needed an utterance which, however obscure, might bring what had occurred back into an inhabited world and make it, however appalling, a human task to deal with. Indeed almost any movement which Elizabeth made could have constituted such a help. Only Elizabeth made no movement.

When Muriel had appeared, speechless and capable only of kneeling on the floor and drooping her head, Elizabeth had seemed to notice nothing, and had simply behaved as usual, talking trivialities, complaining a little, shifting peevishly about, and fiddling with the jigsaw puzzle. Muriel had gradually lifted her head and with an effort which almost made her pant and grit her teeth had entered into the business of replying with an equal casualness and appearance of calm. She did not know what to think. Elizabeth must have heard that desperate cry of "Carel! Carel!" must have understood the meaning of Muriel's presence in the next room. If she had not understood she would surely have asked, have exclaimed. Her very silence implied her understanding. Yet with so odd a girl could one be sure? Perhaps Elizabeth had not understood and had already dismissed the matter. Elizabeth seemed to live on so many different levels, in so many different dimensions. Perhaps some crack or fault in the structure of her mind had simply, and maybe mercifully, shut off from consciousness all memory of an incident which should surely have seemed frightening and appalling. But what, given that which Muriel had certainly and indubitably seen, could the inside of her cousin's mind be like?

About Carel Muriel could not think clearly at all. There had always been an area of darkness in her relationship with her father, something which prevented her from seeing him properly and prevented her utterly from judging him. He had never quite, for her, belonged to the ordinary human scene, and although he was a stranger to her and the strangest thing that she knew, he was so intimately a part of her own consciousness that she was almost surprised that he was visible to other people. She could not now reflect upon him or attribute willed action to him, she could not think of him as a person with a policy, as someone who had made decisions and taken risks. He was too large to be included in her thoughts. He bulked beside them, impenetrable and ineluctably present. It was not exactly that Muriel thought about him all the time. She wore him, she carried him, she endured him all the time.

No new communication came to lessen or make bearable the shock which she had received. She remained shocked, like someone who holds a live electric wire and cannot let go. What did become, with the passage of hours, of a day, more positive was her own sense of guilt. She was guilty of seeing, of knowing. She had committed the crime of looking. Something had been destroyed, smashed, and she herself was the destroyer, the blasphemer, the defiler. She struggled for her reason. Then with the idea of guilt came the idea of absolution and with the idea of absolution came the image of Eugene. It was a surprise as well as a relief to Muriel to find that she was still capable of thinking of Eugene at all. Because he was harmless and kind he remained available and free, outside the mess of her misery. But in some more definite way he had become a necessary presence, an essential counterweight to Carel, the white figure against the black one. She thought again of going to him and telling him everything, and in fact in several imaginary conversations she did this and received much comfort. And she thought about the Russian box and the good tears he had shed for her. She *would* go to Eugene, but not just yet. Eugene was always there. Meanwhile she would wait a little longer watching Elizabeth for a sign.

"Is it still the afternoon?"

"I suppose so. It's hard to tell afternoon from evening in this weather."

"Or morning! I wish the fog would go away. I've only been able to look out of the window two days since we came."

"It'll go soon. It'll have to."

"I don't see why. The weather may have suddenly changed. Perhaps it's something to do with the Bomb."

"It'll go soon."

"Do you think the bomb tests might really have affected the weather?"

"I suppose they might, but not that much."

"What's for supper?"

"I don't know. I haven't shopped yet."

"I suppose there's always eggs."

"You must be getting fed up with eggs."

"I don't mind. There's another piece that fits. Do you know, I think I'm getting better at it."

"I suppose it's a skill like another. You'd be likely to get better."

"Shall we buy a new puzzle when we've finished this one, or shall we jumble this one up and start again?"

"I don't think I could bear to do the same one again."

"No, I suppose not. Even though one knows the picture before-hand one does feel one's discovering it. We'll get another one. May we?"

"Of course if you like we'll get another one."

Muriel closed her eyes and her fingers clawed quietly upon the taut surface of the carpet. Not tears but something like a scream hovered inside her head, moved in there like a bird. Can I stand this degree of pain, Muriel asked herself so specifically that it almost seemed she had said the words aloud.

She opened her eyes and saw a rather strange look upon Elizabeth's face. Elizabeth was not looking at the puzzle but was gazing a little beyond it upon the floor with a tense conscious expression which almost immediately became smooth and vacant. A movement in the air made Muriel stiffen. Then she half turned and sprang to her feet. Carel was standing in the doorway.

He ignored Elizabeth, who did not look up and said in a low voice to Muriel, "Could I talk to you for a moment?"

Muriel had no memory of getting to Carel's study. She was now conscious of the room which was brightly lit for once, with three lamps on and a centre light. The glare made the room look small and mean, inadequately and provisionally furnished. She noticed how threadbare the carpet was. She heard her father closing the door and was conscious of herself with a kind of surprise standing, not fainting, not screaming.

"Sit down, will you, Muriel."

She sat beside the desk. Carel went to the other side of it and sat facing her. She felt him looking at her. She could not look at him.

"I was wondering, Muriel, if you had obtained that appointment yet."

"What appointment?" said Muriel in a thick voice, looking at the floor.

"I mean have you taken any employment, secretarial work."

"Oh. No, I haven't."

Carel's voice was so ordinary, his questions sounded so simple and so familiar, Muriel wondered for a moment whether she had not perhaps made some astonishing mistake. Was it possible that her father too had just not heard her cry out his name or had somehow strangely forgotten it? Or had she ever really cried out at all? Perhaps she had imagined it? Perhaps she had magined what she thought she saw.

"Wouldn't it be a good thing to find work? It shouldn't prove difficult. And some time has passed now."

She tried to look at Carel and got as far as looking at his hands which were laid upon the desk before him, one neatly crossed over the other. Then she saw something else upon the desk beside Carel's hands. It was Eugene's icon of the Trinity represented as angels, the picture foreshortened in her view of it into a golden-blue slit. There was something miraculous and also terrible in the appearance of the icon on Carel's desk. Was there nothing he could not do? Muriel stared at it.

She said, "Yes, I'll soon get a job."

"It's time you were earning money of your own. You can command a good salary."

"In the city, yes."

"Not necessarily in the city."

"I mean it's easy in the city, and since I'm living here—"

"That brings me to another point," said Carel.

Something in his voice made Muriel look at him. "What?"

"I do not desire you to go on living here."

"I beg your pardon," said Muriel.

"I wish you to move out of this house as soon as possible."

Muriel stared at her father. In the very bright light the smooth surface of his face seemed decomposed a little, white and powdery. Only the eyes glistened like damp blue stones and the lank dark hair gleamed as if it were wet.

Muriel said, "I don't understand you."

"I wish you to move out of this house as soon as possible." Carel uttered the words in exactly the same voice as if they were not a repetition.

"You can't mean that," said Muriel.

Carel sat looking at her silently. He moved his hands a little as if to be sure that they were relaxed and comfortable.

"But why?"

Carel cleared his throat. He said, "You know it is most unusual in these days for a young person of your age to live with her parents. You have been leading an abnormal life. I think it is time for you to lead a more normal one. Would you not agree?"

Muriel stared into Carel's eyes, trying to see some movement, some little flicker of a calculating watching consciousness. She could see nothing except the lubricated surface of the eyeball. She blinked, conscious of the steady glow of the icon in the corner of her field of vision.

"What about Elizabeth?"

"Naturally Elizabeth stays here."

"But who will look after her?"

"I will look after her."

Muriel breathed deeply and tried to think. It could not be like this, it could not be. In her wildest imaginings of what her father might do to her it had never occurred to her to conceive that he might try to separate her from Elizabeth.

She said, "I don't think Elizabeth could get on without me." In her heart she said, live without me, breathe without me.

"I have no doubt that she will soon get used to your absence."

Muriel sought for the right words, for some sort of cunning strength, the strength to resist him utterly. Could her father simply make her do what he wished? She said, "If I leave this house I shall take Elizabeth with me."

Carel smiled. The white teeth glistened in the dry face. "I think that would scarcely be practicable, Muriel." He spoke as if it were the most ordinary of suggestions.

Another thought came to Muriel. "But Elizabeth, surely— Does Elizabeth know of this idea? Does she approve?"

"Naturally I have discussed it with Elizabeth and of course she approves."

Muriel stood up. Her father remained motionless, raising his eyes towards her. She meant to say to him, I don't believe you. She said, "I hate you."

Carel continued to look towards her but his face had stiffened and his eyes seemed to glaze over as if he could no longer make the effort of focusing them. He looked as if he were already alone. Muriel made a gesture with her hand as if to dash away too much light from her face. Then with an instinctive movement she leaned forward and snatched the icon up from the desk and hugged it to her breast. She turned and ran from the room.

"Muriel, Muriel, Muriel, not so fast, I want to talk to you. Where are you rushing to?"

Muriel paused half way through the hall. She said to Leo, "I'm going to see your father."

"He isn't there. He's out shopping. Look, I must talk to you."

Muriel laid the icon down on a side table, face downwards. She did not want Leo to see it. The front door bell was ringing and a moment later Pattie could be heard explaining to Anthea Barlow that unfortunately the Rector was busy.

Muriel's first thought on leaving her father's room had been to run straight back to Elizabeth. But a second thought checked her. She needed time to reflect, other help perhaps, before seeing her cousin. Her father's decision to send her away had come to her at first with the flat relentless matter-of-factness of so many of Carel's decisions. So, now what he wanted was that she should go. More slowly she realized exactly why it was that she had to go. Her cousin's silence, her calmness, her so familiar and ordinary peevishness and restlessness, perhaps this most of all, had very nearly convinced Muriel that Elizabeth "knew nothing". Muriel was aware how completely irrational it was to think this. But she had been simply unable to conceive of Elizabeth's silence as a deliberate masquerade, as the initiation of a policy, as part of some terrible revenge.

Now Carel's decision made her see things with a difference. Unless Carel was lying altogether, Elizabeth and Carel must have conferred together about what was to be done. Indeed it was most unlikely that Carel would have told Muriel to go without at least warning Elizabeth; and surely Elizabeth could have stopped him if she had wished to. Elizabeth and Carel had discussed her, conferred about her and coldly decided her fate. She had placed them in a new situation and in this situation they had acted. In her own state of shock it had simply not occurred to her to ask: what will they do?

Even more than what had gone before, this drawing of them together against her altered the whole world. Even the past was changed. Muriel began to ask herself questions of a terrible precision. How long? What was it like? How had it started? Why had it happened? She felt unable now to confront Elizabeth. There ought to be tears, screams and shame. But suppose Elizabeth were cold? Suppose she behaved just like Carel? How very alike they are, Muriel thought for the first time in her life.

She had picked up the icon automatically, by instinct, but now she saw its presence as a sign. The icon had been upon its miraculous progress and now it had come back and it would lead her to Eugene. To take it back to him was the only significant action that was left to her. As she imagined giving it to him and then losing herself in a storm of tears she felt at last in every aching cell of her body how utterly wretched she was.

"Muriel, what's the matter with you? I've been talking to you and you aren't listening."

"Did you say your father wasn't in?"

"He's out shopping. He'll be back soon. Look, we can't talk here, let's go up to your room."

Muriel turned and began to mount the stairs. She entered her room and switched the light on and almost shut the door in Leo's face. The room was icy cold. The fire was rarely lit there, since Muriel spent so much time in Elizabeth's room. Muriel sat down on the bed and covered her face with her hands.

"What's the matter, Muriel?"

"Nothing. What did you want to say?"

"Well, two things. First I've got to confess to you that I'm in a terrible fix. It's like this—old Marcus—well, you probably know by now it was Marcus I went to to get the money to buy that bloody icon back. But never mind the icon. I told Marcus I was engaged to be married. Next thing he sees is you and me tangling on the floor. Well, that's the least of my troubles. I felt bad about old Marcus. I'm quite fond of the old fool really. I can't be his slave either. It was awful. You remember I said I'd give him that seventy-five pounds. Well, I decided it wasn't enough, that I'd have to give him the whole lot, what he'd have to pay for the icon. So do you know what I've done? I've borrowed two hundred and twenty-five pounds from that older woman, the one I told you about. So now I'm in it again with her up to the neck. What do you think of that?"

Muriel was half listening to Leo. In a little while Eugene would be back and would be holding her in his arms and making her think and feel and become a whole human being again. She said distractedly to Leo, "It's not very important."

"What? It's terribly important, it's disgraceful. Aren't you going to tick me off? Aren't I awful?"

"Why should I believe you anyway? You tell so many lies your remarks just aren't interesting."

"Muriel, I'm not lying to you any more, I swear."

"Well, what was the other thing you wanted to say? I'm in a hurry."

"Oh, all right. We'll leave that. I just had to tell you. The second thing I wanted to say was that I'm in love with you."

"What did you say?"

"I'M IN LOVE WITH YOU."

"Don't shout."

Muriel got up and went to the window. As she crossed the room she saw through the half-open door of the corner cupboard the little blue bottle which contained the sleeping-tablets. She pulled the curtain back a little. There was a pattern of frost on the inside of the pane, thin as tissue paper, and beyond it the darkness. She shivered. Longing for Eugene filled her to the brim, longing for a place where she could break down. She groaned and leaned her head against the glass. The granules of cold gritty frost pitted her forehead.

"You don't seem very pleased," said Leo. "But it's all your fault. You would excite me about that girl. And then it was such a fiasco, and old Marcus arriving like that. What did you see anyway through that crack in the wall? You seemed pretty determined I shouldn't look."

"I told you," said Muriel. "She was naked. Well, no she wasn't exactly naked, she was wearing her surgical corset."

"Her what?"

"She has a permanent illness of the back and she has to wear a sort of metal sheath to keep the centre of her body rigid."

"Why didn't you tell me before?"

"I thought it might put you off."

"It would have put me off. Just as well I'm not in love with *her*, isn't it? I might have had to sue you."

"I did mislead you," said Muriel. "I'm sorry. She isn't even very beautiful."

"I don't understand you, Muriel. Most girls want to keep the boys for themselves, but you wanted to give me away. Anyway, you've got me now. What are you going to do with me?"

Muriel moved her head. It seemed as if her brow was becoming frozen to the window. She stepped back. Icy water ran down into her eyes. She wiped her face with her hand and faced Leo. Leo was hunched inside his overcoat with the collar well turned up and his hands deep in his pockets. His nose was red with cold. His rather small furred head peered out from the bundle of the coat, like an animal looking out of a hole. His legs below the coat, in tight faded jeans, looked weak and spidery. How small he is, thought Muriel.

She said, "You're not really in love with me, Leo. Forget it."

There was silence for a moment. Muriel chafed her frozen brow awkwardly with a stiff cold hand.

Leo said in a slower deeper voice, "I don't think you've quite understood me. This is serious."

Muriel thought, what is this idiocy. She could scarcely attend, scarcely understand. She said, "I'm sorry, I can't love you. I've got troubles of my own anyway. You're too young. And I'm in love with someone else." Was that true? Saying it seemed suddenly to make it true.

"I don't believe you," said Leo.

"I must go now," she said. "Please forget about all this." She began to move past him to the door.

"Wait, my girl," said Leo. "I told you it was all your fault. You've got to suffer a bit, too, you know."

"Get out of the way, please."

"Perhaps you don't understand English. I told you I'm in love. It's a kind of sickness, Muriel, don't you know? Like to feel how my heart's beating? Do you really think I'm going to let you get out of that door without touching you?"

"Leo, please, there's something urgent—"

"It can wait. I love you, Muriel. And you're going to undergo my love. And you're going to love me. I wanted a terribly special girl. Well, you're it." He gripped Muriel's arm, digging his fingers in fiercely.

"Let go, you're hurting me."

"That's better. Now you're going to sit down and I'm going to tell you how wonderful and unusual you are."

Leo pushed Muriel so that she sat down heavily upon the bed. He leaned over her, with one arm scooping underneath her knees, and she felt the chill of his hand against her leg above the stocking. She began to struggle but his other hand, pressing heavily on her shoulder, forced her to lean awkwardly back against the wall.

"Naughty, naughty, you're kicking. I'll tell you another nice thing about you, Muriel. You're a virgin. I know. Men always know. So you see— Now kiss me. You didn't do it too badly last time." He thrust his face towards her.

Weakness and disgust made Muriel want to whimper. She sat still in his imprisoning grasp, turning her head away. The misery of her body mounted in a physical paroxysm. She said in a low clear voice, "Don't touch me. I am in love with your father."

As Muriel went through the door of her room she thought: but where is the icon? She remembered that she had left it down below on the side table in the hall. A new buoyancy took her down the stairs. Now she would fly straight to Eugene as to her salvation and make him happy and grateful. The miraculous return of the icon would open the gates of communication between them. This time the privilege of tears would be hers and in those tears the world would begin again. If she could touch Eugene, if she could utter a single word to him about her situation, she would be automatically set free from *them*.

Muriel stopped dead in the middle of the hall. The icon was not there. She approached the table. Was it there that she had left it? She was certain. Fear licked her like an agonizing flame. It was gone. In a futile helpless way she looked about on the floor, peering under the chairs. It was gone, it was lost, someone had stolen it again. It was all her fault. She had had it in her hand, how could she have been so insane as to put it down for a single second? She looked at the front door. It was bolted. Had her father come down and taken it back to his study?

"What are you looking for?" said Pattie.

Pattie's black face was looking out from under the stairs. Behind her the kitchen door stood open.

Muriel moved slowly past Pattie into the kitchen. She said in a dull voice, "I left something on that table."

"Oh, that picture," said Pattie. "Eugene's icon. Yes, I found it there and gave it back to him."

"*You* gave it back to him?"

"Yes, of course. What did you expect me to do with it?"

"But it was *mine*." Muriel's voice had become a high wail. Her hands clawed the air. "I found it. I was going to give it back to him. You should have left it where you found it. It was none of your business. I was going to give it to him."

"Well, you can't now," said Pattie. She turned her back on Muriel and began to stir a saucepan of soup which was steaming upon the hot plate of the cooker.

"You *knew* it was mine!"

"I knew nothing of the sort," said Pattie. "It isn't yours, anyway. I just found it there. You shouldn't have left it lying about. It might have got stolen again."

"You did it on purpose. I found it, I wanted so much to give it to him. You took it from me on purpose."

"Oh, don't be so *childish*," said Pattie. "What does it matter who gave it to him, so long as he's got it back." She went on stirring the soup. She added, "He was very pleased."

Hysteria had now taken hold of Muriel. A high whining sound came out of her, seeming not to issue from her mouth but to emerge from her whole head. She shouted to Pattie, "Listen to me!"

"Don't make that horrible noise," said Pattie. "Someone'll hear you."

"Listen to me, damn you!"

"Get out of my kitchen," said Pattie, turning round, hands on hips.

"It's not your kitchen. You're just a common servant and don't you forget it."

"You little brat," said Pattie, beginning to raise her voice. "Get out of here before I slap you."

Muriel advanced on Pattie, who backed away. "Don't you dare to touch me, Pattie O'Driscoll, I'll tear you in pieces." Muriel picked up the saucepan of soup by its handle.

"Stop that, you vile ill-bred little monkey! Get out of my kitchen, I tell you!"

"You killed my mother," said Muriel. "You killed my mother, you black bitch out of hell."

Pattie, who was still backing away, stopped and bared her teeth. Both rows of teeth flashed. She cried out, "You stopped your father from marrying me. You ruined me, you ruined my whole life. I hate you for it, I'll always hate you."

Muriel swung the heavy saucepan. Pattie screamed as the hot soup came out in a swooping brown stream. Most of the soup went on to the floor, but some of it splashed on to Pattie's stockings and her apron. Pattie continued to scream. Muriel hurled the empty saucepan across the kitchen.

Carel entered the room followed by Eugene. Pattie's screams turned to sobs. Carel took in the scene. He said to Muriel, "The sooner you are out of this house the better. See to it." He said to Pattie, "Be quiet, Pattie. Miss Muriel is leaving us soon. We must try to be kind to her in the time that remains. There, there, my Pattikins, you aren't really hurt, are you?" Carel put an arm round the sobbing Pattie.

Muriel walked past Eugene and out of the kitchen.

# Chapter Nineteen

MARCUS FISHER was in a state approaching ecstasy. He was ensconced in Norah Shadox-Brown's sitting-room in front of a roaring fire. The curtains were drawn against the steely grey afternoon. Under a soft lamp the Irish linen table-cloth was covered with a golden strewing of crumbs from the Madeira cake. Marcus put his empty tea-cup down among the streaks of cranberry jelly upon his white plate in the way in which Norah had often asked him not to. He said, "But it's his *seriousness* that matters, his passion."

Norah leaned to put Marcus's cup back on to his saucer. She said, "Nothing you've told me persuades me he's serious. He's either mad or else amusing himself at your expense."

"Oh, you don't understand!" Marcus sneezed.

"There, I told you you were developing a cold."

"I'm not developing a cold."

Marcus had done his best to explain to Norah the experience, he was tempted to think of it as the mystical experience, of his meeting with Carel. In explaining Carel's arguments he had presented the scene, he was aware not quite accurately, as a sober discussion between the two brothers in which he had played his own part. This was not entirely misleading of course in that Marcus had *thought* quite a lot of answers while Carel was talking, or at any rate he had thought of them afterwards. What he did not tell Norah was that Carel had struck him. That blow was something very private. Norah would not be able to understand it, she would think of it in a crude way as a further proof of Carel's unbalance. Whereas it was in fact a blow designed to produce enlightenment. It was more than that, it seemed to Marcus in his later thoughts. It was a mark of love. His brother had made him exist, had wanted him to exist, for a moment in an intense presence of each to each. Love was the name of such a presence.

Marcus, he had to admit, was now in a condition which could only be described as being in love with Carel. He had been too overwhelmed by Carel's dreadful eloquence and too shocked by the blow to realize this at first. But as he walked away from the house through the intense cold of the evening his whole physical being had seemed changed. He felt radiant, as if he were exuding warmth and light. He felt the kind of happiness which seems to bubble out through the top of the head, making the eyes stare and the lips fall apart in an imbecile smile. The condition was so involuntary that at first he simply could not understand it. Then he apprehended it as in some way caused by Carel having struck him. Then a glorified image of Carel rose up before him and this had absorbed him ever since.

He found when he got home to his room in Earls Court that all his anxieties had vanished. He tested the room, like an electrician looking for a fault. The room had changed, as if some sinister cobwebby litter had been removed from it. Something which had dimmed the lights, something which had sat in the corner and threatened him, had gone away. Marcus filled the room with the radiance of his new being, Marcus and the room floated over London like a gay balloon. Marcus stood in the room and laughed.

He had been right then to imagine that a frank talk with Carel would drive his nightmares away. Even his worry about Elizabeth had ceased. Poor innocent Elizabeth, how distressed, or how amused, she would be if she knew what an awesome little goddess she had been made into in Marcus's imagination! An infirmity of his own mind had inflated that image which had now been blown quite away. He could think again with rational sympathy and affection of a child he had known and of a sick girl he was soon to meet. Out of a number of coincidences he had invented a conspiracy. Why should Elizabeth see him at any time when he chose to turn up, why should she reply promptly to his messages? It was perfectly true that she was ill. He ought to have been more considerate. Of course, Carel didn't make things any easier by his manners of a mysterious recluse. Certainly Carel was difficult, but Carel had always been difficult. Marcus went to bed and had happy dreams of a benevolent figure which seemed to be half Carel and half his younger brother Julian on whom he had so much doted when he was young.

Even his relations with Leo had benefited from the new enlightenment. In a separate compartment of his mind Marcus had become distinctly worried about Leo. That he should feel a bit emotional about Leo did not in itself surprise or distress him. He had often had small passions for his pupils but had always and quite easily managed to keep them sealed up. What troubled him here was that Leo so patently knew of this weakness. Marcus was stung too by the suspicion that Leo was not only prepared to exploit him but did so with mockery and without affection. Marcus had become uneasy, especially after their last interview, about the image of himself in Leo's mind. In a way he was ready enough to be exploited, in a way he liked it. It is part of any teacher's duty to be moderately exploitable by his pupils. But here Marcus felt his dignity rather especially endangered, and his dignity was precious to him. Also he was disturbed by the sheer magnitude of his affection for the boy, increased in quantity after these recent adventures. Marcus was beginning to need a friendship with Leo which he saw little prospect of achieving.

However, on the day after his momentous meeting with Carel he had had a very satisfactory encounter with Leo. Leo had rung him up at Earls Court and had later come round. He had brought with him, much to Marcus's surprise, the sum of three hundred pounds in cash, the price of the icon, and had laid it on the table. When Marcus had questioned him closely about how he got the money he had confessed that on the previous occasion he had told Marcus a lie. The story of his engagement to a girl whose father demanded the production of seventy-five pounds had been a complete fabrication. The truth was that he had acquired a very expensive motor bicycle for which he had partly paid and had sold the icon in desperation in order to pay off the remainder. He had not told Marcus this for fear that Marcus would insist on his selling the bike. Keeping a stern face Marcus agreed that he would indeed have insisted. Since then, accused by conscience, Leo had sold the machine for quite a good price and had taken the proceeds to the White City where he had had a lucky evening with the dogs. That was why he was so happily able to repay Marcus the three hundred pounds. Leo also brought, and very prettily said, the effusive thanks of his father for Marcus's great kindness to them both.

Marcus concealed his pleasure at the breakdown of Leo's ingenious attempt to lie to him, and at the greater frankness between them which Leo's confession had brought about. He lectured Leo sternly upon the importance of truthfulness and threw in a few words about the dangers of gambling. He went on to discuss Leo's future in general and suggested forcibly that he should give up the technical college and return to his and Marcus's earlier plan of doing a university degree in French and Russian. Marcus suggested that if Leo did so change his mind the three hundred pounds which he had so correctly repaid might be earmarked as a sort of education fund to help him over any financial difficulties involved in the changeover. Leo, who appeared chastened, listened seriously and gratefully and said that he would think the matter over. They parted with a warm handshake and Marcus concluded that he had been mistaken to think that Leo had no affection for him. The boy was thoroughly fond of him after all. Now that Leo was grown up there was no reason why they should not be friends.

"You seem very pleased with yourself," said Norah. "More tea?"

"No thanks."

"As far as I can gather from your garbled version of Carel's tirade, he stated not only that there was no God and human life was senseless, but also that the precarious reign of morality, itself of course an illusion, is now at an end and that henceforth human-kind is to be the victim of irresponsible psychological forces which your brother picturesquely designates as angels. This I should have thought rather grim news seems to have raised you to a seventh heaven of delight. I wonder why?"

Marcus shook his head. "You don't see," he said. "It's partly that what Carel says is true, and the truth is always a bit exhilarat-ing even when it's awful. Kant understood that. It's partly that there is a sort of hope, a difficult hope, in what he said. He himself saw this although he denied it at once."

"The notion that the truth is always exhilarating seems to me romantic nonsense and I'm surprised to hear you attribute it to Kant. If I'm told tomorrow that I've got incurable cancer I won't be exhilarated. But what's this hope you speak of?"

"Well, I suppose those two ideas are really one. The situation is terrible, but nevertheless or perhaps because—I mean the human spirit can respond."

"Sometimes it can, sometimes it can't. Cigarette?"

"Thanks. Of course, Carel's right about the absurd optimism of all philosophy up to the present, and he's right that people who pretend to dispense with the idea of God don't really do so. One's got to learn to live without the idea of the Good being somehow One. That's what's hard."

"Well, you've had a philosophical training and I haven't," said Norah, "but I don't see any point in either affirming or denying that the Good is One. I still ought to pay my bills. Ordinary morality goes on and always will go on whatever the philosophers and theologians have to say."

"I wonder," said Marcus. "I wonder." He added, "For you common sense takes the place of faith. In a way I envy you."

"No you don't. You just feel superior to me. Anyway, I'm the many, thank God."

"The many live off the great few in the long run."

"The many decide who are the great few in the long run. I'm not going to worry because someone like Carel loses his nerve. And I'd say that even if I thought he was a genius, instead of being just a poor crackpot who needs a few electric shocks."

Was Carel mad? Marcus asked himself again. He might know the truth even if he were technically insane. What a passion! Marcus realized now that he had never even sighted that spiritual ocean upon which his brother was seemingly suffering shipwreck. He wished he could share Norah's sturdy confidence in the world of common sense. Or rather, she was right, he did not wish it.

"Has this conversation with Carel wrecked your book?" said Norah.

"Yes."

Since the talk with Carel, indeed since fully apprehending the existence of Carel, Marcus had known that his book just wouldn't do. It was as Carel said, milk-and-water theology. Of course he would write another book, a better truer one with real passion in it. But this one was no use. His version of the ontological proof simply wouldn't work. "The angels get in the way," he said.

"You'll soon be as batty as your brother," said Norah.

Marcus recalled Norah's words about the twilight of a dying mythology driving people mad. Yet if one went far enough along that road there must be an issue. Or was that "must" just the old delusion inevitably recurring? Did not the removal of God make real goodness possible at last, the goodness that is good, as it were, for nothing? Or was Carel right that this was an ideal so far beyond our reach that we could not even significantly name it? Was there no answer to Carel? Was there nothing which was both good and real?

"What are you going to do about Carel anyway?" said Norah, uttering a question she had now uttered a great many times.

Marcus took a deep breath. "Save him," he said.

"Save him? How, pray?"

"By love," said Marcus. It was now clear to him that this was the answer. His great book would not be about good, it would be about love. In the case of love the ontological proof would work. Because love was a real human activity. He would save his brother by loving him. Carel would be made to recognize the reality of love. "Is Love One, I wonder?" he said to Norah.

"Marcus, I really think you're taking leave of your senses," said Norah. "And there you go again, sneezing all over the tea-table."

# Chapter Twenty

EUGENE PESHKOV awoke, turned on an electric torch and looked at his watch. No need to get up yet. He turned over and began to fall slowly through a grey shadowy shaft of space and time. The sun is shining brightly on a huge meadow of long grass. The flowers of the grass upon their very thin stalks are reddish and cast a mobile rosy light over the green expanse of the grass which is softly moved by a warm wind. A single birch tree stands in the middle of the grass, its slim trunk elegantly twisted inside its translucent fall of faint greenery. A little white dog is barking and barking.

A lady in a striped dress emerges from a golden haze into a sphere of light. The narrow stripes of her dress are white and green and the hem of her dress has a dark terminal line where it has been sweeping the dusty verandah. "Dickory, dickory dock, the mouse ran up the clock!" Eugene laughs and tries to lift up the lady's skirt. He is the little mouse that runs up the clock. He lifts the edge of the skirt a little bit. Underneath there is a grey petticoat of silk with a heavy fringe. He lifts the fringe. There is another petticoat below made of creamy lace. He thrusts his hands down to lift it up. There is another petticoat, white as milk, and below it there is another. Eugene utters sharp cries now as he digs and thrusts. He is half suffocated inside a wardrobe which seems to have no back but to go on and on. He pushes forward through a forest of clinging flimsy dresses reeking of old perfume. The dresses press closely about him, impeding his limbs. They will stifle him. He cannot breathe. He gasps, and sees his mother weeping in a room in Prague. Her gauzy grey dress extends in a long train, filling the room with a clutter of grey ectoplasm. The little white dog barks and barks.

Eugene woke up to find that he had buried his face in the

pillow. He tried to catch the tail of his dream. He caught a quick glimpse of the sunny meadow and the verandah of their country house near Petersburg, and then it was gone. Even that fell from his memory although he knew that he had remembered it just the second before. He knew the dream had concerned his English governess, Miss Alison, but he could not recall anything which had happened in the dream. Miss Alison had always been there, a stiff figure who moved about very slowly and uttered little shrieks if anything fast occurred such as a dog jumping up or a child leaping. He had talked English with Miss Alison as soon as he could speak. She had taught him English nursery rhymes which she sang in a tiny high voice beating time with her finger. And she had introduced him to a new world of puzzlement and fear when he had found her one day in her room weeping uncontrollably. It was the first time he had ever seen a grown-up weep. He did not know that grown-ups could cry at all, let alone cry like that. He had wept too then, noisily, in terror. If grown-ups could cry like that then there was no safety in the world. He had not till much later wondered about the cause of her tears. Probably she was just homesick and alone, a lost little English lady in a robust alien world which scarcely noticed her. She spoke a little French. She never learnt Russian. She had accompanied them on their flight as far as Riga, and then taken the ship for England. Could she be still alive? Eugene had never had any notion of her age. She might have been twenty, thirty, forty. More likely she was dead now.

Eugene got up and switched the light on. He was late again. It was so hard to wake up in winter. He dressed quickly. As he was dressing his eye fell upon the painted Russian box which was sitting upon the table. The dream had had something to do with that box, something very sad, the something which had made him weep and which he was still unable to remember. He stared hard at the box, trying to make his mind vague and receptive, but could recall nothing. He transferred his gaze to the icon and smiled. He saw in a clear image, like a little oval picture, the icon in his mother's bedroom in Petersburg. It had been surrounded then by a heavy frame of black painted wood picked out in gilt squares. At the bottom of the frame there was an extended bracket intended to hold a lamp, but Eugene's mother, whose piety was tempered by a concern for *objets d'art*, especially those belonging to her own family, would never allow a lamp to be lighted in case the fumes should damage the icon. With the image of the icon in its ponderous dark frame came a vague apparition of Eugene's mother, all softness and dove-greyness, her voluminous pale fair hair pinned up in a high crown, a flimsy grey dress, or was it a négligé, falling vaguely about her and making a shadowy pool about her feet.

It was a miracle that the icon had come back and that it was Pattie who had brought it. He felt that the icon itself must somehow have determined how it all fell out. It had been on a miraculous progress and now it had come back to him. Neither he nor Pattie had any idea how it had come back. Pattie had simply found it lying on a table in the hall and had rushed in to give it to him. Eugene really did not want to know any more. It was a happy augury.

Pattie's significant appearance with the icon had completed the circle of his good fortune. Pattie had made him believe in happiness. He was well aware how dangerous this belief was and that it was new. But he was aware too that the grace of happiness comes to those who have faith in it. He had been indifferent to it for almost all of his life, had not conceived of it as one of his possibilities. It seemed that he had had his life's ration of happiness before he was six. Now he wanted a happy future. And he saw Pattie wanting it too, and suspected that this desire was coming to her for the first time. To be the cause that another person desires to be happy is a grave responsibility. Eugene wore his seriously but with an increasingly light heart. He was becoming sure that he and Pattie would get married.

Not that Pattie had said or done anything clear. She seemed confused. She had asked him to wait and not to trouble her. She had said, "I can't say yes," but her dark faintly reddish eyes had said yes, yes, yes, and she could not resist touching him to take away any hurt her words might have caused. Eugene believed her eyes and her hands. He and she had been taken in charge by the involuntary chemistry of love. While nothing specific was said Eugene felt day by day and more and more the arrival of Pattie. Like a weight slowly subsiding he could feel the steady increase of her reliance on him. Every day there was more of her for him to care for.

Sometimes it seemed to him that she was worried and upset about something and he tried to make it as easy as possible for her to talk to him about it, but she would always fall silent. He began to speculate about Pattie. She had told him that she had no history, but could this be true? Trying to picture the worst he conjectured that she might have had an illegitimate child when she was very young. Or it might be simply that she could not get over the belief that her colour was repugnant to him. Whatever the barrier was, he longed to know it so that he could sweep it away with the force of love. Meanwhile this little crestfallenness in Pattie made her but the more attractive to him. He cherished her diffidence, her doubt. It was not that he was confident of her innocence, he *saw* her innocence. She was the innocent, the undiscovered America, the good dark continent.

His cheerfulness in waiting made it easy for him to behave to her with a quiet constant loving kindness. Love made an artist of him. He bought little presents, invented treats. It was years since he had seen himself making anybody happy. He had lived selfishly for far too long and flattered himself that his dull simplicity was a merit. Leo was right, he ought to have fought for a place in English society. He had drifted weakly into a senseless isolation and called it unworldliness. But if he tried he could do ordinary things at last, he and Pattie together.

His happiness overflowed on to her, and although she seemed sometimes with a half-hearted gesture to brush it away she could not escape its influence. She often sang now. And she was easy with him. With a tact which he hoped he could maintain he still restrained a boisterousness which he often felt. He would have liked to seize Pattie, to slap her and set her on his knee. As it was their physical contacts remained like those of affectionate children. Only sometimes would he allow himself to kiss her seriously or hug her in bear-like transports of joy.

If there was anything which his years as a hermit had given him it was a quality of the affections which he hesitated to call purity. It was more like novelty. He felt as if he were a boy in love for the first time. He had never really been in love with poor Tanya. His only loves had been those of his childhood and he had seemed all his life until now incapable of any other.

"I dreamt about my English governess last night. Miss Alison was her name."

"Were you fond of her?"

"Oh yes. I loved everybody. Children always do."

"Some children."

"What did you dream last night, Pattie?"

"I never dream. What happened in your dream?"

"I can't remember. I think it was at our country house."

"What was that house called? You did tell me."

"It was called Byelaya Doleena. That means White Glen or White Glade in English. It was called for the birch trees. You see birch trees have white trunks."

"I know birch trees have white trunks, silly! There are birch trees in England."

"Are there? Yes, I suppose there are. I don't remember ever having seen any in England. Oh, Pattie, you aren't going are you?"

"I must go. It's past my shopping time."

"Have you got your sugar mouse?"

"It's jumped into my pocket. Shall I wear my new boots?"

"Yes, of course. They make you look Russian."

"They're a bit tight. Suppose they start hurting on the way along?"

"What a worrier it is! You wear your new boots like a brave girl."

"I won't be long."

"Be careful crossing the roads. Buy me something nice."

"Come with me to put on my boots."

Pattie and Eugene went into the kitchen. Pattie seemed in a happier mood than usual and they had been laughing a lot.

"Let me put on the boots for you. Sit down there."

Eugene knelt and took off Pattie's frayed tartan slippers. For a moment he held her warm plump foot in his hand. It was like holding a big bird. He held the boot for her and with pointed toe she pressed a foot in. The boots, which Eugene had encouraged her to buy and which had been much discussed between them, were of black leather, almost knee length and lined with wool. Pattie had never had such boots before.

"They're too tight, I told you so."

"You always complain your shoes are too big for you!"

"They aren't at first. First they're too tight, then they're too big."

"Come on, push."

"I can't get in."

"You don't know how to put a boot on. It's just a matter of getting round the corner. Push."

Pattie's foot entered the foot of the boot and Eugene could feel her heel press firmly down into its place. "Good. Now the other."

With much pushing and hauling Pattie donned the other boot.

"Now your fur coat. Now you're a real Russian!"

Wrapped up in her rabbity fur coat and her head scarf Pattie looked spherical, just such a dear bundle as might be seen any snowy morning on the Nevsky Prospect. Eugene laughed at her and then out of sheer happiness hugged her to him, whirling her round. Over her shoulder he saw standing in the kitchen doorway Muriel Fisher who was regarding them both with an expression of malevolence.

Eugene released Pattie, dropping his hands hastily to his sides. Pattie turned and saw Muriel too. She hesitated and then walked boldly towards the door. Muriel stood aside. Eugene, mumbling "Good morning" followed Pattie into the hall. Pattie went to the front door and opened it. A wave of icy air came in, biting hands and faces. There was much less fog today but little could be seen outside except a thick dark grey light.

"Ouf, Pattie, it's cold. Better not keep that door open long."

"Come outside a moment," said Pattie.

Coatless and shivering, Eugene stood out on the step while Pattie half closed the door behind him. The sudden cold had nipped and reddened their faces and they peered at each other in the bitter dark light. Their faces which had been two flowers each to each were blighted and closed. "What is it, Pattie? I'm freezing."

"I wanted to say—Oh it doesn't matter."

"Say it when you come back."

"I will come back, won't I?"

"What do you mean? Of course you'll come back."

"And you'll be there, won't you?"

"Of course I'll be there."

"You'll always be there, won't you, Eugene, always?"

"Always! Now you be careful, Pattie, and don't fall down in your new boots."

Pattie disappeared into the cold obscurity of the morning, walking rather cautiously on the pavement upon which the snow was frozen in iron-grey lumps. Eugene dodged back into the comparative warmth of the hall. Perhaps he should have gone with her. His few tasks could have waited. He was glad of her words though. She had never said "always" to him before.

Smiling he crossed the kitchen and opened the door of his room. Muriel Fisher who had been sitting down beside the table rose to her feet. Eugene entered more slowly. "Miss Muriel—"

"I'm sorry," said Muriel in a very low voice. "May I talk to you for a moment?"

Eugene stared at Muriel's face. He thought at first that she must be grimacing at him. Her face was wrinkled up and drawn as if it was hung upon hooks. She had always had for him a certain repellant quality of ghastliness. Now she had the air of a demon in torment and he shrank from her.

Eugene had never liked Muriel, who seemed to him unwomanly and hard. He classified her in his mind with Miss Shadox-Brown, as that thin brusque efficient type of Englishwoman who has good intentions but cannot help being patronising. Some kind of tough self-confidence built into such women made them more insufferably superior than a man could ever be. Eugene, still sensitive to the tones and accents with which society addressed him, could detect the little strain of contempt in the midst of the most unassuming cordiality. Muriel had questioned him about his past with a quick thoroughness which did not seem like compassion or even curiosity. He felt that Muriel just wanted to "place" him tidily, to sum him up so as to be able to deal with him briskly and appropriately.

The gift of the Russian box had simply upset him. He forgave the box but not Muriel. The act was condescending or familiar and in either case offensive; while the choice of that particular present was an intrusion into a privacy and a mystery she could know nothing of. That she had thereby clumsily touched a nerve in his hidden past, acting on him in a way which he himself could not understand, was an added insult. He resented this, he resented her having witnessed his tears, and he resented her rude treatment of Leo in his presence, as if she could wield over the son an authority which was lacking in the father. He had early realized that she was Pattie's foe. And since the odious scene of the saucepan of soup he had thought the girl both detestable and dangerous.

Eugene steadied himself now. His immediate thought was that Muriel had come to complain about something which Leo had done.

"Shut the door, please," said Muriel.

"What is it, Miss Muriel?"

Muriel sat down again. She stared at him, her mouth open in a drooping arc. Her narrow glaring eyes burnt through the squeezed-up mask of her face.

Eugene, very uneasy, said, "I expect you want to—there's something wrong—I expect Leo—"

"I want your help," said Muriel in a sepulchral growl. She had some difficulty in speaking.

"I'm afraid I don't understand."

Muriel swallowed hard, took hold of the tablecloth, and bowed her head, shutting her eyes tightly for a moment in a grimacing frown. Then she said, "I found your icon for you."

"What?"

"I found your icon for you. I brought it back. Pattie just found it in the hall. I should have brought it to you."

"But did you have it then? Did you get it from—What do you mean?"

"It's too complicated. I tell you I found it. I was just going to bring it back to you only Pattie stole it."

"Stole it? I'm afraid I don't know what you're talking about," said Eugene. She is dangerous, dangerous, he thought to himself. He looked at her with hostility.

Muriel regarded him with screwed-up burning eyes. Her face seemed to express hatred. She said, "When are the wedding bells going to ring out for you and Pattie?"

Eugene felt anger, a small red spot in the middle of his field of vision. He said, "That is our affair I think, Pattie's and mine."

"So you are getting married? You're in love? That happy scene I saw in the kitchen—"

"Will you leave us alone, please? What did you come here to say? Say it please and then leave me to get on with my work."

"You have no work," said Muriel. She leaned back in the chair. Her face had suddenly become smooth and hard and cold, like ivory, like alabaster. She looked up at the icon. She said, "I think there are one or two things you ought to know about Pattie."

A prophetic fear clutched Eugene's heart. "I don't want to talk to you—"

"Just listen then. You realize of course that Pattie is my father's whore?"

Muriel's gaze slowly returned to Eugene. Her eyes were large now and dreadfully calm.

Eugene stared at her. He tried to speak. "I don't want—I don't—"

"She has been my father's mistress for years," said Muriel, with a slow clear enunciation as if lecturing. "She took my father away from my mother and drove my mother to despair and to death. She has been at my father's disposal ever since. They were at it only last week, making love on the floor of his study last Friday afternoon. I heard them at it, like two animals. Just you ask Pattie and see what she says."

Eugene put his hand to his heart. He pressed his hand very hard against his chest and swallowed some blackness which was coming up from inside him. He said, but the words were little dry wisps, rustling and crackling in his mouth, "It's not true."

"Just you ask her."

"Please go away."

The conviction had fallen from her and she was thin and cold and hard as a needle. He hardly saw her go through the door.

# Chapter Twenty-one

"Excuse me, dear, it's Anthea again. I'm sorry to be so persistent—"

"He won't see you."

"I just wanted to explain to you—"

"He won't see you. Can't you understand English?"

"If I may be just the tiniest bit critical—"

"Go away."

"I realize Father Carel is ill—"

"Mind your own business."

"And the Bishop is—"

"Shut up and be off with you."

"But Pattie, you see, Father Carel is—"

"Miss O'Driscoll to you."

"But, Pattie, my dear, I know all about you—"

"No, you don't. Nobody knows about me, nobody."

"Poor Pattie, I can see you're in some sort of trouble. Wouldn't you like to tell me—"

"Go away, you interfering bitch. Take your bloody foot out of the door.'

With tears starting again, Pattie pushed with all her might. The Persian lamb gave ground. In a brown haze Mrs Barlow slithered and expostulated on the grey ridges of the frozen snow. The door banged.

Pattie, who was on her way to Muriel's room, turned back into the empty hall and forgot the incident instantaneously. Misery filled her mouth and her eyes. Head drooping, she mounted the stairs. Near the top she lost a shoe and did not stop to pick it up.

Eugene had rejected her. She could not but tell him the truth, or rather admit the truth of what he already knew. She had tried to explain that last Friday, that was exceptional, it was just that once, it hadn't happened before for a long time—But to speak of a date, of a happening at all, was something fatal. Even as she stammered to say how it was she was accusing herself. A destructive demon of despair seemed to leap out of her own mouth. This was not anything which could be explained and seen not to matter. She was unclean, she was unworthy, she was black, and she belonged to another, it was all true. Even if Carel had not taken her then he could have taken her at any hour, at any minute. Her will was his. He was the Lord God and she was the inert and silent earth which moves in perfect obedience. How much, how hopelessly, she did belong to Carel she realized as she faced Eugene's anguished but relentless questioning. She had been bought long ago and could never now be ransomed.

It was not that Eugene would never forgive her or that his disgust would last forever or that he was not perhaps good enough to redeem her from the place in which she was fixed. It was that indeed she belonged there. What he charged her with clung to her and no gracious wedding-ring could change her now. Her feet could not run to reach him, the innocence of their converse had been a fake. Pattie did not even appeal to Eugene. He turned from her and she released him. It was the end.

She had known that Muriel had done it, and what Muriel had done, as soon as she had seen Eugene's face on her return. The betrayal by Muriel now seemed to her inevitable. Could she have forestalled that betrayal by any words of her own and drawn its sting? It had seemed impossible, the confession itself would have shown her to him as unattainable and untouchable and treacherous. In speaking to him she would have had to admit to herself the impossibility of her love for him. Crying frenziedly in her own room, hatred for Muriel seemed to exist as something separate, growing by itself, a great black plant rising up beside her. She herself was to blame. But Muriel was hateful. As she got up to go to Muriel there was a kind of relief in it as if to talk to her would be almost a consolation.

Muriel was sitting in her bedroom in an armchair muffled up in her overcoat. She greeted Pattie almost absently and then returned to staring fixedly in front of her, breathing just audibly through her lips with a soft whistling sound. The breath formed smokily about her mouth in the icy atmosphere. The curtains were drawn back and the window pane behind her displayed a huge frost picture which obscured the dim morning light, so that it was quite dark in the room.

Pattie sat down on the bed. Muriel's physical presence intimidated her, as it had always done .She felt empty and wretched, felt little more than a desire to cry piteously. She said, half whimpering, "Why did you do that to me?"

Muriel did not reply and seemed not to have heard. Then after a while and as if she had been thinking it over she said, "I'm sorry about it now. But it doesn't matter."

Pattie was shivering with cold. She said, "It was wicked—"

After an equally long silence Muriel said absently, "Possibly." She continued to sit immobile, her hands in her pockets, staring away and uttering the soft sibilant breaths.

"I hate you," said Pattie. She wanted to touch Muriel, to pluck at her, to strike her, but she could not move from the bed.

Muriel shifted, crossed her legs, and began to look at Pattie with a curiously bland interested expression. "Oh, do shut up, Pattie. Don't cry. We're all in the same boat, in a way."

"You're all right. You just did that to hurt me out of sheer wickedness. I might have got right away and been happy and you deliberately spoilt it all. I loathe you. I'd like to kill you."

"Oh, stop it. Can't you see I'm wrecked, ruined."

Pattie looked at the bland smooth face. "What do you mean? You're all right."

Muriel gazed at Pattie thoughtfully, her hands still deep inside her overcoat. She said, "You know that my father has told me to go away, to live somewhere else?"

"I heard him say that."

"Do you know why?"

Pattie, who had heard Carel's words with pleasure, had immediately interpreted them as a salve to herself. Muriel had been cruel to Pattie so Muriel must go. Later she had been less certain and inclined to think Carel had not meant it at all. She said without conviction, "Because you were unkind to me."

"You! You don't matter. No, no, there is another reason. Do you really not know it?"

Pattie looked at Muriel with suspicion, with mounting horror. She had never before talked of Carel with Muriel and her whole body knew the danger of it. She ought to run from the room, she ought not to listen. "What do you mean?"

"You didn't know that my father is having a love affair with Elizabeth?"

Pattie said, "*Elizabeth. No.*"

"It's true. I know it's hard to believe, but I actually saw them through a crack in the wall. I just believed my eyes at first. Then there was so much other evidence. I can't think why it didn't occur to me before. They must have been lovers for some time. Poor Elizabeth." Muriel spoke with a cool weariness. She looked vaguely away from Pattie now, showing no interest in her reception of the news.

Pattie sat hunched up on the bed with her eyes closed. She tried to say "You're lying," but the words stayed in her mouth like stones. In fact she believed Muriel instantly. It was as if a veil had been taken from something whose form had long been familiar to her.

Muriel went on in the same cool slightly drawling voice, "I don't know whether it's right to tell you, but everything's collapsed, the house has fallen down, the only thing that's left seems to be the truth and one may as well look it in the face. I hope you believe me. Ask Carel if you don't."

"I believe you," Pattie mumbled, head down, curled over the

words. She felt as if she were holding Carel and that he had shrunk into a little thing the size of a nut.

When Carel had asked for the assurance of her love she had thought that he knew of her relations with Eugene. When he had said "Will you suffer for me, will you be crucified for me?" she had thought that he meant ordinary suffering of the kind she was familiar with. In all her imagination of what she might suffer for Carel she had not conceived of this. This was the one thing in the world which she could not bear.

"It's so cold and hard and organized," said Muriel, rambling on as if she were thinking aloud. "That's what strikes me. And I can *see* it now in Elizabeth, she sort of wears it all. If it was something momentary and impulsive it would be different. But I don't think it is. I feel it's deep, it's already become like an institution. And then telling me to go away like that. He's settling down with Elizabeth. They'll be like a married couple. They're like it now."

They'll be like a married couple, thought Pattie. And I shall be their servant.

"Well, I'm going," said Muriel. "I'm clearing out. And I advise you to go too, Pattie. Leave them to it. I think that's the kindest thing I've ever said to you. One must keep one's sanity. One *ought* to."

Pattie lifted her head. "I don't think I can keep my sanity," she said. She put her hand over her mouth as if she were going to be sick. Her whole body felt in tatters of wretchedness. After all there was no salvation, no one to call the lapséd soul or weep in the evening dew. The house had fallen down. Nothing was left to Pattie except a last desire to tear and to destroy. The world had finally punished her for her blackness. She said, "Now I'm going to tell you something which is so secret I had almost forgotten it."

"What?"

"He made me swear never never to tell and I locked it so away in my mind I hardly remembered it any more."

"What is it?"

"Do you know who Elizabeth is?"

"What do you mean?"

"Elizabeth is your sister."

Muriel sprang up. She came and shook Pattie violently by the shoulders. Between her hands Pattie jolted inertly to and fro.

"Pattie, what are you talking about? You're saying mad things—"

"Leave me. I'm telling you the truth. You should be grateful. You said you wanted the truth. Elizabeth isn't Julian's daughter, she's Carel's daughter. Julian never had a child. Julian and Carel quarrelled over some girl, it was after they were both married. Carel was in love with the girl, but Julian ran away with her and left his wife. Carel seduced Julian's wife just out of spite, for revenge. When Julian knew that his wife was pregnant he killed himself." Pattie added after a moment. "He told me all this— long ago—when he loved me." Her voice became a sob.

Muriel was standing quite still with her head turned away in an awkward deformed attitude. Her whole body seemed to have been wrenched. Then she sat down rather carefully on an upright chair, her head still turned. "Do you swear that this is true, Pattie?"

"I swear it. As you said yourself, ask him."

"I suppose there was no doubt—who the father was?"

"No doubt."

"You're sure he didn't invent it all?"

"No. He always told me the truth in those days. And I found some letters too. He destroyed them later. But ask him, ask him."

"Do you think Elizabeth knows?"

"I don't know. Ask her."

"How *can* he then—"

"Just for that very reason. With him, it had to happen. I should have known. He thinks I'll stand anything. But I won't stand this."

"I think you'd better go now, Pattie," said Muriel. "I'll talk to you about this again later."

As Pattie rose, Muriel came and stretched herself out on the bed and closed her eyes. She lay there inert and pale, her arms straight by her sides, the little plume of breath hanging above her lips. She seemed already to have lost consciousness.

Pattie stumbled out of the door, leaving it open. She crawled along the wall of the corridor like a bat. Tears gushed from her eyes and nose and mouth. She would have to go, she would have to leave him at last. She loved him, but she could do nothing with her love. It was for her own torment only and not for his salvation. She did not love him enough to save him, not that much, not with that suffering. She could not stay and see him with Elizabeth. She could not love him that much. She could not make his miracle of redemption.

# Chapter Twenty-two

MURIEL was almost ready to leave. She had not spoken to Pattie again. She had not seen Elizabeth again. She believed what Pattie had said. She preferred not to speak more of it, she wanted no discussions or assurances or proofs. She wanted nothing which would further enforce into her mind this thought which she would have to live with for the rest of her life. Better to leave it quiet and hope that in the end, like Pattie, she would seem to forget it.

Muriel had spent most of the previous day, after Pattie's revelation, lying upon her bed in a state of coma. The intense cold seemed to dim and lower her consciousness until there was nothing except a faint flickering awareness which was scarcely aware of itself. Something lay upon her, pinning her to the bed. Perhaps it was an angel of death that lay there, slowly chilling the inert body. The little daylight went soon and darkness came. Time passed. Footsteps passed. A light turned on in the corridor shone in through the half-open door of the room. But nobody came to her. Pattie did not come. Carel did not come. And Elizabeth did not ring her old familiar bell. The house fell silent.

Muriel thought she must have slept a little. Her limbs were long and stiff with cold, the joints frozen. She could not bend her legs or her arms. She rolled a little to and fro on the bed. Pain passed through her body like an alien distilment, a sensation she could hardly recognize. She knew objectively that this must be pain which her awakening body felt. She made it return again and again. She felt that if she continued to lie still she would soon die of cold and of the extinction of the will. The will, returning to her, was pain too and she closed her eyes and bared her teeth upon it. At the end of a long time she managed to sit up and put her feet down to the ground. Her feet seemed curled and cramped into balls which would not flatten to meet the floor. She moved them awkwardly about upon her ankles, and the blood forced its way onward in anguish. She was able at last to stand, take her overcoat off and put on an extra jersey. Putting the coat on again was an almost impossible feat but she got it on after a lot of slow struggling. She looked at her watch in the light from the corridor and found that it was only ten o'clock. She went quietly downstairs, left the house, walked to the nearest telephone box, and telephoned Norah Shadox-Brown.

Her relief at hearing Norah's voice was so intense that she could hardly speak at first. During this time Norah, who seemed somehow immediately to understand, kept up a monologue of sensible soothing remarks. When Muriel started incoherently to talk Norah forestalled her explanations. Of course Muriel wanted to leave her father's house and to leave it early tomorrow morning. What could be more natural? Of course Muriel could come and stay with Norah for as long as she liked. In fact, what Muriel really needed was a holiday. Norah was going off in a few days to stay with a cousin who had a villa at San Remo. Why shouldn't Muriel come along too? They might even get some sunshine, though of course even in Italy at this time of year one couldn't be sure. She would expect Muriel early tomorrow morning. Muriel left the telephone box murmuring "San Remo, San Remo." Perhaps after all there was a world elsewhere.

She could not really believe it though. Her misery was waiting for her in the house. Here was the machine in which she belonged. Here was the stuff she was made of and running away could make no difference. She got into bed with her coat on and lay there shivering. She tried to think about Elizabeth but the familiar image was so altered that it was not like thinking about her any more. The iron maiden. She pictured Elizabeth's room with the fire flickering and the jigsaw puzzle laid out on the floor. Perhaps it was finished now. She pictured the flickering fire and Elizabeth's eyes open in the half dark and she dreaded the sound of Elizabeth's bell like a summons from the dead.

She could not sleep, turning and turning in her bed, there was no warmth in her. What was Elizabeth thinking now, what could she be thinking? Did she regard Muriel as a spy, a traitor who had for a long time watched and suspected and schemed? Muriel thought: I must be hated for my knowledge. Oh God, if only I had never known. If only I had taken Elizabeth away without ever having known. But would Elizabeth have come? It was impossible now to think of taking Elizabeth away; and yet to what was she being left? Muriel could not conceive of Elizabeth as a victim. But had she no pity for her cousin? Had the long years of their friendship suffered a metamorphosis so that even their childhood was changed? She thought: poor Elizabeth. But the thought was empty. She thought: my sister, but she could not give the words a meaning. The only thing which at last stirred her with a warm shudder of emotion was the realization that she had not fed Elizabeth. Would her cousin die there in the house like a neglected animal? Her bell had not rung. It was unspeakably weird to think that someone else must have fed her. Muriel fell asleep and dreamed of her father as he had been long ago.

When the morning came it felt like the end of the world. Muriel thought, this is the worst day of my life, let me just stiffly live through it. She opened the window to a paler twilight. The fog seemed to be clearing. It was no colder out there than it was in her bedroom. Nothing spoke in her now, not even the little voice of self-preservation which continues after reason is silent. She just remembered, as if from long ago, that she had somehow decided she must go. The notion that she could even now if she chose walk to Elizabeth's room and open the door was present to her mind painfully but remotely like a detailed and academic hypothesis of a torture. She moved about mechanically and her teeth chattered with a localized self-pity.

It was already nearly nine o'clock. She began to pack a suitcase, picking things up with clumsy frozen hands. She put her note-books into the bottom of the case, and the loose sheets on which her long poem was written. She glanced at the poem as she put it in and saw in a flash that it was no good. She quickly stuffed some jerseys and a skirt in on top of it. Her fingers were too cold to fold anything and she was now almost weeping with exasperation. The case would not shut. She must be making a lot of noise. She jammed the case down on the bed, half sitting on it, and got one lock to snap. She looked for her overcoat and found that she was wearing it. She did not look round the room but went straight out of the door. The electric light was still burning on the landing. She moved with long quiet strides along the landing and down the stairs. She could hear the gramophone playing in her father's study. She opened the front door.

"Excuse me," said Anthea Barlow, "for calling so early in the morning. I was just wondering if I could see the Rector."

Muriel stared at Mrs Barlow who had materialized, huge as a bear, in the pale brown light of the doorway. Mrs Barlow was too big, too material. Muriel felt like a spirit before her, and for a moment it did not occur to her that they could communicate.

"It is rather an early call, but I do rather urgently want to see him. You see—"

Muriel made a tremendous effort to speak. Her voice came out precise and clear. "I'm afraid my father is not here."

"Oh, really? Could you tell me—"

"He has gone," said Muriel, "to stay at his villa at San Remo." Her voice piped, thin and high.

"Really? Could you—"

Muriel closed the door. She waited in the hall until she heard the slow footsteps going away. Then as she was about to open the door again she paused. There was something which she had forgotten. The sleeping-tablets.

It occurred to Muriel to notice, and she noticed it grimly, that during all her recent pain she had never for a moment considered leaving a world which had become so appalling. She evidently preferred the agony of consciousness. She had packed her poem and forgotten the tablets. Perhaps she would survive after all. She half decided to leave the tablets behind, but some old prudence turned her back. About the future, one never knew.

She put her suitcase down beside the hall door and mounted the stairs again very softly two at a time. The music was still playing in her father's room. She reached her own room and quickly opened the cupboard where the tablets were kept. They were gone.

It took Muriel a little time to be absolutely certain that they were gone. She blinked her eyes. She looked at the other shelves and ran her hands all over the surfaces. The tablets were simply not there.

Muriel had been in a sort of hysterical coma ever since she had woken up. Now she became entirely cool and clear-headed. Had she moved the sleeping tablets from that place? No. They had been there a little while ago, she was sure, and she had not moved them. Muriel stood frowning into the cupboard. Had someone borrowed them innocently? No one in the house used sleeping-pills. Even Elizabeth was a fairly good sleeper, and though her father kept odd hours he could sleep when he wanted to.

Muriel slowly closed the cupboard door. It was odd and disconcerting. But she supposed there was nothing she could do about it. There must be some simple explanation, though she was not able to think of it at the moment. She had better go now. This problem was not the only or the worst one that she was leaving behind her. She had better go, before she met her father, before Elizabeth rang her dreadful bell. Muriel moved slowly out of the room and as far as the head of the stairs.

The sound of the music still continued. It was Swan Lake. Muriel recognized the Dance of the Cygnets. Surely all was well. She put her foot on a stair. Then she turned and walked quickly along the landing to her father's door. She knocked. There was no reply. She waited a moment, knocked again, and then very cautiously opened the door.

It was dark inside. The curtains were still drawn and the lamp upon the desk had been covered by a cloth. Muriel stood still, frozen, expecting a sudden voice to speak to her out of the dark. Nothing happened. Then she heard, through the soft drone of the music, another sound, a sound of heavy breathing. Her father must be asleep.

Now she could see a little more inside the room. She moved forward through the doorway, setting her feet down very softly and peering into the corner. Her father, wearing his cassock, was lying upon the couch with his head supported on a cushion. His breathing was clearly audible, a long guttural snoring sound, then a long pause, and then another one. Muriel closed the door behind her. She moved closer to look at her father.

For a moment, with cold horror, she thought that his eyes were open and that he was looking at her. But it was only a trick of the light. His eyes were closed. His lips were slightly apart, their corners drooping in a sort of sneer. One hand hung down to the floor and lay relaxed upon the carpet, palm upward. Muriel stood still, staring down at him. What was she doing here? Suppose he were to wake up and find her looking at him? But an anxiety which she could no longer master had taken control of her. Very cautiously she shifted the cloth from the lamp and let the light shine upon Carel. She stood rigid again. He did not stir. Then she saw the little blue bottle which had contained the sleeping-tablets. It was lying on the floor near the foot of the couch and it was empty.

Muriel had known this from the moment of leaving her own room, but the knowledge had been numb and dead in her. She stood there now beside the desk, breathing very quickly, and wondering if she was going to faint. She managed to sit down on a chair. She thought, he is gone. And she closed her eyes.

She opened them wide a moment later. The music. Carel must have put the record on. He must have been conscious just a few minutes ago. She got up and went to the couch. She could hardly bring herself to touch him. She put her hand on his shoulder. She gathered the thick stuff of the cassock and as her grip tightened felt the bone of the shoulder within. She shook him, and said "Carel!" The closed eyes did not flicker, the body showed no awareness, the regular breathing continued. Muriel shook him again, much more violently this time, trying to pull him up by both shoulders and digging her fingers in. She called into his ear "Carel! Carel!" The inert body fell back from her hands.

Muriel thought, I must call for help. I must get to the telephone quickly and ring up the hospital. He is only just unconscious. He can't have swallowed the tablets very long ago. They can still treat him, they can bring him back, he will be all right. She started for the door. Then, as if she had been plucked from behind, she hesitated and stopped. And as she stopped she moaned in an agony of pity for herself. This, this, this, she was not to escape this. Ought Carel to be brought back?

She turned and stared at his face. Already it had changed a bit. The enamelled skin which had glowed with whiteness was like grey wax now, the colour of trodden snow which had lost its glitter. The features seemed to be sinking into the bone. Even Carel's hair, spread a little upon the cushion, had lost its glossiness and looked like a relic, some scarcely recognizable stuff found in a tomb or a casket. Muriel gritted her teeth. She must *think* now, think as she had never thought in her life before. But could she, in the presence of this, think?

Carel had made a decision. Was it for her to alter it? A privilege she had claimed for herself, could she deny it to him, to go when and how he pleased? He had his reasons for going, reasons perhaps more dreadful and compelling than she could conceive of. She could not be responsible for dragging him wretchedly, piteously, back into a consciousness he had rejected and thought to annihilate.

She could not do that to her father, to his authority and to his dignity. Carel was not to be hauled back by his heels into a hateful life. She could not at this last moment assume that power over him.

Yet she *had* the power, and could not deny it, the power of life and death. Now and for a little time she could decide to make him live. Should she not forget who he was and simply save him? But she could not forget who he was. Should she not return him to his freedom? He could make the decision again, she would not be condemning him to live. He had always done what he wished. Should she contrary him now? How could she decide this awful thing when she was stricken and sick herself, sick with the presence of death, the death that was in Carel, which was slowly taking him away, and which she could check if she would by a cry?

Muriel sat down and laid her head on Carel's desk. The music continued, airy, substanceless, clear and mercilessly beautiful. The music continued cut off and far away in a beyond where nothing was sick or mortal. Here in the room Carel's breathing was guttural and regular, a sort of quiet self-absorbed discourse. Muriel thought, if I do nothing these sounds are numbered now, in a little while they will simply cease, there will be a last breath and then no more. Mechanically she began counting. Then she thought, all breaths, all heart-beats of all humans are numbered. My life is as finite as his. Was she thinking and had she decided? No thoughts could help her now. She had never more positively felt the utter and complete absence of God. She was alone and rested on nothing and had recourse to nothing. There was no rock of ages.

She got up again and walked about a little. She came near to him and looked down upon the sleeping face. It seemed a terrible intrusion to look upon that face. The peace which it had desired had not yet come to it. The sleeping face was anxious. Oh God, does he want to be waked, does he want to be rescued, thought Muriel. If I could only know, if he could only tell me. If he had told me before I would have obeyed him. She leaned over him, staring, but the anxious sunken face had no message. Then suddenly she saw something white, held in Carel's right hand which was resting between his side and the back of the couch. It was a piece of crumpled paper. Muriel reached out, hesitated, and then very gingerly plucked at the paper. What dreadful awakening was she now afraid of? That he should wake and know her act? Surely he knew even now. His fingers seemed to resist her. The paper came away.

Muriel smoothed it out.

My dear this is so awful I can hardly write it, I have to go, and if I saw you I couldn't. You know I said I would never go dear. I wouldn't have ever honest I wouldn't. You know I love you my dear. Only this other thing I couldn't bear. How could you have done it. You know what I mean about Elizabeth. Muriel told me. It has killed me. You have had the years of my life, all there was of me. You know I love you and I've been your slave only I couldn't stay on with her you know and the only way to go is like this suddenly. When you get this I'll have gone away and don't try to find me, well you couldn't, I'm going right away out of the country I think. Don't worry of me I have money saved dear. You know I will be miserable and thinking of you always, I will be miserable all of my life for you. I could not be what you wanted of me, it was too hard for me. Forgive me please. You know it is all because I do love you so much, you know that. I love you and I can hardly write this letter. Goodbye.

Pattie

Muriel read the letter through twice and then tore it up into very small pieces. The letter steadied her, it was something to think about. So Pattie had had the resolution to get out. She had acted even faster than Muriel had. So it was for Pattie's sake that he lay there. He knew that Pattie knew and he knew who had told her. What did he think of me, what did he ever think of me, Muriel wondered. Is he dreaming of me now? Are there strange huge dreams perhaps at the end in such a slumber? She began to look around the room. Perhaps there was a letter, perhaps he had written her a letter, left some scrap of message for her? He must have known that sooner or later it was she who would find him. She looked on the desk and searched the floor and all about the couch. At last she saw a piece of white paper lying a little under the couch near his head and quickly picked it up. It was a paper dart.

Muriel began to cry. She cried silently in a hot blinding stream of tears. She loved her father and she had loved him only. Why had she not known this earlier? There had always been a darkness in her relationship with her father and in that darkness her love had lain asleep. If only there had been no Pattie. If only there had been no Elizabeth. If only there could have been just herself and Carel together. She seemed now so strongly to remember a time when it had been so. She had loved him so much. She could have made him happy, she could have saved him from the demons. But Elizabeth had always intervened. All Muriel's connections with the world, her connection with her father had had to pass through Elizabeth. She knew now that a special pain which Elizabeth had caused her, and to which she had become so accustomed that she scarcely noticed it, was the pain of jealousy.

Muriel's tears continued and she moaned a little, very softly, and trembled, standing there in the lamp-lit room beside the sleeping figure. Would there be love again? Love was dying and she could not save it. She could not wake her father and tell him she loved him. Her love only existed in this awful interim between dark and dark. It was a love immured, sealed up. It could only have this demonic issue. To let him go was all that she could do for him now. She would not wake him to a consciousness which he had judged unbearable. She would not wake him like Lazarus from a dream of hell to hell itself, a place where love was powerless to redeem and save. She had been given her knowledge too late, and perhaps in the corruption of her heart could only have accepted it too late. And now she was condemned to be divided forever from the world of simple innocent things, thoughtless affections and free happy laughter and dogs passing by in the street.

The Swan music came abruptly to an end. Moving trance-like, Muriel leaned to put the record back to the beginning again. Her tears fell on to the drooping folds of the cassock. He had gone, and he had left her Elizabeth. There would be no parting from Elizabeth now. As she turned back to the sleeper she saw a bright streak of light between the curtains. Wearily, heavily she pulled the curtains back. The fog had gone away. There was a little blue sky and the sun was shining. Against a mass of moving clouds she saw the towers of St Botolph and St Edmund and St Dunstan and the great dome of St Paul's. There would be no parting from Elizabeth now. Carel had riveted them together, each to be the damnation of the other until the end of the world.

# *Chapter Twenty-three*

"MARCUS."

    "Yes, Norah."

"Are you going down to see them out at the Rectory?"

"There's nothing I could do."

"Are the girls going straight to the new house?"

"I believe so."

"Where is it, Bromley or some such curious place?"

"Bromley."

"I do wish Muriel would take a holiday, now the spring's come."

"She could afford to."

"They're both quite well-off now, aren't they?"

"I do think Carel ought to have left something to Pattie."

"Pattie's all right. If you write to her again don't forget to call her Patricia."

"She seems to be enjoying her African refugee camp."

"Misfortunes of others soon cheer us up."

"Is that a cynical remark, Norah?"

"No."

"Pattie took it well, don't you think?"

"There's a streak of ruthlessness in Pattie."

"There's a streak of ruthlessness in all of us."

"You say the girls took it well."

"Muriel did. I still haven't seen Elizabeth."

"Not a feather ruffled?"

"Not a feather ruffled."

"Odd young woman."

"You didn't write to her again?"

"I'm through with trying to see Muriel."

"They'll be pulling the Rectory down next week."

"Did you see in *The Times* about the Wren tower?"

"Yes, too bad. Found a new place for Eugene Peshkov yet?"

"Not yet."

"I suppose his refugee pension will go on?"

"Don't worry. I'm his pension."

"What do you mean?"

"I pay him that pittance. He thinks it's from a fund."

"Norah, you're extraordinary."

"One must be rational about charity. I don't think you are."

"You mean about Leo. Don't forget he's coming to tea, by the way."

"Do you think he really means to do that degree in French and Russian?"

"Yes."

"Well, there was no need to give him three hundred pounds."

"I told you, we'd earmarked it as an education fund."

"He exploits you."

"Nonsense. I think maybe I will go down to the Rectory after all."

"You'll stay here tonight?"

"No, I must get back to Earls Court. I want to work late."

"So you *are* going on with the book?"

"Yes, but it's all different now."

"Have you arranged to have your furniture moved yet?"

"No, not yet, actually."

"Would you like me to arrange it?"

"Oh, please don't trouble, I'll—Look, it's stopped raining."

"Well, I suppose you'd better go now if you're going."

"Sure you won't come, Norah?"

"No. Muffins for tea."

"Muffins. Goodie."

The building site crawled with men and machines and over it a continuous mingled din of machinery and voices and transistor sets rose up into the weak blue sunshiny air. The recent rain had covered the black surface with little glassy pools, each of which reflected a faintly bluish silver light. Orange monsters with huge claws scored the sticky earth and cement tumbled noisily in huge revolving drums. In the distance a steel skeleton was already rising.

The Rectory could be seen from afar, a red blob beneath the soaring solid grace of Wren's grey tower. Marcus picked his way along the muddied pavement past singing, shouting men in striped jerseys and slowly manœuvring lorries. What did he want at the Rectory? why on earth was he going there? In the course of the grim rituals after Carel's death, and in the month and more that followed, he had seen a certain amount of Muriel, but nothing of Elizabeth. Muriel had been formal and polite and constantly refused his offers of assistance. She was decisive and calm and efficient and seemed entirely unmoved by her father's suicide. She would not allow anyone to help, and there was nothing today which Marcus could do for her. He was come simply as a spectator to indulge some painful craving of his own.

Marcus had been living in a new time, the time since Carel died. It already seemed a long, long time, long enough to grow old in. After the first awful shock of the news Marcus had felt lost, deprived of use and purpose. Carel had been a great sign. Marcus had been ready to meditate on Carel, to fight with Carel, to be hurt by Carel, perhaps to redeem Carel. He had no resources to deal with this sudden parting. He was left with an old love for his brother which he could do nothing with. He wondered if with a greater show of affection, with a little more understanding, even with a kind of brutality he might have saved him? He was tormented by the idea that Carel had needed something from him.

What had Carel died of? What demon, what apparition, become too terrible to bear had quenched that dreadful vitality? Had Carel despaired, and what could that despair have been like? Or had his departure been something cool, another act and as it happened the last one in some long pattern of quiet cynicism? How did this act relate, how could it relate, to that passion in Carel which Marcus had been ready to revere? Had chance, sheer contingency choked Carel in the end? Had he died of a mood?

Marcus could not bear to think of his brother as defeated. He needed, and he realized how far this need stretched back into his childhood, to see Carel as a man of power. He himself had lived on that power, even when he had condemned it, perhaps especially when he had condemned it. In fact he had come to think Carel wise, a witch doctor, but wise. Carel's black philosophy had cut him with an edge of truth. Truth almost always hurts a bit and that is why we know so little of it. Carel's truth was an agony. But can such truths be borne, and if they cannot are they really truths? Carel had lived this, perhaps been maddened by it and perhaps died of it. Marcus had felt its faint touch and had started back, had felt only just enough to know the falsity of what he had written in his book. He had imagined that he had time to learn from Carel, to help Carel. This sudden ending left him aching with puzzlement and with a recurring doubt. Was it all dust and ashes, Carel's passion and his own reflection? Did this death prove it? Perhaps any death proved it.

A very large furniture-van was standing outside the Rectory and the last of the furniture was just being carried out. Marcus stood a little way off rather wistfully and watched. He recognized some of the pieces as having been long ago in his father's house. Things, things, they outlive us and go to scenes that we know nothing of. He was hurt that Muriel had not consulted him about the disposal of the furniture, not all of which was going to Bromley. He felt too that she should have offered him something of Carel's as a keepsake. Now it was as if Carel too were being packed up and carted briskly away. The mystery of Carel had shrunk to the size of a footstool.

The back of the van was closed up with a loud clang and the men climbed up into the front. Slowly the van drew away. Its big square shadow passed along the red brick façade and touched the grey base of Wren's tower. The door of the Rectory remained open, and from where he stood Marcus could see into the empty hall. The house had become a vacant shell whose significant spaces would soon be merged into the empty air. It would soon exist only in memory; and indeed in the faint clear sunshine it looked like a memory already. It seemed unreal, vivid and yet not truly present, like a coloured photograph projected in a dark room. Marcus wondered if he should go in, but he was afraid to. He was sure that Muriel and Elizabeth were still inside.

As he waited, and the sounds from the building site flew chattering upward over his head into the big rivery air, another shadow fell beside him. A taxi had arrived and was now drawing up outside the house. The taximan got out and went to the open door and rang the bell. The bell sounded loud and differently in the empty house. Marcus watched. From far within there was an echo of slow strangely heavy footsteps. Then framed in the doorway he saw the two girls, immobile as if they had been there for some time, their two pale heads close together, their bodies seemingly entwined. With a shock he realized that Muriel was carrying Elizabeth in her arms. The taximan ran forward. Gingerly Elizabeth's feet touched the slippery pavement. Marcus saw her face turned towards him, long and without colour, half hidden in the drooping metallic hair which gleamed in the sunlight a faintly greenish silver. It was and was not the face of the nymph he had known. The large grey-blue eyes blinked painfully in the bright light and met his vacantly and without interest. Now she was being helped into the taxi. Muriel followed her and the door slammed. The taxi moved away, diminishing through the lanes of the building site until it disappeared into the narrow labyrinth of the city. Elizabeth had not recognized him.

Marcus sighed and for a moment felt his beating heart. Then almost automatically he walked to the open door and entered the Rectory. There could be no peril now, no ghost even which he could encounter there. Those dangerous presences were gone. The girls had taken elsewhere their mysterious solidarity, their pale impenetrability. And *he* he, had ceased to be. From that great light, smoky and lurid, the central incandescence had been removed and the glow would slowly fade away. The old fear would fade, and the love would fade too or else unrecognizably change. The relentless vegetable vitality of human life would grow in this case as in all others to eclipse the dead.

Standing in the middle of the hall Marcus had a sudden eerie sensation. Somebody was near, looking, moving. He turned slightly and saw with the corner of his eye the shade of a disappearing figure. It was Eugene Peshkov who had seen Marcus and who was now gliding away under the stairs hoping not to be observed. For a moment Marcus thought to call to him but then decided not to. He felt a little hurt and sad that Eugene should hide from him. But he had never troubled to make friends with Leo's father. He wondered if he should tip Eugene, give him a pound, say. Had the girls remembered to? But no, it was impossible. On this day all they could do was avoid each other, not know each other, and turn away as if ashamed.

Marcus began to mount the stairs. He trod softly but his footsteps made little echoes. He turned at the top and made for what he thought had been Carel's study. The door was open and the sun was shining through it. The room was completely empty and dust was already thick upon the floor. Nothing that Marcus could see identified it as the dark cluttered cavern where he had last seen his brother alive and where Carel had struck him that blow which had seemed to him such an indubitable proof of love. Had he been right? It was better not to ask.

He went to the window and looked out. The spires of the city twinkled a little in the light as if just faintly visible stars had alighted upon them and were moving elusively from place to place. Marcus began to think about Julian. He pictured him vividly, as he had not done for years, clothed in all the grace of a barely grown-up boy. They had loved him. Indeed they had loved each other, all three. Now Carel was gone too and seemed already to recede so fast, as if he were in haste to find his way back to Julian in some distant land of youth. Only Marcus remained, heavy with these deaths, these lives. Only within him did all that was singular of them upon this earth live and grow now.

There was a sound behind him and he turned sharply. A woman was standing in the doorway. She was dressed in a smart blue tweed coat and her greyish fair hair was fluffy under a diminutive blue hat. Her sudden appearance, her stillness, her staring face gave her for an instant the quality of a ghost. Then she moved. Marcus stared at her. Something in those wide rather ecstatic eyes was familiar to him. In a contortion and shock of memory he spoke.

"Anthea!"

"Marcus!"

"I can hardly believe my eyes! Wherever did you spring from? Is it really you? You haven't changed a bit."

"Neither have you, not a bit!"

"But where have you been all these years? And whatever in the world are you doing here? You're the last person I expected to see."

"I work in this area now. I'm a psychiatric social worker."

"A psychiatric social worker! But why haven't I come across you or heard about you?"

"Well, you might have heard of me as Mrs Barlow. I don't think you ever knew my married name."

"Good heavens, are you Mrs Barlow?"

"I expect you've heard I'm ghastly!"

"No, no! Not still in the C.P. are you, Anthea?"

"Dear me no. I'm not even a proper Christian any more I'm afraid. I suppose I'm a sort of Buddhist now really."

"But why didn't you get in touch with me? I know it's been a long time—"

"And one does hesitate with old friends. Well, I've only lately come back to London. And since I've been here I've had a rather special job. You see, it concerned Carel—"

"Carel?"

"Yes. You see, the Bishop specially asked me to see Carel and, well, make a sort of report on his sanity. It was to be quite confidential. I was just to say that I was attached to the pastorate. The Bishop was terribly worried—"

"But how extraordinary that he should have asked you, I mean what a coincidence—"

"It wasn't exactly a coincidence because the Bishop knew I'd known Carel before. He thought it might help. Oh, the Bishop knows all about little me!"

"How fearfully odd though. Carel was very keen on you in the old days, you know! Well, we all were, Julian, myself—You caused us quite a lot of trouble!"

"I know. I was *awful*!"

"Whatever did you make of Carel now?"

"I never got to see him."

"But you must have written to him?"

"Yes, but I don't think he ever got the letters. He had cut himself off completely."

"How strange. And how very sad."

"So you see, he never knew."

Marcus looked at Anthea. Of course she had changed. Yet it was still the same ecstatic, slightly crazy, trouble-making girl. And now she was in psychology. It seemed quite suitable. He had told Norah that he found her funny. He still did find her funny. But he had loved her.

"I'm sorry I didn't write to you, Marcus. You see, Carel was—"

"I understand."

"I was just going to write to you now. I got plenty of news of you from Leo, actually."

"Leo? So you know young Leo, do you?"

"Oh yes. We're great friends, Leo and me."

"But how do you come to be acquainted with Leo?"

"Oh, it's a long story. He comes to me with all his little troubles, you know. He misses that mother that he never had. And I've been able to help him with a small loan now and then."

"A loan? What was that for, I wonder? Something to do with girls or motor bikes?"

"No, no, it was for his work in Leicester."

"What work in Leicester?"

"You know, his work in Leicester with delinquent boys. Such a worthy project."

"Delinquent boys! I see! Well, Anthea, so you're married."

"*Divorcée.*" She breathed it.

"Oh, good. I mean— Come to dinner with me, Anthea. Come next Monday, come to my flat."

"I'd love to. I already know where you live. I looked you up in the telephone book. But aren't you just moving from there? Someone said—"

"No," said Marcus. "I'm not moving. I'm definitely not moving."

"Look, I must fly. I'm nearly due at the clinic."

"Monday then. Half-past seven."

"Au revoir, Marcus."

When he had heard her footsteps recede and the front door close Marcus began to laugh. He remembered that she had always made him laugh. It was not so much that she was absurd, a kind of electric vitality in her seemed automatically to produce laughter. Carel had laughed for her too, abandoning himself to just such relaxed inexplicable mirth.

How confoundedly odd it was, Anthea turning up again, and how extremely invigorating he found this oddness. There was a kind of silly innocence about it all, a kind of thoroughly cheering innocence. He looked forward to seeing her again. With her the ordinary world seemed to resume its power, the world where human beings make simple claims on one another and where things are small and odd and touching and funny.

Marcus found that he had left Carel's room and was walking down the stairs. Would he go on working on his book? Perhaps it was a book which only a genius could write, and he was not a genius. It might be that what he wanted to say about love and about humanity was true but simply could not be expressed as a theory. Well, he would think about all that later on. What he needed now was relaxation, perhaps a holiday.

He emerged into the street. He smiled at the feeble sunshine and at the big bustling scene of men at work. He moved out into the gay din of ringing voices and babbling transistor sets. Fancy old Anthea turning up again like that. A psychiatric social worker forsooth! Well, it was odd, it was all confoundedly odd.

# Chapter Twenty-four

EUGENE PESHKOV whistled softly as he packed his suitcase. It was good to have few possessions. It made moving so easy. Miss Shadox-Brown had arranged for him to move into a church hostel in West Bermondsey. They said he would have to share a room at first, but they were confident they would soon manage to give him one to himself.

Eugene had been alone now for several days at the Rectory. The furniture had gone, the girls had gone. Leo, who seemed suddenly to have money in his pocket, had gone off on holiday to Spain. Eugene was sorry to leave the place. It had been a snug hole, especially in winter. Of course it was quite deathly now that it was empty, and the last two days were unbearably noisy since they had been demolishing the Wren tower. Today was happily Sunday.

His belongings filled three large suitcases. His clothes were in one, the second contained the crockery wrapped in towels, and this third case was to hold the oddments, his shaving things, his wireless set, the Russian box, the icon, the photograph of Tanya. His paperback books had been deposited in a box in the hall to be collected by Mrs Barlow for Oxfam. The potted plant and its stand had already gone to the hostel on a handcart.

Well, he was on the move again. That was how it was. On from one camp to the next. He thrust the photograph of Tanya into the bottom of the case and then pulled it out again for a moment to look at it. It was not a very good one. It showed her in one of her tragedy queen moods. He looked at the wooden hut behind her, trying to remember it more exactly. Tanya was a ghost. He looked through her into the hut. They had shared it with another married couple. They had been reckoned lucky. Perhaps they had been lucky. Perhaps he had been lucky. After all the world was just a camp with its good corners and its bad corners. His corners had never been too bad. The world was just a transit camp. The only certain thing was that one was not in it for long.

He wished he had been kinder to Tanya. He had felt trapped by her somehow. She had died young in bewilderment and misery and he had been too preoccupied with Leo and with his own future to attend properly to her dying. He had given people cigarettes to sit with her. He was very sorry for her, but he was anxious for it to be over. She was not a brave sufferer and he did not want to undergo her terror of death. He resented this test of the stoicism he had made for himself. He had dropped no tear for his mother, for his sister, persons infinitely dearer to him than Tanya. He had been hard with Tanya and she had not understood. Did it matter now, now that she was nothing?

He dropped the photograph into the case and turned to lift down the icon. The milky blue angels were infinitely sad. They had travelled a long way. When Eugene was gone they would still travel on and on, until one day no one knew who they were any more. There was only this travelling. Did it matter now, Eugene wondered, his unkindness to Tanya, since there was no God? He felt that it mattered. But that was just a feeling, a heaviness within him. He shook the crumbs of toast and sugar cake off the furry green tablecloth and wrapped the cloth round the icon.

Pattie seemed distant now almost as if she too belonged to a remote era of time. He was already insulated, closed against the pain of thinking of her. The pain existed somewhere separately, and all that came to him bodily was sadness. He had loved Pattie because she was a misfit like himself. But she was a misfit of some quite other kind. They could not really have met each other's needs. He could not have let Pattie into his past, and he was his past, that sombre egg which had grown around the jewel of his childhood. He could not have contained Pattie. It was too late now for him to contain anybody. Of course he would have forgiven Pattie, he would have come round, he would have tried at least to understand. Only when she suddenly went he was relieved in a way and soon began to think of it as inevitable. The happiness she had represented to him was merely something dangerous. To grow old is to know that not circumstances but consciousness makes the happy and the sad. He was a sad man and he would never make the happiness of others or live in a house like ordinary people.

His foot touched something which was lying just underneath the bunk and he stooped to look. It was a paperback detective story which he had overlooked. He picked it up and opened the door and began to walk slowly toward the hall to put it in the box with the other books. He stepped softly through the stripped empty kitchen. The sound of living footsteps seemed inappropriate, the waking of echoes which were already moribund. He passed through the darkness under stairs and then stopped abruptly. There was somebody in the hall. Then he saw that it was only Mrs Barlow. He was about to speak to her when he saw that she was behaving oddly. She knelt down beside the crate of books, then sat upon the floor leaning her head back against the crate. He heard a faint whimpering sound. Mrs Barlow was crying.

Eugene backed quietly away and tiptoed back through the kitchen. He left the book behind him on the kitchen floor. He did not want to be involved with Mrs Barlow's grief. For whom or for what she was weeping there alone in the empty hall he did not know, he had never really thought about her, and the mystery of her tears soon passed from his mind. He returned to his packing. The third suitcase was nearly full. He packed his little wireless set next to the icon and tucked newspapers in around it. There was only the Russian box left to be put in now.

Eugene picked up the Russian box. As he did so, with a rush of memory which made him gasp and brought the blood to his face he recalled what it was. There had been in the drawing-room of their country house a box identical with this one in which he had kept lumps of sugar for his little white English terrier. The little dog had been killed one day by one of the half-savage mastiffs that guarded the house. He could still picture the footman who had brought it in, hanging limp like a little rat. So the tears which had so mysteriously come to him, and which rose again now to his eyes, were not for his mother or his sister after all. Or perhaps indeed they were. For they were tears for himself. It had been the first tragedy of his life.